PATH TO
THE SILENT
COUNTRY

Also by

Lynne Reid Banks

THE L-SHAPED ROOM
HOUSE OF HOPE
CHILDREN AT THE GATE
THE BACKWARD SHADOW
TWO IS LONELY
ONE MORE RIVER
SARAH AND AFTER
DARK QUARTET

PATH TO THE SILENT COUNTRY

Charlotte Brontë's Years of Fame

LYNNE REID BANKS

DELACORTE PRESS/NEW YORK

Published by
Delacorte Press
1 Dag Hammarskjold Plaza
New York, New York 10017

Originally published in Great Britain
by George Weidenfeld & Nicolson Limited

Manufactured in the United States of America
First U.S.A. printing

Designed by Oksana Kushnir

LIBRARY OF CONGRESS CATALOGING IN PUBLICATION DATA
Banks, Lynne Reid.
        Path to the silent country.
        1. Brontë, Charlotte, 1816–1855, in fiction. drama,
poetry, etc. I. Title.
PZ4.B2173Pat   [PR6003.A528]   823'.9'12   77-20290
ISBN 0-440-06985-8

TO MY DEAR UNMET FRIEND
LOIS TUCKER

Strew with laurels the grave
Of the early-dying!—Alas,
Early she goes on the path
To the silent country, and leaves
Half her laurels unwon,
Dying too soon!—yet green
Laurels she had, and a course
Short, but redoubled by fame....

Matthew Arnold, "Haworth Churchyard"

CONTENTS

FOREWORD

*J*n my previous work on the Brontës, *Dark Quartet*, I offered my appreciation to those scholars who had gone before me, providing the stepping-stones of fact which enabled me to chart my course through all the imponderables of the lives of Charlotte, Emily, Anne, and Branwell. Well documented though they are (to a point where to seek new original sources would surely be fruitless), the unanswerable questions remain. My speculations in this, the story of Charlotte's last years, take an overtly fictional form, for which I make no apology. I have stuck to the truth wherever it was known, and have kept my imagination harnessed to it. I have also, as before, employed the convention of quoting wherever appropriate from letters, as if the words had been spoken in dialogue, in order to give as genuine a rendition of Charlotte's thoughts as possible.

I acknowledge my continuing debt to Mrs. Gaskell, every Brontë student's *sine qua non*; Winifred Gerin; Phyllis Bentley; Margaret Lane; and now Margot Peters, whose really excellent new book *Unquiet Soul* gave me deeper insights into Charlotte's approach to death.

LYNNE REID BANKS
London 1977

PREFACE

*C*harlotte Brontë had been well advanced in the writing of her third novel when the three people closest to her—her brother and her two surviving sisters—were torn out of her life within a few months of each other.

"Torn" was the appropriate word. Their deaths had left a gaping hole in the fabric of her own life, and if her new novel, *Shirley*, had not been already established in all essentials in her mind, it could not have been employed as a patch, however inadequate, to keep the harsh winds of sorrow and loss from rending her to shreds.

As it was, by the time her sister Anne died in April of 1849, Charlotte's plot was formed, her characters set upon their courses. It was possible to lay some of the burden of continuation upon *them*—those creatures of her mind's making now imbued with a will and a life-force of their own. They helped her—Shirley, Caroline, the militant Mr. Helstone—all of them. During the long summer evenings Charlotte was able, with their assistance, to push her tale forward and her grief back.

"Moments as dark as this I have never known"—so she had written to her friend Ellen Nussey while watching her beloved sister Emily die. But as her book grew toward completion she began to hope that after all she was triumphing over bereavement, that her later words to Ellen had not been mere whistling in the dark: "Still I have some strength to fight the battle of life."

Courage was her only companion as she worked on her manuscript—the courage Anne had wished her with her dying words. Now the home they had all shared, Haworth Parsonage, was little more than a bleak square pile of empty boxes, stacked upon the flank of the Yorkshire moors. In winter it would be terrible in its cold, silent loneliness. Yet in summer it was less terrible, especially when she was able to escape through the "inner door," into her work. Then she could sometimes remember her brother and sisters as they had been in the days when that pile of boxes had been rooms, holding treasures of companionship, warmth, shared endeavor, and mutual support.

Few siblings can ever have been more intimately bound up with each other than Charlotte had been with Emily and Anne, and perhaps particularly with their only brother, Branwell. He had been kin to her in a special way. They were soul-twins in their childhood and youth, all their burgeoning creativity interdependent and interacting, producing enormous quantities of collaborative stories, histories, and magazines based on the inhabitants of a country of their own which they had called Angria. Emily and Anne had had their private world, too—Gondal. Less fabulous than Angria, it was no less real to them, and they had played at it until they were grown up.

From such secret and prolific sources had sprung their adult writing, seriously entered upon by the sisters only when all other means of earning independent livings had come to nothing. Branwell, in whom their youthful hopes had been invested, had come to nothing, too—worse than nothing: all his brilliant promise sunk in pitiful weakness and misfortune which, in the end, had destroyed him.

But by that time his sisters had secretly published, first, an anthology of their poetry, which had sold precisely two copies, and subsequently several three-volume novels. Emily's *Wuthering Heights* and Anne's *Agnes Grey* and *The Tenant of Wildfell Hall* had been somewhat harshly reviewed, but had sold well. Charlotte's *Jane Eyre*, written after the failure of her first book to find a publisher at all, had been a *succès de scandale*, establishing her in a few months as the most talked-of writer of the day.

The talking was due not only to the book itself, but to the mystery surrounding its authorship. All the sisters, at Emily's particular insistence, had published under pseudonyms, aimed at disguising not only their identities but their gender. Keeping their initials, they had called themselves Currer, Ellis, and Acton Bell, and there had been very much gossip and speculation in the salons of Mayfair and elsewhere as to who these three might be. Were they brothers? Were they, in fact, all one person? Emily had held the other two to their promise of anonymity to the end, but now Charlotte had begun to suspect that she might not be able to keep their secret indefinitely.

In some unacknowledged part of her mind lay a willingness that her true identity should become known. Since her early childhood she had yearned for a different life from that of a poor, plain, and socially restricted country parson's daughter—a role in the great urbane world of social, literary, and political events. This was the world she and Branwell had striven to create for themselves in their childhood writings. The very smallness and unchanging parochial dullness of Haworth were a blight on her spirits, though, ironically, she fled back to it eagerly after each excursion, for shyness still inhibited her dealings with all but her few intimate friends.

London, which she had visited only twice, contained much that fascinated and attracted her. Her two publishers, George Smith and the older and gentler Mr. Williams, were full of fondness and admiration for her; Mr. Smith had made clear his eagerness to open new doors for her and to show her (and show her off to) such men of letters and of "the world" as he felt would interest her and enlarge her horizons.

All this was very fine, and Charlotte, shy or not, would have been happy to take advantage of these offers, if only as palliatives for her grief, had it not been for the strong Calvinist conscience which had always harassed her. In the first place, it forbade her to indulge in unmerited outings and pleasures until she had provided her publishers with the new novel they required. In the second, it reminded her continually that there was one still left at home who depended on her and missed her cruelly if she were away for even one night—her father.

The Reverend Patrick Brontë was now over seventy. He had survived—incomprehensibly to himself, as he believed he was forever ailing and certain never to get through another winter—the deaths of five of his six children (his two eldest daughters, Maria and Elizabeth, having succumbed to consumption in childhood). Now, after the unendurable visitations of the past year, he was left with just this one last ewe lamb.

The thought of losing *her* was more than his aged mind could tolerate. He would look at her—so tiny in physique, so frail in constitution, as burdened by grief as himself, and with the additional burden (which the old man sensed) of a twofold responsibility: to be his prop, and to fulfill her God-given talent. She looked too fragile to sustain the cruel elements without, the turbulence within. Surely, surely she would be taken from him! Yet how, in the name of pity, could God rob him of his last support? He must retain hope. Nothing else could now sustain him in his age.

But the hope was thin, and it was threatened by every little cough, every twinge, every slight degree of pallor on his dear child's face. His irresistible compulsion to pester her about her health made living with him harder than it need have been.

Yet Charlotte could hardly be said to live with him in a normal family way. Clinging to the habits of many years, he did not take meals with her, other than afternoon tea, and in fact Charlotte saw more of Tabitha Ackroyd and Martha Brown, the parsonage servants, than she did of him. Old Tabby, who had been the family housekeeper since Charlotte's childhood, and had seen her family through all but its earliest losses, was now so crotchety and decrepit that she could be little more than an added burden on Charlotte. True, Martha was as devoted and sturdy as ever, but she was hardly a companion.

Charlotte's domain lay on the left side of the parsonage, the little front room which was dining-room and work-room combined, while across the flagstone passage the Reverend Patrick pursued his concerns in the parlor, which was also his study, with an old John Martin etching in its gilt frame still on the wall behind him and Emily's small upright piano, now silent, near his table.

Patrick was still nominally the incumbent of Haworth parish, though over his declining years his curate, Mr. Nicholls, had gradually taken over most of the visiting and much of the service-taking. But Patrick was not idle. He still wrote all his own sermons, studied his health assiduously through the medium of home medical books, and took a burning interest in the struggle of a few enlightened men of his village to improve the general health of their small community by rectifying the appalling drainage and sewage systems. The fight, largely waged by letter, to arouse a glimmering of official interest in this last project was exactly suited to Patrick's taste. He had always relished a battle with authority.

Charlotte for her part was glad that her poor, bereft father was able to maintain an interest in anything other than herself. It oppressed her inexpressibly to feel the strength of his devotion and dependence upon her, to have him fussing about her, exacerbating her own anxieties by pouncing upon every trivial symptom. And she was grateful, too, at not having to spend too much of her time keeping him company. Lonely and desolate as she was, it was not *old* company she craved, but that of contemporaries.

Yet whom could she turn to? She had no friends in the village, for she and the local girls had little in common beyond church-going. Her only real friends, apart from her sisters, had been Ellen Nussey and Mary Taylor, both of whom she had met at school. Now Mary was gone to New Zealand, fulfilling her bizarre but admirable dream of an independence right outside the narrow constriction of English society which would have confined her (as it had Charlotte until her success with *Jane Eyre*) to genteel poverty and the drudging life of a governess or teacher. As for Ellen, she had a life of her own of sorts, caring for her mother and acting housekeeper for one or other of her "twenty" brothers, as Mary would say—there were actually nine. She could not often visit; and, indeed, it was not often that Charlotte considered herself fit to receive her. She was frequently—despite her titanic efforts to master her grief—so overborne by depression and low spirits that she felt it would be an insult to friendship to inflict herself on Ellen.

Yet as *Shirley* progressed toward completion, Charlotte began, almost stealthily, to anticipate a reward for her determination to oppose her will for life against the forces of death which had sought to defeat her. If she could write this all-important book under these wretched circumstances, surely she could do anything she chose! It was the apparent triumph of her will, and of her creative part, which allowed her to face the dark days of coming winter without terror; but the future might also hold some element of the "life and stir" which Mary had always said she needed —trips to London . . . new people, new ideas to feed and stimulate her. . . . When the book was complete, she could put her conscience in her pocket.

Perhaps the darkest moments were truly over.

PART I
The Years of Fame
1849–1852

chapter 1 THE SECRET IS OUT

*I*n October, Charlotte went to Brook-royd to visit Ellen Nussey, her childhood friend. She felt she had deserved a break; she had kept her promises to herself—made work her palliative to keep her from brooding about her brother and sisters, and held herself rigorously just above the surface of despair.

Ellen, determined to make her visit a lively one, broadcast invitations far and wide among Charlotte's former acquaintances. Many expupils of the Misses Wooler, who had taught Charlotte at Roe Head School, still lived in the neighborhood; among them the prospect of her visit aroused tremendous excitement. Despite Ellen's disclaimers it was widely believed that Charlotte and the controversial and mysterious Currer Bell were one. Currer Bell was, indeed, Charlotte's pen-name. She, Emily, and Anne had determined on anonymity when they had had their first joint literary effort—a book of their poetry—published. Fearing that they would be undervalued if they were known to be women, they deliberately chose ambiguous first names, while retaining their true initials, and became Currer, Ellis, and Acton Bell.

Adding to the fascination of the mystery was the fact that many, especially among the older generation, regarded *Jane Eyre* as a shocking novel. One of these was Charlotte's godmother, Mrs. Atkinson. She called upon Charlotte at Brookroyd a few days after her arrival, and, greeting her with marked chilliness, asked for a few moments of her time alone.

With sinking heart, Charlotte led her into one of the less ornate and lofty chambers of the house, where she felt more in scale with her surroundings, and they sat down facing each other.

"Charlotte," Mrs. Atkinson began at once, "did you write a certain book? I beg you will grant me a truthful answer."

"I would prefer not to commit myself," said Charlotte. "But let us say I did. What then?"

Mrs. Atkinson drew herself up and fixed Charlotte with eyes hitherto warm and affectionate, but now filled with displeasure.

"I have read it," she said, "and so has the Reverend Atkinson. We have known your family for a long time, Charlotte, or I would not comment on the matter—I would simply withdraw from your acquaintance without the unpleasantness of an explanation. I owe it to your father, however, to voice what must be his own true feelings as a man of the cloth, though perhaps he has not told them to you." She paused and took a deep breath. "It is a *wicked* book. It is a book that should never be intruded upon a Christian family circle, and I would not have read it to the end but for the unwelcome rumors I had heard about its authorship."

Charlotte was now sitting bolt upright, with clenched hands and clenched teeth, staring through her spectacles at her godmother. A weaker woman might have quailed before that look, but Mrs. Atkinson merely swallowed and went on.

"Though you have been raised in somewhat peculiar circumstances, you have not been deprived of good breeding. Your father is an upright and pious man, your mother was almost a saint—*she* must be turning in her grave at your depravity."

"My *what?*" ejaculated Charlotte.

"Well . . . that of your principal characters. Does it not come to the same thing? I say, you have been given the benefits of a gentle-woman's education and that with this bold and irreligious effusion you have disgraced not only your background, but your whole sex. This is not only my opinion," she continued hastily, for Charlotte had turned very pale. "One reviewer wrote that if you were in-deed a woman, you must be one who for good reason had long forfeited the society of other females. That proves that I am not merely expressing the prejudices of a provincial minister's wife. The cream of intellectual society has been shocked by the vulgar-ity, the unwomanliness, and, worst of all, the unchristian traits in your work. I am appalled when I contemplate the harm such a book could do in the hands of young, impressionable girls—the very governesses whom your heroine claimed to speak for!"

Charlotte was on her feet by now, and breathing heavily.

"Is that all you have to say, Mrs. Atkinson?"

"Only this remains—that I consider you have forfeited *my* soci-ety at all events, and I desire no more acquaintance of you."

With that she swept from the room, leaving Charlotte in such a rage as to be absolutely incapable of speech or movement for sev-eral minutes. When Ellen came to find her she was lying on the windowseat, stifling her outrage in a cushion.

When she had calmed her down a little and heard the story, Ellen said in her placid way, "Well, darling, you should have expected it. People don't look to see those sorts of things written down—at least not in English books. With French ones it's different—vice is expected among them."

"Vice? What vice? *What vice?*"

"Well! It wasn't Rochester's having a—I mean, Adèle being a—I mean, it wasn't *him* so much; it was the way Jane took it so calmly when he told her."

"Did that shock you?"

"Perhaps a little . . ."

"But unchristian, Ellen! That is surely unjust! Is it unchristian to forgive, to have hope of regeneration? Is not every word Jane utters the word of a Christian? Is it not her Christianity that urges her to leave him, despite her own strongest longings?"

"Of course *I* saw that, because I know you. But you know she doesn't say so in so many words. One might think she was doing right for its own sake, or for *her* own sake, without reference to God at all."

Charlotte was silent.

"And then," Ellen ventured to add, "the nominal Christians in the book—the horrid Mr. Brocklehurst, for instance, and St. John Rivers—are so unsympathetically depicted, and Mr. Rochester, who is so attractive that half the girls in England are in love with him, has not a Christian sentiment put into his mouth from first to last. I'm afraid, dear, that you may find many clergymen and their families glowering at you if the truth comes out—as it must soon."

"Then I shall brace myself to stand up to their glowering, let it be as grim as it may," said Charlotte. "I have had the bitterest taste of it this morning. I fell back before it, but now I am armed to withstand as much more of the same as they care to throw at me. Only those we love can truly sting us; that's why my godmother's strictures hurt me so much. But I am convinced that all who really know me will not condemn, however they might criticize."

There was another blow coming, however, of a subtler sort. Dear Miss Wooler, her old headmistress, now middle-aged and graying but as honest and generous as ever, laid her hand over Charlotte's when she called, and delivered her dart thus: "Many will attack you, my dear, and I cannot say it will be without cause. But I wish you to know that nothing is changed between us, *despite all!*"

"I thought she would be gratified by my achievements!" Charlotte exclaimed later to Ellen. "I simply cannot understand what she is talking about! Must one pretend life is entirely different than it is, must one coat one's characters with whitewash until they are featureless, before one can win unstinted approval from *good* people?"

"Be comforted," said Ellen. "My family adored the book, and the young are on your side to a man—and woman! Tomorrow you will be assailed by winks, nudges, and heavy hints of adulation from none other than your old schoolmate Amelia Walker, who is wild to offer you her patronage—she is quite a grand lady these days."

"The praise of fools is no comfort at all," said Charlotte glumly. "Oh, this is dreadful, Ellen! Emily was right. I never realized I knew so many people, or that so many knew me! I never dreamt the entire district would read the book and connect it with me in this way. And now, oh, heavens! When *Shirley* appears, and people begin to recognize themselves in it, what then? It will be all over with me. What a fool I was not to set it in New Zealand, using Mary's colorful letters as a base! Then I might have been safe."

"Bear up, Charlotte, this is the price of fame—and fame, my dear, is just what you most need."

"Well, Williams. What do you think of it?"

The two publishers were seated in the small office in the back of the bookship at Cornhill, with the manuscript of *Shirley* between them on the desk.

Mr. Williams could see plainly that George Smith was disappointed, and a great flood of affection and protectiveness for their "little authoress," Charlotte Brontë, came over him.

"I think it a great achievement," he said, with such emphasis that Smith raised his eyebrows. His partner was so seldom emphatic. "Not merely—if that is the word—because of the heartbreaking circumstances under which she wrote it, but because of the nature of the book itself. She has taken to heart every informed criticism of *Jane Eyre*—"

"Too much so, possibly. The supposed 'coarseness' and 'sensations' castigated by the more conservative critics had, let us face up to it, a fair amount to do with its popularity."

"Nonsense! It was the conflicts, the depths of character, the grip she placed upon the sympathies of the reader. And in this second tale she does the same again. Did you not come near to weeping when Caroline struggles to subdue her unrequited love for Moore? And again, what originality—who since Shakespeare ever wrote of a girl like Shirley, so feminine and yet so soldierly, so high-principled and at the same time so free-thinking and independent? She is all I would like my own daughters to be. You know," he went on, to Smith's secret impatience, "I wrote to Miss Brontë recently, asking her advice about careers for them. I don't believe such a notion would have crossed my mind had I never known her; but she has taught me to realize that every woman has a right to independence. How might *she* have got on, lonely and isolated as she is, had Providence never given her courage to adopt a career? Well, my girls shall not have to depend on Providence, I assure you! I intend—"

"Yes, yes, Williams," interposed Mr. Smith, for the older man was drifting from the point. "But to the novel. Are you happy about the Yorkshire milieu? I find it a trifle dreary after the gothic background of *Jane Eyre*. Also, I fear the whole may be too work-a-day, too lacking in drama and excitement."

"The power of feeling will more than make up for that," said Mr. Williams firmly. "I found the details of locale most engaging."

"They are very specific, certainly, and, unless I mistake, she has lifted many more of her characters from life this time than last. My guess is that her days of anonymity are numbered."

"She will hate exposure . . . I wish one might spare her. . . . Yet the secret must out in the end, I suppose."

"Intriguing, Williams! What will those stiff, narrow Yorkshire folk make of it? What, by the bye, did our stiff, narrow Scot make of *her*?"

The firm had a new member, a small, dry, sandy-haired young man called James Taylor. He had been appointed to go to

Haworth on his way back from a visit to Scotland to collect the manuscript of *Shirley*.

"He said very little, except to express amazement at the remoteness and gloom of the place."

"And she?"

"After all her prior anxieties about her inability to entertain him suitably, she made no comment at all. I think all her thoughts are turned to our reaction to her manuscript. And there she sits now, anxiously waiting! Is it agreed that I write our warmest approval?"

"Yes," said Smith slowly. "Yes. It *is* a good book, I don't deny it. But not a great one. It is flawed somehow—"

"A flawed masterpiece," said Mr. Williams severely, "is not to be confused with 'a good book.' "

Shirley came out while Charlotte was still at Ellen's, but she did not receive her complimentary copies until she got back to Haworth.

Their covers pleased her, as always, and she wrote thanking Mr. Williams. But although she tried to await the reviews calmly, in fact she was in a fever of suspense. She knew that the ongoing career, on which she was depending to sustain her through the years to come, hung on the reaction to this all-important second book. Another anxiety was that she might let her publishers down. But the worst terror concerned her dawning realization that soon she would "walk invisible" no longer.

All she had done, believing no one she knew would ever read it, or if they did would not see the connection, she now saw as if through the eyes of all her acquaintances. The Yorkes in *Shirley* were close likenesses of the Taylors; the contemptible curates were all taken from real ones in the neighborhood—the least grotesque was actually a portrait of their own Mr. Nicholls! Charlotte shuddered when she thought of his reading it, recognizing himself, and knowing she had written it.

The first review that reached her, early in November, struck her like a pailful of iced water. She judged it ignorant, incompetent, flippant—yet for all that it wounded her deeply. She dared not show it to Papa, and so had to digest her sorrow and indignation alone.

"Were my sisters alive, they and I would laugh over the notice," she wrote to Mr. Williams. "But they sleep, they will wake no more for me, and I am a fool to be so moved by what is not worth a sigh."

Their deaths had left her with only a scant third of her former strength and resistance to harsh attacks from outside. Together the three of them had supported and sustained each other's morale; they had been safe, too, behind their *noms de plume*. Now she felt naked, vulnerable, exposed; she had dreams of being fastened in stocks in the market-place, with cruel, stupid people abusing her and hurling stones.

However, the first harbinger of critical opinion luckily proved unrepresentative. Most critics warmly approved, and those who did criticize often did so constructively. Charlotte had never craved blind adulation, but only wanted to be treated seriously by minds she could respect.

There was one which she actively longed to submit her work to for judgment, and that was Harriet Martineau, the famous writer and activist. Charlotte's awe for this great woman was such that at first, when Mr. Williams asked if there was anyone to whom she wished a copy of *Shirley* sent, she hardly dared suggest her name. Miss Martineau was unquestionably the greatest woman writer of her day. She deserved this epithet in all senses, to Charlotte's mind, for she was not merely famous from one end of England to the other and scarcely less well known in America; she was great because she had earned her renown through herculean efforts to improve society. She had not only reached the minds of many important men, in parliament and out of it, through her prolific writings, but had also influenced them to the extent of getting laws changed and so materially lessening the injustices and abuses from which so many poor and unrepresented people suffered. Now in her late forties, she had devoted all her adult life to the flaws in legislature, to publicizing, through a series of highly readable pamphlets, the sufferings which these weaknesses—in laws relating to education, agriculture, taxation, population, et cetera—laid upon the common people, and which the more prosperous had managed to ignore until Miss Martineau forced them to take notice.

She had written one novel, which Charlotte had enjoyed, but her main point of admiration was that at which her own gift diverged from Miss Martineau's. For she was all Charlotte would have liked to be—strong, fearless, independent, blazingly intellectual—and not only gifted as a writer, but determined to use the weapon of her pen in the service of humanity.

When Charlotte had first read of Miss Martineau's early life—a nervous, insecure, introverted childhood—she felt as if she were meeting herself as she had been at school. Since then she had felt a deep, awed longing to meet this woman—perhaps currently the most famous of her sex—face to face.

So she plucked up courage to have a copy of her book sent to her. Then she dwelt for several days on the idea of her receiving it, and her possible reactions. A woman so large-minded, humane, and free of bigotry would see nothing "disgusting" in Charlotte's humor, nothing "coarse" or "unwomanly" in her characterizations —of this she felt sure; and there was comfort in that, although she feared her work might be judged unimportant and inward-looking by someone whose whole life had been a bold crusade.

As the lonely evenings drew out and Charlotte sat alone, the thought of another visit to London took shape in her mind. The prospect of the long lonely winter frightened her; the stimulation of town offered at least a postponement.

"What do you think, Papa?" she asked Patrick. "Could you spare me? I shall not be gone longer than a week, or perhaps two."

He cogitated. "Go, my dear," he said at last. "You deserve it. But don't forget to write to me about all that you do, and especially the people you meet. You'll not avoid being shown off a little this time."

Charlotte looked at him sharply. What was this? Could this quiet, retiring father of hers be relishing the prospect of enjoying, at one remove, the social life of a celebrity? She suppressed a smile, and kissed his forehead. "I shall bring it all home to you, Papa."

chapter 2 HIGH-LIFE

Though the idea of a little high-life in London was appealing, the approach of the real thing was a formidable challenge, and by the time Charlotte—her box full of new dresses, all deep black for she was still in mourning, but at least not shabby—arrived at the Smiths' home where she was to stay, she was in a finely wrought-up state of nerves.

There had been some idea of her staying with the Wheelwrights, old family friends whose three daughters had been her pupils in Brussels, but when Mr. Smith heard of this he made his disappointment so apparent that the plan was hastily changed. Now when Mrs. Smith and her daughters, Eliza and Sarah, welcomed Charlotte into their elegant home, she felt at first very stiff and strange. It was obvious that young Mr. Smith had issued his womenfolk the most explicit directions as to how she was to be received, for the hostesses seemed fully as nervous as the guest. She was shown to a beautifully appointed bedroom, lit by wax tapers and a blazing fire, and they all twittered around her before an imperious signal from "Mama" abruptly cleared the room, leaving Charlotte alone. Clearly Mr. Smith had ordered them not to fuss her too much or be officious in her entertainment until she had settled in.

When the young man of the house himself returned from the city, and they all sat down to dinner, Charlotte began to reassess him. George Smith, son and brother, was an altogether warmer, more attractive person than George Smith, hardheaded publisher. Not that he lacked attractions in either role; tall, well-dressed, with warm, sagacious eyes and a virile dark beard, he had a dashingly handsome appearance. Seeing him as a figure in this lively family interior made Charlotte like him more; and in his presence the ladies relaxed and all of them felt more at ease. His affectionate way of teasing his mother and sisters soon had them all laughing, and despite her headache, Charlotte began to be confident that they would get on together and that the strain would not be too much for her after all.

The next few days seemed to her a positive kaleidoscope of new impressions and new experiences. The Smiths put themselves out in every way to amuse her. They took her to the theater, to the National Gallery, and, best of all, to a wonderful exhibition of Turner's paintings which made her forget everything—sorrows, apprehensions, nervousness—in the contemplation of a talent she could wholly admire.

The kindness of Mrs. Smith and her daughters soon thawed the ice of Charlotte's reserve; and her own unpretentious manners and deep gratitude had a similar effect on their first feelings of almost fearful deference. It was obvious to Charlotte that they knew who she was, but were far too well-bred to refer to it in any way—she only knew it because of the awed looks she caught in the eyes of the girls.

One person she seemed to see a lot of was James Taylor, the third member of the house of Smith, Elder. She had been unimpressed when he had come to Haworth to collect the manuscript.

His red hair, his freckled skin, and his "determined, dreadful nose" (as she wrote to Ellen) quite put her off. In fact, he repelled her; but because Mr. Williams obviously respected him, she did her best to overcome her aversion, though she and Mr. Smith sometimes made less-than-kind remarks about him privately.

She was dismayed to notice that Mr. Taylor seemed to like her. He made excuses to call at the Smith home, accompanied her on sight-seeing trips, took her arm as often as convention allowed and held it after convention decreed it should be released. The worst was his blunt attempt at sympathy for her recent losses. These raw wounds she could not bear to have touched, especially by one toward whom she could feel so little sympathy, and she was always glad to return to the gentler and more sensitive company of his two colleagues.

So it was with mixed feelings that she heard, after about a week, that her "swain," as Mr. Smith *would* call him, had been laid low by an attack of rheumatic fever. She was sorry for his sake, for he was not a bad little man, but she was still glad to have him out of her way.

One evening at dinner, George Smith casually mentioned that he had invited William Thackeray to dinner the following day, "together with some others, so that the Titan's formidable presence shall be watered down a trifle. Is this within our compact, Miss Brontë?" (They had agreed he should not show her off without her express permission.)

"I shall be honored," she said, summoning her courage. "There is only one thing." And she whispered to him, "The matter of my identity."

"Madam! You need not give *that* another thought."

Charlotte had already arranged to visit her friends the Wheelwrights next morning. Mrs. Smith's carriage drove her to Kensington shortly after breakfast.

The three Wheelwright sisters were on the doorstep to greet her. When she had last seen them they had been little girls and her pupils; now Laetitia was twenty-one, and Frances and Sarah-Anne (whom Emily had taught piano) were eighteen and fifteen.

They all kissed her, there in the street, and Sarah-Anne cried: "Why, Miss Brontë, see! Even I am taller than you!"

"I am suitably cowed," returned Charlotte.

The ensuing laughter eliminated any residual teacher–pupil shyness. Soon they were sitting together in the Wheelwrights' delightful, airy morning-room, drinking chocolate and "getting unbuttoned with each other," as Frances (the naughty one, as Charlotte recalled) put it.

There was inevitably some constraint, though, when they spoke of Emily.

"We were so dreadfully shocked to hear of her passing away," said Laetitia. "Both my sisters cried."

"For my part, I was somewhat surprised by how deeply I felt it," said Frances. Ignoring her elder sister's pointed look, she went on, "No, let me be frank. I was afraid of her when she taught me. She was so very closed in, and that made her seem stricter than she really was. Also, it must be said she lacked something in patience; but when I remember how little I practiced and how maddeningly slow my progress was in consequence, I can't blame her for that! But the truth is, her effect on me seems to have been deeper than I realized, for when I heard she was dead I could scarcely believe it, and I burst into tears as if she had been very close to me."

Charlotte cringed inwardly, waiting for the inevitable pain. But as the conversation went on, she found herself able to listen, and even join in, with no more than a twinge of the acute pangs she suffered when thinking about Emily in the solitude of Haworth. It actually seemed to help to talk about her with these fresh, healthy-minded young girls who viewed death with the wholesome incredulity it merited in creatures so distanced from it. Yet they could view it and speak about it, in connection with Emily, with an openness and lack of morbidity which Charlotte found oddly soothing.

And there was something else which modified her usual pain. The memories these girls had of Emily (and those she had of them) were all linked with the Pensionnat Héger in Brussels—the girls' finishing school where Charlotte and Emily had first been pupils and later teachers. Charlotte had her own memories of that time which—she was startled to find—were poignant enough, even now, to take the sharpest edge off her anguish about Emily.

For it was in Brussels, at that school, that Charlotte had fallen profoundly and devastatingly in love for the only time, with Monsieur Héger, the husband of the principal of the school. It was over now, of course—long over. He whom Mary had called her "little black professor," black of beard, black of hair, black (Charlotte had come to believe in her suffering) of heart, had killed it by neglect. Not that Charlotte had expected, nor wanted, more than "the crumbs from the rich man's table"—or rather, the rich woman's, for it seemed to her still that Madame Héger was blessed very far beyond her deserts. Charlotte, irresistibly brought, by the sight of these girls, to remember the whole bittersweet succession of events, suddenly knew that she would never wholly forgive Madame for her cruelty. What threat had Charlotte ever posed to Monsieur's beloved wife, the mother of his children? Yet Madame had ousted her from the school, torn her from the most innocent association with her master, and even when she was "safely" back in England, had (Charlotte was sure of it) basely intercepted her perfectly innocuous letters or otherwise prevented Monsieur from answering them. Thus she had brought about some of the worst misery of Charlotte's life, for Charlotte persisted in believing that a correspondence between her and Monsieur Héger would adequately have fed her love and prevented the slow withering of her heart.

Of course there was no question of easing *that* torment with frank and simple conversation. Now that Emily and Anne were dead, no one but Mary Taylor, far away in the antipodes, knew of her love, and Charlotte felt the safer for that. She tried never to think of Monsieur Héger; but that he lived on within her heart nonetheless was made plain at moments like this when some association revived her memories. One day, she thought as she sat there listening to the girls reminiscing about their schooldays, one day I will rid myself of him in the only way I can—by writing him out of my system.

Abruptly her deeply private thoughts were broken into.

"And now," said Frances, turning to her with a mischievous look in her eye, "that we are *fully* unbuttoned, I am going to ask Miss Brontë The Question."

Charlotte stiffened. Surely they could not guess—could not have divined her thoughts? By their giggles and by Laetitia's unconvincing attempts to bring them to order, Charlotte was reassured that the Wheelwright sisters were not thinking of Monsieur.

"We wish to know—*all* of us, including Laetitia, no matter how she pretends to be controlled on the point of curiosity—whether you are, or are not, Currer Bell."

Charlotte blushed deeply. The two younger girls pointed long fingers at her face and uttered shrieks of glee. "Look—look—look at her! Is any further answer needful? It's true then! Our teacher is the great Currer Bell!"

Charlotte pulled herself together sharply. "Nonsense," she said in her best schoolroom manner. "No such thing is to be said or dreamed of! Don't be absurd. Whatever put such a silly idea into your heads?"

"It is so obvious!" cried Laetitia, forgetting her reticence. "I spotted it first. Robert Moore's sister Hortense was a perfect portrait, to the life, of Mademoiselle Haussé who taught us at the Pensionnat! I recognized her instantly, with all her little quirks and fancies. You even quoted her in places. And I remember you once telling us the story about your sister's courage when the mad dog bit her, and she told no one but went straight away to the kitchen, heated an iron, and burned the wound. It was I who noticed the scar on her arm and asked you about it. Don't you remember? And the very same thing happened to Shirley! Oh, come, dear Miss Brontë, don't deny it to us. We won't tell, will we, girls?"

"Not if you *want* it kept secret," said Sarah-Anne wistfully, "though *why* you should wish to walk unknown, when you could be so famous that all London would be gazing at you, I cannot understand!"

"Not everybody likes to be gazed at," said Charlotte with a shudder.

"There! That's an admission!" exclaimed Frances. "Confess, confess!" And she and Sarah-Anne so far forgot dignity as to begin dancing round her, chorusing, until she threw up her hands and covered her ears.

"Enough, sit down now, you are behaving shockingly and upsetting our guest," said Laetitia sharply. "If Miss Brontë wishes to keep her secret, we shouldn't pester her. Good gracious, just look at the time! We must go and change for luncheon. It's very late, Miss Brontë—won't you stay and have a bite with us?"

But Charlotte was too flustered to think of eating. Besides, she had remembered that she was to meet her great idol, Mr. Thackeray, that very evening. The mere thought of that drove away any vestige of appetite.

By the time the carriage had returned her to the Smiths, luncheon was over. Assuring them that she had eaten, she hurried to her room to try and rest; but hunger had now returned and was added to her trials. She felt a headache coming on, compared with which her ordinary ones were trifling. Too restless to lie down, she went walking in the park, got lost, and by the time she found her way back through the bewildering cacophony of traffic she barely had time to change and tidy herself before she was called down to the drawing room.

Her agitation at the thought of meeting Mr. Thackeray was by now almost unbearable. She had once, all unwittingly, given him cause almost to hate her. By dedicating the second edition of *Jane Eyre* to him (after hearing that he had been moved to tears by her book) she had caused the tongues in the London salons to wag with all manner of wild surmises. Was the author of the book Mr. Thackeray's governess? Was Mr. Rochester based upon Mr. Thackeray himself—Mr. Thackeray, who, like Rochester, *had a mad wife*? Naturally Charlotte had not known this; the great man himself was obliged to tell her about it in a note of acknowledgment sent to Currer Bell in care of his publisher. Of course he had been large-minded enough to realize that she had harmed him unintentionally; doubtless he would not hold a grudge against her—even if he knew who she was—which he wouldn't, she concluded firmly. After all, hadn't Mr. Smith promised that he wouldn't?

By this time she felt quite faint with hunger. At home, supper was eaten at six—in London, not till eight or even later. Now it was seven, the doorbell was ringing, and Charlotte felt the drawing-room and its occupants whirling around her.

Did he know her? Would anything be said? All she wanted was to observe him from some hidden vantage point, drink in his wit and brilliance, absorb the overspill of his high moral purpose: in a word, worship him from a safe distance. The knowledge that this would be impossible in such a small gathering filled her with nervous dread.

"Mr. William Makepeace Thackeray."

The announcement caused an audible rustle among the ladies in the room, and George Smith, impeccable in evening dress, hurried to greet his distinguished guest. Charlotte, sitting in the remotest part of the room, clasped her hands in their little half-fingered, black lace gloves and felt the blood pulsing in her temples. There he stood, tall as a tree and broad as a church door, his strange features—like a face modeled in dough—marred with a cynicism she had not expected. Why, he was almost ugly! His satirical black eyes raked the room the moment he was clear of the door, and rested for one quizzical second upon her. Then he was engulfed by the bright satin dresses of the ladies, and Charlotte's moment of terror was over—for the time.

She had begged her host not to introduce her, and he did not; but when—not one instant too soon for poor Charlotte—they all rose to go in to dinner, the great man suddenly loomed before her.

"Shake hands," he said quietly.

He knows! thought Charlotte instantly, and wished the ground would give way under her—indeed, her knees threatened to do so. But she kept command of herself, and offered her tiny hand, which was swallowed, it seemed, to halfway up her arm by his enormous fist.

At dinner she kept very quiet, ate ravenously, and listened

acutely to the conversation. Mr. Thackeray kept throwing little knowing glances at her and trying to draw her out, but she could not manage anything like a sparkle. In listening to him, she found herself hard put not to be shocked at the degree of cynicism he showed. Was he speaking in jest or in earnest when he mocked religion and questioned the most fundamental tenets of domestic morality? He did it all in the wittiest and most brilliant vein, but it was not what Charlotte had looked for from the lips of the author of *Vanity Fair*, and she was a little scandalized. This, as much as her shyness and sense of awe, kept her silent, and she was painfully aware of the looks that Mr. Thackeray exchanged with his host which seemed to say, "What a little mouse it is! Are you sure there is no case here of mistaken identity?"

After dinner the ladies withdrew, and Charlotte had a short time to quiet her nerves before the gentlemen rejoined them. When they did, Mr. Thackeray strolled up to her and quizzed her with what seemed to her an entirely enigmatic remark, "Did not a *warning fragrance* announce my imminence, Miss—er—Brontë?"

She had not the least notion what he meant, and looked around desperately, catching as she did so a stiffening of Mr. Smith's features in the direction of the speaker which baffled her more than ever. It was only when kind Mrs. Smith leaned over to her with a smile she could not repress and said, "Mr. Thackeray is referring to the fragrance of *cigars*," that it came to Charlotte in a flash that he had been quoting from *Jane Eyre*. She flushed hotly, and with a gaucheness that later made her blush again, muttered something about its being a smell she did not mind. No one laughed, but the almost malevolent gleam in the eye of Mr. Thackeray was worse than laughter to her. She threw an accusing look at Mr. Smith, who had the grace to blush.

At last the party ended. Mr. Thackeray, after a further handshake, accompanied by a more kindly smile, departed, and Charlotte took her host to task.

"You told him!"

"My dear, dear Miss Brontë, I assure you—"

"He knew. Did not his allusion to Rochester's cigar prove it?"

Mr. Smith threw out his hands and attempted a winning smile.

"I was about to assure you that it was not my doing. The coteries of London have already seized upon your name, among others, as a possibility. And if your presence here led Mr. Thackeray to jump to a right conclusion, am I to blame?"

"Why did you give him that angry look when he was indiscreet? That argued some prior collusion between you."

"I may have begged him beforehand not to mention Currer Bell or his works—"

"That was tantamount to exposing me! And now no doubt he has gone straight to his club, where he is bandying my name about. . . . Oh, it is too mortifying!"

"How could you think such a thing? He will do nothing of the sort," Smith insisted, though privately he thought it extremely likely.

"And I behaved so stupidly before him. Oh! I am such a block in company."

"Nonsense, you were perfect. Nothing could be more charming, more intriguing than your quiet manners. The whole of London will soon be abuzz with you," he enthused, entirely forgetting caution.

Charlotte threw up her hands in wordless dismay.

But for her, the climax of her visit was yet to come.

"Miss Brontë, I bring news," said her host one day. "Harriet Martineau is in London. Ah! I thought that would interest you. She is staying with her cousin Richard in Westbourne Street."

"Is it possible I might meet her?"

"Well, now. I am, alas, unacquainted with her. But it would be perfectly proper for you to send her a note asking if you may call."

"How shall I sign myself?"

George Smith smiled mischievously. "If you sign yourself Miss Brontë, she will suppose you a mere curiosity-seeker and refuse to see you. If on the other hand you sign yourself Currer Bell . . ."

Charlotte was too excited to consider carefully the inevitable results of this course. In some part of her mind she had already acknowledged that her secret was out, and begun to adjust herself to the new situation. Some of Mr. Smith's impish spirit must have rubbed off on her too: the temptation to intrigue Miss Martineau was quite irresistible. So she wrote her a note and signed it with her *nom de plume*.

The response was immediate. By return messenger came an invitation to tea the following day at six. Charlotte did not fail to notice that although the note was addressed to "Currer Bell, Esq." it began, "Dear Madam."

At precisely six o'clock, Mrs. Smith's carriage deposited Charlotte on the front steps of Richard Martineau's house, and Charlotte, inwardly shaking but outwardly composed, rang the bell. A servant answered.

"I wish to see Miss Martineau. I have an appointment."

"Who shall I say, Madam?"

Charlotte had not foreseen this! "Miss—Brontë," she said faintly.

The servant preceded her majestically to the door of the drawing-room, threw it open, and announced, "Miss Brogden!"

Charlotte's sharp ear caught an agitated whisper from one of the women in the room: "No, no, it is Brontë—I have heard the name —they are of the Nelson family, I believe!" She looked toward the whisperer, but *she* could not be Miss Martineau. Ah! There she was—that tall, unconventional-looking woman with an ear-trumpet, gazing at her in undisguised astonishment.

She was as devoid of beauty as Charlotte herself, and about ten years her senior. Charlotte immediately recognized in her a kindred soul. Her fluttering pulse calmed instantly, as if she had come into some secure harbor; and without shyness or hesitation she walked directly to her and offered her hand.

"My dear Mr. Bell," said Miss Martineau solemnly, looking down at her, "this is a great honor."

"My real name is Charlotte Brontë."

"And may I now drop the ambiguity and greet you as a fellow authoress?"

"Pray do."

"I feel highly privileged to be let in to such a well-kept secret."

Charlotte smiled ruefully. "I begin to fear it is not much of a secret any longer."

Miss Martineau and her cousins entertained Charlotte very pleasantly, and after tea the two women were tactfully left alone. Miss Martineau, seated beside Charlotte on the sofa, looked down at her. Charlotte was the smallest woman she had ever seen, and beside herself seemed even smaller. A wave of protectiveness flooded warmly over the older woman. Charlotte was returning the look, but in her fine, glowing eyes—a feature so striking as to make her look, at moments, almost beautiful—there was an expression of the most touching appeal, almost of love. The deep black Quaker-like dress, the smooth wings of shining brown hair, the submissively folded hands, as delicate as a child's, all moved Miss Martineau inexpressibly; she recognized something of her former self, tortured by nerves, ill-health, religious oppression.

"You are in mourning," she said. "May I ask for whom?"

"For my sisters and my brother."

"Are you then the sole survivor of your family?"

"But for my father, who is now an old man."

Miss Martineau turned her head away. She had seen much suffering in the course of her researches—suffering had been, to an extent, her stock-in-trade; yet she had never become inured to it, and seeing it now, so evident to her perceptions though well disguised, she had much ado to keep her composure. She was startled to find herself wanting to cry.

Charlotte saw and rejoiced inwardly at this evidence of mutual sympathy, but she felt obliged to change the subject. "I'm glad of this opportunity to consult you," she said. "I have been distressed by some of the criticisms of my work—"

"Have not we all!"

"Only yesterday—"

"Oh, dear! *The Times*, of course. Savage brutes—I felt for you, though I did not know you then."

"It was touching how my host's whole family strove to keep the paper out of my hands. At last I realized it had been hidden, and why. I told my host's mother that I understood her motives, but that I would rather not be shielded. Dear Mrs. Smith acknowledged the concealment, and begged me to go out on our planned excursion before reading it . . . she feared the review might spoil my pleasure."

"And did it?"

"Yes, I'm ashamed to say it did. I held the paper up to hide my face, but I'm afraid Mrs. Smith noticed the tears of pain I could not hold back. It made it worse, reading it in the home of my kind publisher, for it emphasized my fear that such a severe review would impede sales—"

"You need not worry about that! The whole of London is buying it."

"Mr. Thackeray called in the afternoon. He never took his eyes off me. I felt sure he had come especially to see how I had taken the blow. I contrived to appear tolerably composed, but his strange, sardonic manner did nothing to soothe my feelings."

"No. Mr. Thackeray's presence is seldom soothing."

"It is not your sympathy I want, but your elucidation! The critics in general puzzle me much. I acknowledge they have treated me generously upon the whole—it would be churlish to complain—and yet some of their strictures do not so much anger as bewilder me. What am I to think when people accuse me of coarseness, impiety, unwomanliness? All these are anathema to me! I *cannot* see anything coarse or scandalous in *Jane Eyre!* What is there in it to shock anybody? In what manner is Jane irreligious or unmaidenly? My aim was the exact opposite! Tell me, am I blind to my own true nature? Am I betraying something deep in myself which I do not recognize but which others can perceive through my books?"

Miss Martineau was silent for some time. She understood that this strange little sprite of a woman had opened her heart to her in a unique fashion, partly through loneliness no doubt, but also because there had been, from the first, a mutual instinct of trust. She did not want to damage this budding intimacy between them, for she wanted Charlotte Brontë for a friend. Yet she was too wedded to forthrightness to begin friendship on a basis of false-hood.

"Madam," she said at last, "I will be truthful with you. God knows I'm much older than you and I have lived—as you never have—in what we call 'the world' in the French meaning: that is, the world of society, the world which sets itself up as the arbiter of fashion and morality. Certain modes of speech and writing have gained acceptance in this society as 'proper'—God save us! We've been lulled by the fact that most of our—shall I say—entertainers, novelists, speechifiers, essayists, journalists, et cetera, conform, largely through fear of ostracism, to these arbitrary standards. We've come to expect this conformity as if we had a right never to be jolted or shocked by having certain polite veils torn aside. Do you smoke? How stupid of me, of course you don't. Forgive me if I do."

To Charlotte's astonishment she produced, from an oriental-looking box on the table, a thin black cigar, which she proceeded to trim and light. Never having seen or even dreamt of a woman smoking, Charlotte felt shocked at first; but the scent of the cigar was so pleasingly exotic, the sight of Miss Martineau puffing at it so novel, that Charlotte's shock modified to fascination.

"It is a habit I acquired in the East. I once crossed the Sinai desert on camelback, and the beastly odor of those ignoble creatures, not to mention the need to keep the flies at bay, forced me to attempt the Bedouin remedy. This box was given me by a pasha whose harem I visited in Egypt . . . a paltry compensation for the hideous sights I witnessed there. I'll tell you all about it one day. But to get back to your writing.

"You and your sisters, knowing nothing of these rules I spoke of, put before us tales of things which exist—we all know they exist—but for which there are no acceptable words. Bastardy, for example."

Charlotte jumped. Miss Martineau smiled.

"Well, you see! If you had called Adèle a bastard in your novel, you would not have been surprised to be rebuked for coarseness.

But the fact is that the inhabitants of this self-protected world of which I spoke, of which the critics are the representatives, while they know that children can be born out of wedlock as the result of an intrigue between a reprobate and a woman of loose morals, do not wish to—no, I must not say that! Clearly, they *do* wish to read about it, but they cannot do so without saying that they find it outrageous. Just as I broke *your* personal rules of what is proper by saying the word I used just now, you broke polite society's rules by introducing the *fact* into your book, bringing this *fact* into the life not of your villian but of your hero, and allowing your heroine to learn of it from his own lips without it damaging her opinion of him. Even when Jane discovers that Rochester tried to involve her in the crime of bigamy, she loves him as much as ever and only leaves him because she believes it wrong to live in sin— *not* out of disgust that he tried to commit this crime. Her morals are not the morals of the polite world the critics inhabit, where such things may happen—nay, do happen—but are morally unacceptable. You accept Rochester; you tempt us to accept him; you dare to make him loveable, pitiable, strong, and masculine—in a word, a hero—and although you punish him by making him a cripple, you reward him with happiness at last. Are we to understand from this that such sins as his are not damnable in the eyes of God? That they will be forgiven, and heaven reached after passing through the purifying fires? *This* is what scandalizes, for Rochester is, by his deeds, a wicked man, and the wicked should die and go to hell—yes, to hell, Miss Brontë, for where do you show him repenting? You have gone counter to the teachings of the Church, and for doing so you must expect to be frowned upon."

Charlotte, who had kept her eyes fixed on Miss Martineau's throughout this long exposition, now said suddenly, "Yet you smile as you say so. What is your own view?"

"My own view is well known. I reject the Church and all its superstition and hypocrisy. I have freed myself of it. In the course of my life and my researches for my books I have seen what God allows, and I would not stoop to beg favors of a Being whose notion of justice to His children is so uneven—if God existed, He would be a monster of cruelty and partiality, and I find it insufferable to thank Him for being good to me when He lets millions, as worthy and far worthier than I, rot in misery. I prefer to believe that life is what we make of it, that we have a duty to follow our consciences and to help each other for our own sakes. That is why I loved your book, for Jane believes in goodness for its own sake; her uprightness is something she has developed from within, through hardship and loneliness; all the nightmares of her childhood—with which I felt the strongest kinship, incidentally—have not embittered but strengthened her. You may call her a Christian, if you wish. I call her a woman of deep, hard-won, independent and personal *principle*. Such a woman I admire more than any who is good through fear of divine retribution. And her love for and acceptance of Rochester—her whole relationship with him from beginning to end—accord perfectly with my ideas of what love should be. Except when she leaves him, of course—I would not have done that! Yet I respected that inner principle of hers so much by that time that I could only anguish, not quarrel with her about it."

"So you are saying the book *is* unchristian?"

"Yes. And all the better for it in my eyes."

Charlotte put her face into her hands and for a moment her companion thought she had made her cry. But when she looked up it was clear she was struggling to control a fit of wild laughter.

"Oh, dear, oh, dear!" she exclaimed, wiping her eyes under her spectacles. "Well, I don't know what to say or feel now! You offer consolation in such a strange form. It should distress me more than ever, and yet it delights me—and about my delight, too, I feel ambiguous and a little guilty! And are you truly a—an atheist?"

"Yes!" cried Miss Martineau, her eyes dancing with mischief. "Furthermore, I smoke cigars—I blaspheme—and I believe in women's suffrage! What have you to say now? Can you be friends with me?"

"Quite impossible! And yet—I am. I feel it, I know it. It is out of the question—and yet it is going to be. What am I to make of that?"

chapter 3 SOLITUDE AND SOCIETY

*I*t was hard to settle down to parsonage life again after London, although initially Charlotte returned to her remote abode with relief. Patrick was overjoyed to see her, and for days his routine was bent, if not broken, by his all-conquering desire to hear and hear again every detail of her trip—whom she'd met, what they'd said, where she had been, and how everyone had treated her.

This last seemed to dominate his thoughts. When he heard of Mr. Thackeray's intrusive visit to see how she had taken the unfavorable *Times* review, how he had watched her quizzically without offering sympathy, Patrick scowled. "Sensation-seeker! Ill-mannered fellow!" When Charlotte regaled him with a description of her last night at the Smiths', when at dinner they had entertained some of the most formidable critics in London, all of whom had treated her civilly and even with deference, his brow cleared and he rubbed his hands together with glee.

Because of his obsessive desire that she should be "appreciated," she found it quite impossible to share with him the bitter draft she had to swallow in January. Of all critics, she had been most anxious to hear the opinion of G. H. Lewes, whose commendation of *Jane Eyre* had given her such encouragement. Since then they had had some correspondence, and she had gone so far as to stress, in a letter to him just before *Shirley* appeared, that what mattered to her was that he should give her work honest treatment *without reference to her sex*. But what should she find, on eagerly tearing the wrapper off the *Edinburgh Review*, but a long notice which was nothing but references, and reproaches, and even labored jokes on the subject of women writers in general and Currer Bell in particular. Words such as "coarse," "over-masculine," "rude," "harsh," "vulgar," even "flippant" splashed the lengthy article as with vitriol. He culminated the whole outrageous attack by quoting what Schiller wrote of Madame de Staël: "This person wants everything that is graceful in a woman, and nevertheless, the faults of her book are altogether womanly faults. She steps out of her sex—without elevating herself above it."

Charlotte laid down the periodical feeling ill. Her face was cold, her throat dry. She did not cry as she had at *The Times*'s effusion. She was too angry to cry. If Mr. Lewes had stood before her at that moment, she felt she could have struck him—yet was this impulse not a sort of confirmation of all the evil things he had said about her? Oh, but it was infamous! Was this man not her sworn friend and admirer, and was he not—what was far more to the point—a rebel against convention, a man emancipated from the narrow constrictions of what Miss Martineau had called "the world"? If *he* could not rise above the thick filter of antifemale prejudice that prevented so many from clearly and fairly judging her work, what hope had *she* of ever gaining rational appreciation, now that the secret of her sex was known?

She flung herself at her desk and penned him a single line: "I can be on guard against my enemies, but God deliver me from my friends."

For several days she raged inwardly, longing for someone to share her indignation, to dilute it with mockery or sympathy. The first anniversary of Emily's death had only recently been got over ... a whole year gone by, a year she should be able to take satisfaction in, and yet the sharpness was not blunted, the longing not one whit mitigated. At moments like this, when she *needed* her sisters for something specific, it seemed utterly impossible to believe that a cry, loud and desperate enough, would not reach and summon them to her side. "Listen, only let me read you what this so-called enlightened male is not ashamed to have printed! The superiority, the *stupidity* of men beggars all belief!" How easily she could imagine Emily's snort of "Fool!" and Anne's "Don't take it to heart, love, he is not worth it." But it was not real. They were gone....

At last she summoned Ellen, who swiftly came, as always when Charlotte needed her and let her need be known. She was escorted up the lane from the top of the main street (the cabby who had brought her from Keighley Station would not trust his conveyance on the narrow cobbled lane) by Mr. Nicholls, who happened to be paying one of his oddly frequent calls on his superior. Charlotte, who was watching from the window, noticed how easily the curate shouldered Ellen's heavy box, and the courteous way he handed her through the narrow gate and up the front steps. It was seldom enough that Charlotte noticed anything about him. After so many years, his massive, rather dour presence about the parsonage and neighborhood scarcely impinged on her consciousness; yet now she thought, as if surprised, "He is a good man in his way, and has nice manners . . . yet fancy Ellen smiling at him so gratefully, as if curates were not all of a piece!"

A gloomy tribe, she had always thought them, smug, and priggish—all except dear Willie Weightman. Poor, doomed Willie, dead now these eight years, yet still shining from afar, a bright little lamp in the dark halls of her memories. She saw Mr. Nicholls's broad black back retreating to the gate, saw him turn there unaccountably and gaze back at the house. But the doorbell was jangling and Charlotte, running to greet Ellen, forgot the dead and the living curates.

They were girls again together, sitting on the hearthrug drying their hair and gossiping. Charlotte actually forgot about Lewes. They talked instead about Mary Taylor.

"How she mocks us in her letters!" exclaimed Ellen. "Even her sympathy for my dependent situation is galling. She offers me all manner of advice, on how to 'get my living' and so forth, knowing full well that nobody, not even she herself, could take it in England. Why else did she leave? In the last letter I had from her, she warmly recommends me to join her in New Zealand if you please, and take up a trade—she seemed particularly to recommend taking in *washing* as the best paid, the least unhealthy, and the freest occupation for a woman, at least in England."

"She once talked to me about our opening a shop together. I thought it a joke at the time. Now I wouldn't be at all astonished if she really did it."

"Nor I! And I'll tell you something else. My namesake, Mary's cousin Ellen, is thinking of joining her, and speaks quite seriously of shopkeeping as a possible joint enterprise. How can she contemplate it? Did Mary write to you about the earthquake? Half the houses in Wellington were brought down by it. And then there are the Maoris—one might as well be in darkest Africa! Of course Mary admits that of cultured society there is none, and in that at least we might be allowed to feel we have the edge on her independent and adventurous life. But even that small satisfaction she undermines, saying 'It's all my eye, seeking society without the means to enjoy it.' "

"She is right in that," said Charlotte emphatically. "When I see what the earnest courtship of society has wrought upon a giant like Mr. Thackeray, fairly bringing him low in many respects, I want none of it, even if I had the means, as he has. The greater the means, the greater the downfall!"

"Not that Mary would understand that. She is not interested in money anyway. Her description of her home, with the bench-seats and fires built on the earth floor, and all her absorption with the buying of cows and the getting of calves. . . . It's a marvel to me how she stands the crudity of the life."

"I admire her greatly for that. *I* could not put up with such a want of comfort, even for independence."

Ellen could not help glancing around the humble dining-room where they sat, with its plain gray walls and cold flagstone floors. Even now that Charlotte had put up some crimson curtains where before there had been only shutters, the room, the whole parsonage, was stark, bare, and comfortless indeed by comparison with Ellen's elegant home and those of her married brothers. She could almost as soon imagine living in Mary's pioneer shack as in this remote, cramped, Spartan house, especially now it was so sadly silent and empty. She had not noticed its simplicity so much in the old days when Anne, Emily, Branwell, and that sweet young curate Willie had filled the little place with bustle and music and laughter.

"I see Mr. Nicholls is still with you. He has lasted longer than most, hasn't he? How do you get on with him?"

"Well enough. He at least has the merit of unobtrusiveness, and he is a great help to Papa."

"When I met him I detected in him some interesting germs of goodness."

"If shameless bigotry is the same as goodness, I agree with you. He is a very tyrant against any who diverge by a hair's-breadth from the straight and narrow path of Anglicanism."

"Ah! So he is Mr. Macarthey in *Shirley*? The one who is all diligence, charity, and rationality till it comes to burying an unbaptized fellow-creature in consecrated ground, or however you put it?" Ellen shook her head. "You're a brave spirit, Charlotte. What if he reads it? Will not relations be very awkward, even though you treated him more kindly than the others?"

"Horrors! But he surely won't. Mr. Nicholls, reading novels? He would as soon be caught dancing in our graveyard at midnight or putting gilded candlesticks upon our altar!"

"Yet you chose his middle name for your *nom de plume*. That argues some respect for him."

"It argues the opposite. We did it out of irreverence, knowing how he would disapprove of parsons' daughters producing books of poetry."

Ellen sighed. No romance there—a pity, for on the other side there was feeling, Ellen had long sensed that. She wondered if Charlotte truly did not know.

"So what of Mr. Smith and James Taylor?" But Charlotte would have none of that either.

"No doubt Mrs. Smith is keeping a sharp eye on me, as upon every woman to whom her precious son pays the least attention. But if you could see the elegant beauties who surround him, you would soon put your notions back in your pocket. I marvel his mama can suppose him so strange in his tastes as to afford me a second glance in that way. As to 'the little Scot'—he was very attentive, it's true—and now I'm far from him, I confess to thinking more kindly of him. He is fearfully intelligent and sagacious and puts on most masterful airs, as if he were one of the lesser curates trying to ape Mr. Rochester . . ." They both burst into giggles. "But Ellen, when I am near him, I can scarcely abide him somehow, so nothing could come of it."

"So you entirely discount romantic prospects. Therefore I must ask about your career, which you notice I—unlike Mary—am still old-fashioned enough to put second. Will you begin writing another book?"

"I don't think so. I have so little material. I've exhausted Brussels—I've exhausted Yorkshire. What else is there?"

"London?"

Charlotte smiled. "Well . . . watching the Smiths and their circle, several little seeds were sown. Whether they will germinate is another thing."

"And apart from that? How do you foresee your life?"

Charlotte was silent, staring into the fire.

"As a protracted emptiness," she said at last.

"Fie, Charlotte! Imagine what Mary would say if she heard you! You are famous now, all doors could be open to you. Have you not received invitations?"

"Oh . . . yes. Miss Martineau kindly said I may visit her home in the Lake District. I will probably not go, but it is pleasant to think about. And then someone called Sir James Kay-Shuttleworth this morning sent me an invitation to his home in Gawthorpe."

Ellen pricked up her ears at this name, which she knew well as among the most illustrious in the district. Sir James was a baronet, no less, having earned his title rather recently for services to the ministry. Before that he had had a remarkable career as a surgeon, from which he had branched out into public life, taking an energetic interest in education in its broadest sense. Only a short time previously, however, his health had given way under the strain of his many activities and he had now been ordered to take life more quietly. This in turn had obliged him—since to live in idleness or retirement would have been anathema to him—to cast about for interests which would not overtax his strength. The chief of these was celebrity-hunting.

Ellen knew something of his reputation, and slyly said, "Gawthorpe Hall is only ten miles away, as the crow flies. He could launch you in society, Charlotte."

Charlotte laughed outright and resumed brushing her hair.

"Oh, really! As if I wanted to be launched in society, as if I could bear the thought of it! I would do almost anything to avoid such a fate, as you well know, you minx. I declined as neatly as I knew how, and I pray that *that* would-be sponsor at least will desist."

"From what I have heard of the gentleman, he will not be so easily put off. Did you employ your poor health as an excuse?"

"I believe I did mention it—"

Ellen hugged herself. "Then you may expect to be visited momentarily, for he is a doctor by profession and your refusal on those grounds will challenge the physician in him as strongly as your fame challenges the lion-hunter."

"I shall take to the moors."

"That won't help you! I'll live to see you a glittering star in the London firmament—oh, what news to tell Mary in my next letter!"

"I shall live quietly here until I die."

"We shall see. Meanwhile, even here you may not live as quietly as you wish. I had a letter this morning, too—from our vicar at Birstall, who wishes me to find out from you by stealth 'the secret of the company he has got into.' It's no use looking innocent! He has recognized the excellent portrait of himself in *Shirley*—'black, bilious, of dismal aspect' et cetera. You blush now, as well you may! But he is not offended. He simply wishes to be able to crow over fellow-victims."

Charlotte sat dumbly, staring at her. Ellen put back her head and rocked with laughter. Then she shook her finger at her friend. "My guess is, it is coming home to you, Charlotte, with the speed of a tornado! Brace yourself, for this quiet roof above our heads is about to be blasted away, leaving you crouched under the great peering eye of the world like a rabbit in a ploughed-up burrow!"

Indeed, only a few days after Ellen's departure, Martha Brown came puffing and panting into the quiet parlor, her red face shining, her eyes wide and mouth agape.

"I've heard such news!" she began.

"What about?"

"Please, ma'am, you've been and written two books, the grandest books that ever was seen. My father heard it at Halifax, and Mr. George Taylor and Mr. Greenwood and Mr. Merrall at Bradford, and they are going to have a meeting at the Mechanics' Institute, to settle about ordering them."

Charlotte fell into a cold sweat. "Hold your tongue, Martha, and be off!" she cried with quite unwonted asperity. Martha turned tail and fled to the kitchen, where she could be heard braying out the news to Tabby, and soon they both tiptoed back to peep through the half-open door at her, marveling, as if she were translated into some incredible wonder whose like they had never seen before.

They will all read them now, thought Charlotte in utter panic. God help, keep, and deliver me!

And read them they all did, all who could read, and soon the whole district was buzzing with the fame of the parson's daughter.

Martha relentlessly brought her reports, braving her silence or her snappish reactions.

"Father bought *Jane Eyre* and lent it to Mr. Nicholls, our lodger. He fair ate it up, wouldn't come to meals, wouldn't go to bed, two whole nights and half a day he were at it. Then he cried out for t'other, and he's to have it next week—"

"Much good may it do him! Begone, chatterbox, I am busy."

But her guilty nerves gave her no peace until, a week later, Martha was back with the next installment. "Eeh, our mam is that worried about poor Mr. Nicholls! She fears he's gone wrong in his head. He's sitting up in his room above t'parlor, roaring wi' laughter every other minute, clapping his hands and stamping on t'floor like any madman. She's afeard to take his meals up to 'im, and any road he never touches 'em."

"He's *laughing?*" asked Charlotte, utterly astonished. "Mr. Nicholls?"

"Aye!—fit to split himself."

Here was news she had not looked for! And soon Mr. Nicholls was striding up to the front door, with a sinister parcel under his arm. Charlotte fled in panic to her room, but before long she was amazed to hear Mr. Nicholls's sonorous voice in Papa's study below, and there was no note of complaint evident in it. Charlotte crept to the bottom of the stairs, and listened incredulously. Mr. Nicholls was reading aloud a passage from *Shirley* dealing with the maligned curates, and both clerics were choking with mirth!

"Oh, that bad girl, that bad, bad girl!" cried Patrick hilariously at last, and Charlotte could picture him wiping his eyes and hear him blowing his nose. "She never had patience for the breed! I well recall one day when we had some pair or trio of 'em to tea, and they were holding forth in carping vein such as she has them do in those pages, while she was sitting there dispensing dainties and endlessly refilling cups, and of a sudden she rose up and surveyed them with unveiled contempt and said, 'I'll sit here no longer to hear Yorkshire maligned. Those who so scorn the district that gives them bread had better quit it speedily and find lodging in more salubrious climes—if any can be found to receive them.'

What a fluttering amid the clerical doves succeeded her departure from the table! Such tuttings and splutterings and clatterings of cups in saucers! Such meaningful looks of reproach in my direction! Yet I could not blame her—they were indeed insufferable." There was a slight pause, and then the old man added, "But she exceeds bounds in caricaturing *you*, my dear fellow. *You* have been our comfort and support through these troubled years, and deserve better of her."

Charlotte caught her breath in shame, for it was perfectly true. She had to some degree lumped Mr. Nicholls together with the rest of the tiresome tribe of curates, while in truth he had been very kind. His regular calls during Emily's illness came back to her, and the fact that in all weathers he had never failed to take the dogs for their daily walk—an act of charity which had done much to ease Emily's mind at the time, and relieved Charlotte of a tedious duty.

But Mr. Nicholls, far from bearing a grudge, took the whole thing in wonderfully good part.

"Oh, never mind it, sir! I am flattered she found anything in me worth lampooning. I believe she has immortalized me, and what man minds that?" He paused and added more quietly, "I never thought her to have taken sufficient notice of me to have drawn me so plain. I shall take her implied rebukes to heart. It may be that I *am* too rigid in my attitude to unorthodoxy—unhinged for a week by an invitation to tea with a Dissenter—dear me! I must mend my ways."

"You suit me well enough as you are, my boy," said Patrick gruffly.

There was no reply, and for the first time the strange and bizarre notion came to Charlotte that it might be *herself* that Arthur Nicholls aimed to suit. Though she was much relieved not to have hurt him, she hoped heartily that her notion was prompted by vanity alone. Yet she knew vanity was not among her weaknesses, and intuition high among her strengths.

Ellen had been quite right about Sir James Kay-Shuttleworth. He was not a man to take any woman's "no" for an answer. Very shortly he was on the doorstep in person with his lady, pressing Charlotte to step into his carriage and return with them forthwith to Gawthorpe Hall. When Charlotte persisted in backing off, Patrick proved himself an unexpected ally to the baronet.

"Certainly you must go, my darling, it will do you good!"

"But, Papa—I have told Sir James, I cannot leave you—" she began, making passionate eye-signals to him, which he blandly ignored.

"Nonsense! I can manage capitally. Take her, sir, give her a holiday, show her new things! And you can 'bring them home' to me, my dear," he added with a meaning look.

So it was settled, and Charlotte, reluctant, nervous, almost resentful, went off to visit these total strangers.

In the event it was not as oppressive and exhausting as she had feared. The Kay-Shuttleworths made her welcome in a very unpretentious way, and since Sir James enjoyed nothing more than holding forth about himself, Charlotte was not called upon to do much talking—she had only to listen, and very interesting it all was.

"He was a pioneer in education, Papa," she told Patrick on her return. "He believes all must be radically changed. Charity and science are not enough, he says, to cure poverty and disease—only education on a universal scale will have any effect. He's worked among the poorest classes as a doctor and he believes every child must be educated, that illiteracy must be wiped out. Indeed, it is right—why should children in poorhouses not be taught? One thing he did, though, which I was not happy about. In attempting to bring about reforms in a pauper institution in the south about ten years ago, he insisted that children be separated from adults, including their parents, before being taught a trade, for Sir James believes that living with adults of that class depraves them. Surely, I said, there are good and tender parents among them who must grieve if their children are taken from them? But he replied that for the general good there might be no exceptions. And indeed his results were so beneficial upon the whole that the Privy Council set up a national Committee on Education, of which Sir James was appointed First Secretary. He has traveled a great deal to collect ideas from abroad and in fact worn himself out to the point of serious ill-health with his endeavors."

"How does the Church view him?"

"With suspicion and hostility, I'm afraid, Papa. He has promoted special schools to train lay teachers, and this of course might tend to remove mass education from the hands of the Church."

"Does he advocate this? Does he realize its implications?"

"I didn't like to ask him. But he is too intelligent not to."

Patrick shook his head. "These reformers often fail to look ahead to the logical ends of what they instigate," he said. "Lay education for the poor can only weaken established religion and be to their ultimate detriment, however noble the aims of a man like your new friend."

"I wouldn't presume to call him that, Papa."

"Why not? It is very clear he wishes to be so. Did he treat you courteously, my dear? Did he behave as one who realizes your great worth?"

Charlotte smiled, and patted his hand. "Of course, Papa."

"Tell me! Tell me what he said that showed he appreciates that however great a man he may be, you are his equal!"

The Kay-Shuttleworths followed up Charlotte's visit by an invitation to participate in the London season as their guest. Charlotte shrank from such a prospect. But her father was growing addicted to these heady doses of vicarious aggrandizement, and would not easily allow her to forego them.

Charlotte prevaricated and the winter dragged on. The heart-warming enthusiasm for her work which waxed stronger and more exuberant among her own and neighboring villages did something to cheer her (the sexton was by now earning half-crowns by pointing her out to visiting celebrity-hunters in church). Mr. Williams continued to send boxes of books which more than anything else alleviated her solitude. And there was always the postman, with his life-bringing offerings from the outside world.

Yet despite all this, Charlotte felt the emptiness of the parsonage more and more keenly. The blustering storms, buffeting the little stone house unmercifully, struck a gray and gloomy response in her mind and sought out weak places in her health as they sought out cracks in the masonry and loose fittings around the doors and windows. Sitting by the dying fire in the evenings, wrapped in her black shawl, with her fragile hands masked in mittens and still icy due to her poor circulation, she would lower her book and listen to the rampaging wind and to the ticking clock which fought its way through during lulls—the eternal, merciless ticking away of time. Youth—gone—loved ones—gone—work—done—naught—to come. So the remorseless refrain went on. Sometimes the sense of hopelessness and loneliness was so acute that she wished that the specialist she had consulted (at her father's pressing insistence) while in London, had not been so reassuring as to the soundness of her lungs. More often she would strain her ears through the desolate sounds besetting them, trying to hear Anne's and Emily's voices calling her from the moors. She knew the futility, the morbidity of this effort, and was frightened of the habit, yet it grew on her.

Patrick saw her misery, but could not think how to ease it. He was too old now to change his ways, to take his meals with her or sit with her for more than an hour or so in the evenings. He felt he was doing his utmost in urging her to accept opportunities to visit away from home, and considered this a sacrifice on his part, not acknowledging the satisfaction which accrued to him. Besides, he was busy about his parish, and his own health was precarious. He spoke about his concern to his curate.

"What am I to do, Nicholls? She is so apt to sink into despondency. I worry ceaselessly that the delicate state of her nerves will prey upon her frail physique. How can I cheer her?"

Arthur Nicholls was silent for some time and then said, "Perhaps if she could be transported back in time, from the recent past which so oppresses her, to the more distant. Have you any mementos of your youth that might catch at her imagination?"

"I have some letters," said Patrick slowly. "From—her mother. I have never shown them to anyone . . ."

"Perhaps the time has come when they may be helpful."

So Patrick put the small, treasured packet of letters from his Maria into the hands of their only surviving child, and she read them, and was immeasurably touched and, for the time being, lifted up, for she found in these sweet love-letters a fitting echo of the mind which had helped form her own. There was sadness too, that that mind was no more to be known, but for a little while at least Charlotte was relieved of the crushing pressures of her own immediate sorrows.

She knew that if she were ever to write another book she must bestir herself, get out of this place, so empty, not only of what had been, but of any new stimulus whatever. She even wished to go. But she felt, as winter drew into spring at last, that she had no reserves of physical or moral energy left which would be sufficient to sustain her away from her own dismal but undemanding surroundings.

One day in late April she went walking on the moors with the dogs. It was the first time she had done so for months, partly because of the cold, partly due to her reluctance to face the familiar scenes of her childhood, each detail of which would remind her of Emily—or the wide sky and distant views which would cry out the name of Anne. But she could stay indoors no longer, and force of habit led her over the sheep-tracks she had trodden with her sisters until she reached, after an hour's walk, the stone bridge over the beck which had been Emily's special sanctuary and playground. There she sat down on a boulder and gazed at the stream, rushing over its stony bed in spring spate, trying to conquer her sorrow and summon up the power to do what had to be done if she were to go on living.

She knew that if she went up to London as the guest of Sir James and Lady Kay-Shuttleworth she would suffer, in some ways, more than she was suffering now. The infliction of strangers—especially of a sophisticated breed, with their epigrammatic style of conversation and their sharp, sly wit demanding constant ripostes—was an enervating torment to her; she could never be at ease except among those who spoke plainly and intelligently and who liked her for herself. Yet perhaps she was not meant to be at ease. Perhaps this kind of agony was essential to creativity, and in creativity, she recognized clearly, lay her only salvation. The hard road to it must be taken, or she would stagnate, rot away in this place which she had once dwelt in as securely as in her own skin. She must break forth and endure so that she might write, and save herself.

The seeds for a new book, sown in the Smith household, had not germinated, but lay dormant in her brain. She felt some invigorating infusion was needed to bring them to life—perhaps another look at that alien world of London society would do it. But she could not face the pressures Sir James would surely put on her if she placed herself under his wing. Better by far would be another quiet sojourn with the Smiths, who knew her limitations and peculiarities and would protect her from too much exposure.

She wrote a letter, not to George Smith himself, but to James Taylor, with whom she had corresponded intermittently throughout the winter. His letters were so sympathetic that she had allowed herself to forget his repellent person, and confide in him some of the secrets of her loneliness and inability to raise herself above her losses. She knew what would happen. The letter would be shown to George Smith, who would speak to his mother—and sure enough, very soon an invitation arrived which she was doubly free to accept, due to a fortuitous attack of illness suffered by her would-be patron, Sir James. So she traveled down again to London.

Now she admitted to herself that she was seeking material for a novel. She spent every moment in company actively observing, listening, recording. Her wide eyes followed George Smith about, alert to each mannerism, each vocal inflection; she knew she would use him, probably as a key-character, and she meant to use his mother too and so watched her likewise. This would have caused Mrs. Smith some discomfort had she noticed it, but she was far too concerned at what she took to be this unprepossessing little spinster's intense interest in her son: those watchful eyes seemed to her to indicate doglike devotion. So when George suggested, in his authoritative way, the "excellent plan" that Charlotte should accompany him and his sister Eliza to Edinburgh, whence they were shortly going to fetch their younger brother from school, Mrs. Smith could hardly conceal her agitation. Charlotte, of course, saw this and interpreted it rightly.

"I think I had better not," she told her publisher in private. "Your mother is distressed at the idea."

"My mother is not infrequently distressed by my ideas, but she has learned to allow me my head. *You* don't find the plan objectionable, I hope?"

"My dear Mr. Smith—"

"I have had enough of Mr. Smith. You are to call me George."

"George, then. The prospect of a visit with you to *China* would not raise the slightest negative thought in my mind. You and I understand each other. I am only concerned lest your mother should—*mis*understand."

"Will you allow me to worry about that? Come to Edinburgh. You will love it, I promise."

"May I think about it? There is my father to consider, too"—but she knew Papa would urge her to go. And indeed, the prospect was alluring. Though she had no romantic illusions about George, to be with him, unencumbered by his mother's keen-eyed presence, for several days appealed to her.

Meanwhile there were other preoccupations. James Taylor came calling. One look at him in the flesh and the warm feelings accumulated by a winter's correspondence dissipated, leaving a cold, shrinking indifference. But there was no avoiding being squired around London by him, and some of his entertainments did not fail to please. He took her, for instance, to the zoo, and, mindful of Papa waiting eagerly at home, she wrote a long letter about all the animals. But for herself, she was more gratified by a visit to the Houses of Parliament and, one Sunday, a glimpse caught of her old hero—now old indeed—the great Duke of Wellington, attending service in St. James.

All these visits passed off pleasantly enough. But there were three ordeals which she had to pass through. The first was a visit Mr. Thackeray paid her.

She begged George to stay at her side throughout the interview, which he was glad to do, for he regarded it as a meeting of great minds and looked to hear much that was brilliant and memorable. Instead he heard something uncomfortably like a quarrel.

"What the deuce does she mean by it?" Thackeray asked him afterward, mercifully sounding more sardonic than annoyed. "She takes up the posture of an austere little Joan of Arc, riding down upon us from her scouring northern clime, reproaching us with every look and word for our easy lives and easy morals. Did you hear how she took me to task about my 'frivolity'? And while I yet reeled from that thrust, I must needs be asked by that—that—that little black flame of rectitude if I am aware of my *mission*. My mission, forsooth! I declared to her roundly—you heard me, Smith! —that I acknowledged no mission. I am a teller of tales, not a pricker of consciences. Let her thrust upon someone else the horrid burden of crusading!"

"You put her down too roughly, just the same," Smith found courage to say. "To have such a woman at *my* feet, wishing me to step up onto a pedestal for her to admire, would not bring out such a devil of perversity in me as you displayed."

Thackeray bridled, his huge white hand on his breast. "I? I?"

"Certainly! You mocked her unmercifully, turning her earnestness back with the most wicked levity and parrying her solemn reproofs with cynical jests."

The satyr's eyebrows went up, and George thought he had gone too far. But then the big pudgy face broke into something like a schoolboy snicker. "Serve her right! She brought out the villain in me, instead of the gentleman I longed to be to her. Damn me, I like the creature! I adore her work and I want her to admire me. But she must not put upon me the necessity of writing tracts, spouting literary sermons, and modeling my life too closely upon the saints!"

Charlotte, for her part, anathematized Thackeray to Ellen as "a great Turk and a heathen, whose excuses for his literary shortcomings are worse than the crime itself." But her former worship, though tempered sadly by the reality, was not quite done away with, and she was extremely flattered when he invited her to dine at his house.

"You'll be the guest of honor," he said bluffly. "Let's see how Joan of Arc will take on a whole contingent of the devil's advocates."

Prior to this ordeal, however, came one only slightly less onerous—a luncheon party given by the Smiths.

For once, Charlotte was in form—perhaps because, having crossed swords with the Titan and not been worsted, her blood was now up. And it was as well for her that it was, because the first person to arrive was none other than G. H. Lewes, the critic whose notice in the *Edinburgh Review* had so wounded and outraged her.

At first, she contrived rather obviously to ignore him. But whether by accident or mischievous design, George had seated her opposite to Lewes at the dinner table. And there a thing happened which was so unexpected and so strange that instead of being able to summon up indignation to aid her in dialogue, tears rose to her eyes and she could scarcely say a word. For the man whom she had called "at once enthusiastic and implacable, sagacious and careless," the man who had made her want to strike him, stared boldly out at her from a face quite intolerably like her sister Emily's. The nose, the eyes, the cast of mouth—she felt that whatever he did or wrote, she could never hate him.

Yet a moment later she almost did.

Noticing nothing of her sudden stifling distress, he leaned over the table and remarked roguishly, "There ought to be a bond of sympathy between us, Miss Brontë, for we have both written naughty books."

Mrs. Smith gasped and looked quickly at her son, who closed his eyes. In tones of ice, and for once making her voice clearly heard the length of the table, Charlotte replied, "You mistake me for some *masculine* author, Mr. Lewes. I have never stooped to the penning of such a book as you describe. Those who properly comprehend a woman's nature, as distinct from merely being able to detect and expose it, could never confuse what you are pleased to term 'naughtiness' with the workings of love. Such confusion betrays in you something close to crassness."

George Smith bowed his head to hide a grin of pure delight. His mother covered the unfortunate contretemps somehow and by the end of the luncheon Lewes had contrived to smooth down Charlotte's ruffled feelings to some extent. He never knew that only his cast of features, and not his winning tongue, had made this possible.

But the worst was to come—the purgatory of Thackeray's dinner-party.

For once in her life Charlotte was determined to look nice. She could do little about her clothes, for she was still in mourning and considered that the jet and frills and laces which usually embellished mourning-garb in society absolutely negated the somber feelings which underlay the convention. But she had carefully noted the fashion in which ladies wore their hair. Her smooth style, parted in the center and drawn back on either side was unexceptionable, but dull; however, if she should fold a plait around her head, it would add something of smartness and perhaps reduce by a little her perpetual awareness of how plain she looked.

So she wrote to Ellen and asked her to buy her an artificial plait (her own hair being too fine and too short to supply her need). But when it came, it did not quite match, so Charlotte wrote to her again and asked this time for some brown satin ribbon. From this she could make a plaited crown which would not look as if it were supposed to be her own, but would simply, she hoped, enhance her appearance.

For the occasion she wore her best dress of barege, which was not entirely black but had a faint pattern of green moss. Like all her dresses it fastened to the throat and to the wrists with little buttons and its crinoline underskirt was of modest spread. She wore little half-fingered black lace gloves and carried an old-fashioned reticule. She considered removing her glasses—would that be an affectation? No. She would do it, and carry them with her to put on if she needed to see someone in particular.

George was to accompany her. He inspected her before they stepped into the carriage. More than ever, his sympathies were deeply touched by her frail little figure in the childish dress and especially by the efforts she had made to look pretty when—alas!— she never, never could. The brown satin plait was a painfully obvious sop to fashion, yet no more stylish than anything else about her; altogether she looked as plain and countrified, and even a touch eccentric, as ever. But he put his hands upon her little bird-shoulders, smiled straight into her eyes, and cried heartily, "You look splendid!"

"Do not say 'pretty' or I will know you are lying."

"Pretty is as pretty does! You have dignity and charm and a fascination all of your own. They will eat from your little mittened hand. Come, Cinderella-in-a-satin-pigtail—to the ball with your Prince Charming!"

He watched her small solemn face break into a smile. Oh, dear, those teeth—some discolored, some missing. . . . But somehow they made him feel still more affectionate and protective. She would give all her fame to be pretty, he thought, as he handed her gallantly into the carriage.

The first thing to take Charlotte aback on her arrival was the large number of other guests. "Even at the opera, there did not seem to be more people!" she whispered to George, aghast. And how elegant they were, how fashionably dressed and bejeweled! Her eyes flickered among them, looking for a kindred soul, and lit upon what was obviously a governess. She longed to sit in a corner with this little woman and discover things about her life, but that was impossible. Mr. Thackeray was leading her around, introducing her: "Mrs. Elliott, Mr. and Mrs. Carlyle, Miss Perry, Mrs. Proctor . . ." There were two little girls, aged about ten and thirteen, evidently in the charge of the governess but not under her control, for they kept bobbing up at Mr. Thackeray's elbows hissing at him, "May we not be introduced, Papa? *Please* may we sit up to dinner? We will promise not to chatter!"

He was most forbearing, she thought; for her part, the little girls with their eyes agog and their whispered asides (clearly about her) made her feel like a specimen in a cage, and she wished their governess would tell them not to stare. When she failed to do so, Charlotte gave them a meaningful frown herself.

But then everyone was staring, she suddenly noticed. Even the elegant grown-up guests could not keep their eyes from her for long. They seemed to be waiting for something—waiting in vain. When dinner was announced, everyone seemed relieved. Mr. Thackeray offered her his arm, which she could not hold without reaching almost above the level of her own head—she thought she could hear the children tittering behind them, no doubt at the ludicrous discrepancy in their heights.

At the dinner-table she sat in the place of honor at the foot of the long table, opposite the host. She was sorry to be so far from him, and kept leaning forward to catch any sallies he dropped as he carved the joint. The rest of the party, distributed along the sides of the great glowing table, seemed to be attending a tennis-match. When the host spoke, every head turned to his end of the table; when he stopped speaking the heads, attentive, expectant, turned uniformly toward Charlotte. She did not know what they wanted of her; what *she* wanted was to sit quietly and listen to the civilized ebb and flow of conversation, which her brain stood ready to record for future use. But the talk, what there was of it, was all but incomprehensible to her. It was all badinage and quick, racy little anecdotes, full of allusions to personalities of whom she knew nothing; much of it was evidently mere gossip, spiced with wit and cynicism. The two little girls bounced excitedly in their chairs and interjected remarks and questions as often as they found an opening. They reminded Charlotte a little of the Taylor household of long ago; not since had she seen children so freely given their heads in a gathering of adults.

After the meal, the ladies retired to the drawing-room and distributed themselves about it. There was a low murmur of conversation punctuated by little shrills of laughter which seemed to run up Charlotte's spine in shivers. In her unease, she looked around for anyone who might prove a kindred spirit. And there she was on a distant sofa, the little governess; it was herself all over again, with the ubiquitous sewing-basket (that detestable badge of office) at her side. Charlotte made a beeline for her.

"May I sit here?"

The woman looked up in astonishment. "Here? Why—yes, only—"

Charlotte sat. Without thinking she put on her glasses. "I am Charlotte Brontë," she said, and offered her hand.

"I know." Charlotte waited, smiling, and the governess added shyly, "My name is Trulock."

"Do you know everyone here? For I must own I was so nervous when my host introduced me that scarcely one name has stuck in my head."

"I know most of them by sight. They are Mr. Thackeray's particular friends."

"Who is that tall, handsome lady by the fireplace who is turned toward us now?"

"That is Mrs. Brookfield. She is highly regarded in society, I believe. She is received everywhere."

"She needs the services of a good governess, to teach her that it is rude to stare," remarked Charlotte with asperity, for she was heartily embarrassed by the keen observation Mrs. Brookfield had had her under since her arrival.

Miss Trulock suppressed a smile and bowed her head over her sewing.

"Are you hemming?" asked Charlotte. "Oh, dear—when I think of the miles and miles of hem-stitching I have left in my wake—my thimble-finger has a callus to this day! Don't you hate it?"

"Well! But it is part of my duties."

"Are your charges pleasant children? Or oughtn't I to ask?"

Startled, Miss Trulock replied, "They are dear girls both. A little too lively for me to manage, I am afraid. They feel the lack of a mother," she added very softly, bent over her work.

With a shock, Charlotte remembered that Mrs. Thackeray was "put away," and wondered if the hornet's-nest of gossip her dedication of *Jane Eyre* had stirred up had touched this retiring little woman, so akin to herself. Hadn't it even been suggested by some that a governess had written the book?

"How long have you been with Mr. Thackeray's family?"

"Oh, a number of years now—"

"Did he have another governess before you?"

"I don't believe he did."

Charlotte sat staring at her. Had she heard—had she been made to suffer by the idle, inventive tongues as Mr. Thackeray had suffered? But no. Surely not! She could not sit thus placidly at Charlotte's side if she had. Mr. Thackeray would have shielded her.

Nevertheless Charlotte now felt closer than ever to this woman. She could have spent the remainder of the evening quite contentedly in conversation with her, but this was not permitted. The intrusions of the little girls, who wandered about nibbling biscuits and interrupting conversations, eventually became too much, even for their tolerant father.

"They are so dear to him," Miss Trulock murmured, "he cannot be strict. And I am not good at making up the deficiency."

But when her employer signaled to her, she rose and called her charges upstairs. As she left the room, she turned for a brief moment and gave Charlotte a shy, secret smile, an acknowledgment, though tentative, of the bond between them. It was a smile Charlotte cherished more than all the flashing beams and simpering smirks she perceived on all sides as she was led, an unprotesting victim, back into the main body of the drawing-room.

Then the worst part of the evening began.

Everyone present had been invited especially to meet her, and they expected something more than the mere thrill of shaking her hand and examining her appearance. All had anticipated that she and Mr. Thackeray would strike from each other's wits a brilliant display of verbal sparks—and the feeling of disappointment, even of resentment, grew upon the gathering as nothing of the kind developed.

Several people made efforts to draw her out, but the relentless literalness of her replies to witticisms soon damped the conver-

sational energies of all but the most determined. Mrs. Brookfield
was one of these. She made up her mind that she would not depart
without one pearl at least to carry away with her to other salons,
and to this end tried every approach at her command—all without
success. At last, in despair, she threw out the most mundane question she could think of. "Do you like London, Miss Brontë?"

There was a thoughtful pause, and then Charlotte turned her
large, luminous eyes onto her tormentor and said gravely, "Yes
and no."

Mrs. Brookfield all but threw up her hands, and moved away.

Charlotte was left sitting on her own, but she was like the skele-
ton at the feast—no one could be comfortable, no one could talk
freely. For some reason there was only one lamp in the room, and
as darkness fell outside it could be seen to be smoking: the glass
chimney grew sooty and its light dimmer. There was no fire, for it
was summer, and altogether the room grew gloomier and gloomier, while the company did likewise.

At last George Smith, at whom she had been casting appealing
glances for an hour past, came to Charlotte's side.

"Have you had your fill of being a celebrity, Charlotte?" he
murmured.

She looked up at him beseechingly. She knew he must be disappointed in her, but there was no hint of reproach in his face.

"Oh, may we not go home now?" she whispered.

"Soon."

He sat down near her. The evening dragged on, but now Charlotte became interested in George. With his usual social adroitness
he managed to create around the two of them a little area of
warmth and banter, without her having to do much to help.
There was a very pretty young lady at whom George seemed to
look a great deal, and who laughed infectiously at his slightest
sally. So busy was Charlotte observing the two that she hardly
noticed when a handsome young man, rather unconventionally
dressed, strolled up to her and said to George, "Introduce me to
this lady again, Mr. Smith. I think she did not notice me the first
time."

George stood up politely and said, "Miss Brontë—John Everett Millais. Mr. Millais is one of our foremost artists, Charlotte."

Charlotte automatically put up her hand, which was shaken and held. Startled, she looked up, and met the man's eyes fixed on hers.

"May I have the honor of painting you, Miss Brontë?"

With a quick intake of breath Charlotte withdrew her hand. "Why—no—that is to say, I am grateful, but—"

"Miss Brontë has already agreed to sit for Mr. George Richmond," said George.

"He is privileged," said Millais. "I hope he will do justice to a remarkable pair of eyes." He bowed, gave her another penetrating look, and moved away.

"You may be flattered, Miss Brontë!" exclaimed the young lady who had been flirting with George. "In society, you know, we say that to be painted by Mr. Millais is to join the immortals without having to die."

"Perhaps Miss Brontë has joined them already, on her own account, Miss Proctor," remarked George—but it was at the vivacious girl that he looked, even while he paid Charlotte a compliment that would have given her a memory to treasure, had they been alone. But now it was as if she had closed her fingers upon some venomous insect, which stung her painfully—a veritable scorpion.

As if to punish herself for the sting, she pressed it deeper in. Miss Proctor, feeling herself rebuked, tossed her head and drifted away, and as she left Charlotte leaned over and put her hand on George's knee. "She would make you a very nice wife," she said.

George looked startled. "Whom do you mean?"

"You know whom I mean!" returned Charlotte almost roguishly, and sat back again. Oh, she had been right in *Shirley*, when she had written that one must learn "to endure without a sob"! Not only were her eyes dry; they were bright as if with raillery; she felt the poison checked by her own willingness to accept pain and conceal its effects from the world. But what was the nature of the smart?

George was getting up. "I think we may decently take our leave, if you are ready, Charlotte."

Ready! She rose with alacrity. He offered her his hand and she made the rounds of the guests, stiltedly bidding them good evening. Their host, unaccountably, was nowhere to be found.

As soon as she was safely in the carriage Charlotte felt better. But now the full weight of guilt for her failure fell on her.

"I'm so sorry, George!"

"You couldn't be expected to hold up a dying party single-handed," he tersely replied. "Our host behaved shamefully."

"What happened to him? He was not there at the end."

"He absconded," said George grimly. "Such rank cowardice I have never witnessed! I saw him creeping out the door about half an hour ago. He is probably now comfortably in his club."

Charlotte burst out laughing. "Oh, I don't blame him! How I would like to have run away myself!"

"It was entirely his fault you felt so uncomfortable. It was his duty to make you happy and to entertain his guests. Don't be upset, Charlotte. The evening was an unmitigated disaster, but none of it can be laid at your door."

He squeezed her hand and smiled at her, and suddenly she knew what sort of scorpion had stung her.

chapter 4 NEW PLACES, NEW FACES

*M*onsieur Héger had been the unwitting means of teaching Charlotte a lifelong lesson: that to let oneself fall passionately and uncontrollably in love was to court humiliation and fathomless misery. So, when she felt a dim semblance of this same emotion once again threatening to overtake her, she caught hold of it instantly and shaped it after a very different mold.

To begin with, her love for George Smith was guilt-free, and there was neither self-deception nor ultimate expectation in it. She was six or seven years his senior; and even if there had been more congruence in their background and fortune, she fully realized—being as fondly observant of him as she was—that no woman could hope to win him who had no beauty, grace, or sophistication of manner.

There is a measure of pain in all unrequited love, and Charlotte was prepared to accept this; but she made sure there would be no anguish. She had long ago given up all idea of marrying; yet she believed in love for its own sake, in a woman's need to love someone even if it were not returned. That was preferable, she thought, to the barren emptiness of having no one to focus one's affections on.

George was a man Charlotte could admire, talk to, share things with. He was handsome, gallant, and kind—and he had a genuine warmth of heart toward her. She asked no more.

The spell of this controlled emotion could hardly have failed to invest the trip to Scotland with a sort of magic. Charlotte stopped off on the way to see Ellen at Birstall; fresh from the excitements of London, and with the delights of Edinburgh just ahead, she was less guarded than usual.

"You talk a great deal about George," Ellen remarked archly. "And your face lights up most particularly on each recurrence to the subject. Are you quite sure, now, that you are not in love with him?"

"Would you believe me if I said that whether I am or not is irrelevant? He is not in the least in love with me, so there is no need for anyone to be troubled about it—even I. We are friends, that is the best of it."

"And what about poor Mr. Taylor? Is he quite cast off?"

"I'm afraid James became a little too possessive toward the end of my visit. He felt George was claiming too great a share of my time, and he made his feelings plain. I had to be rather firm. You know, Ellen, there are advantages to being thirty-five and ugly— one has no expectations so one is free to choose one's male companions on a rational basis."

"There is a contradiction somewhere," said Ellen. "Here you have two men running after you—one of them patently jealous of the other—and yet you claim to have no expectations."

"No more have I. George deserves, and will eventually marry, a young, beautiful society girl, fit to be his hostess and the mother of his children. As for James—I don't know what he deserves, but what he will get is certainly not me, for I cannot endure to be near him."

She joined George and his sister Eliza, not in Argyllshire as he had decreed, but in Edinburgh, at the end of the Smiths' tour up the West Coast. His first words to her as he met her at the station were, "I am very annoyed with you, Charlotte! Why did you not fall in with my Number One Plan, and meet us in Tarbert?"

"Why didn't I? Because Fate decided otherwise."

"My mother did, you mean! You know full well you cut short your holiday with us in deference to her unspoken wishes."

"Well. I was also having a good time with my friend Ellen. Is it your intention to ruin such time as I *can* spend with you by bending those scowling brows at me? Come—be your own kind self, and forgive your mother and me."

"You—perhaps. It depends on how docile you are now you're here. My mama—never. She shall taste fire and brimstone on my return, never fear!"

But the scowl vanished, and for the next three days Charlotte knew unalloyed pleasure. She had always liked the idea of Scotland—Emily had had an almost mystical attachment to it—and the reality in no way disappointed her. Whether the proximity of this young man whom she was permitting herself to love cast a romantic radiance over the stern old capital, or whether she would have found it beautiful and magical in any case, she neither knew nor cared. Edinburgh Castle, black and lowering, became a fairy edifice, Arthur's Seat a crag of poetry and fable; the broad and elegant streets of the city charmed her, and the surroundings all seemed transmogrified into a landscape of wonders which recalled the unreal, yet more real than life, enchantment of Angria.

"You may keep your London," she declared to George on the third day of sight-seeing. "This place is 'mine own romantic town,' and should I never have the fortune to be here again, it will always glow in my memory with a special radiance. I love every stone of it."

"And every Scotsman who inhabits it? Remember before you answer that I am a Scot myself."

Charlotte blushed, but met his eyes frankly. "Truly, there does seem to me to be something grand about the Scottish national character. No doubt that is what lends the land its essential charm and greatness."

George Smith bowed low over her hand, and kissed it flamboyantly. "That tribute, madam, will glow forever in *my* memory."

"I hope so. It was very sincere."

At Haworth, Patrick, alone but for Tabby and Martha and the dogs, was feeling his age and his bereft situation very sorely. True, he had more or less driven Charlotte from the house to go into the world, but three weeks was altogether "beyond enough," as Tabby would say, and he was feeling very fretful and ill-used.

The truth was, he didn't at all care for the idea of Charlotte going to Scotland with that young man Smith, nor did he relish the lyrical letters she wrote from there. He accepted her assurances that she regarded the relationship as purely one of friendship, but no assurances had reached him as to the young man's intentions.

Patrick's love for his only remaining daughter was concentrated and passionate. In his eyes—they were dim, and mainly functioning by the distorting light of memory—she was still young, even desirable. Any man, however handsome and rising in the world, might, once he got past her shyness as Smith clearly had, seek to steal from Patrick this last great treasure of his heart and carry her away.

When Patrick allowed himself to reflect upon what marriage entailed, his blood ran hot and cold with the flux of emotions that had no name, but which he chose to call fear—fear for Charlotte's health, for her life. Her fragile delicacy—part of her charm, no doubt—must inevitably collapse under the stress of the marital relationship. Patrick convinced himself that it was his absolute duty to circumvent any such thing—if he could. His own comfort was not the issue—he was thinking only of her. A young fellow like that—it must not be!

He was infinitely relieved that the Edinburgh visit was short, and when Charlotte was back at Ellen's, the old man relaxed a little. But not for long. The day he was expecting her home, a letter reached him from Ellen telling him Charlotte was ill.

"I knew it! I knew it!" he cried to Tabby, waving the letter. "The journey, the strain, were too much for her! The young have no thought for any but themselves. If he has ruined her health—"

He wrote a frantic letter authorizing Ellen to spend what money was needed to provide Charlotte with the best care.

Soon, however, she was well enough to come home, and there she found her father in a pitiable state of anxiety.

"But whatever is the matter, Papa? It was nothing serious—I was just a little run down after the excitements of my trip—"

"Then you must never make another such, Charlotte, for I cannot bear it! You are not strong enough—look at you—if you could see yourself! You are pale, and thin, and altogether worn out. It is very plain that it has all been far too much for you."

"Papa, you wished me to go."

"I did, I did, and I blame myself heartily for it. You shall not take such risks ever again, for the strain of such another fright as I have had would be the end of me."

"I *told* Ellen not to alarm you—"

"Oh, it was not only that! I have been in a dreadful state of anxiety since you told me you were going to Scotland."

"But why, Papa?"

Eventually it came out. "Evidently that young man Smith has designs upon you. I must warn you, Charlotte, that you should regard the state of matrimony as being entirely out of the question in your case. You would never stand it."

"Papa! Is that what is worrying you? Then put it from your mind this instant, for no such thing will occur. I have told you I shall never marry, and certainly Mr. Smith would run for a week if he thought he was in any danger from me."

So she soothed him little by little, and the parsonage routine settled back into its old grooves. Patrick was happy again, though he fussed intolerably about Charlotte's health. Tabby, slower and deafer than ever, pottered about in the kitchen, while Martha and

Charlotte did all the real work. Mr. Nicholls and neighboring parish curates came to tea, and the latter gentlemen tried, with varying degrees of subtlety, to prove to Charlotte that she had libeled them unjustly in *Shirley*. And Charlotte, in her plentiful spare time, fell into a depression deeper and more desperate than any she had known before.

Toward the end of the summer, Patrick came home one evening from a visit to a parishioner and caught Charlotte lying on the sofa, so sunk in misery that she had not been able to pull herself together when she heard his step.

"My darling! What is it, what is it?" he exclaimed, wringing his hands and going white in the face with agitation. "Are you feeling ill?"

"Not ill, Papa! Oh, pray don't keep harping on my health, for it distresses me to be always thinking of it—I am well enough in body. But I am so—lonely— Sometimes as the day ends and I face the evenings, when we all used to be so close, so much together, it is too much for me to bear! Forgive me—I shouldn't trouble you— you have your own grief—but I miss them so! Oh, God! I miss them so!"

He drew her to him, and she wept in his arms until all her tears were spent. Then he stroked her hair and said gently, "You must accept Sir James Kay-Shuttleworth's invitation to the Lakes."

Charlotte sat up, catching her breath in after-sobs. "But, Papa— you said I must stay at home. Your bronchitis—"

"A man may change his mind. I must not be selfish."

"But I don't wish to leave you again so soon!"

"If you don't go, Charlotte, you will displease me seriously."

So she went to Windermere, where Sir James had taken a house for the summer. She went reluctantly—so depleted by the savage return of sorrow that she had no hope that temporary pleasures or stimuli would revive her. However, something awaited her there which she had not anticipated.

She had known she was to meet Mrs. Elizabeth Gaskell—Sir James, the cunning celebrity-hunter, had used each woman as bait for the other—but had not guessed how much they would like each other.

Mrs. Gaskell had already gained an enviable reputation as a novelist. Charlotte had been quite worried at one stage whether *Shirley* might appear too similar in background and theme to her "rival's" first novel, *Mary Barton*. The two books were not, in fact, alike; nevertheless, Charlotte had felt from the first that her mind was in some way akin to Mrs. Gaskell's.

The tragedy of *Mary Barton* had bitten deep, with its passsionate concern for individual lives blighted by a social system heavily weighted against those who enter it with too little. Charlotte had been particularly moved by Mrs. Gaskell's obvious compassion for the sins to which poverty can drive such people. Surely all too few as happily placed in life as Mrs. Gaskell herself would have such a strong sympathy and tenderness for the wretched and deprived of a lower class.

Apart from the qualities of mind and literary gifts of her fellow-guest, Charlotte knew little about her before arriving at Briery Close, the lakeside house her hosts had taken for the summer. But no sooner had she settled in than her chatty hostess remedied that. Lady Kay-Shuttleworth was expecting a child and was indisposed, so Charlotte spent hours with her in her room, listening while she regaled her with all manner of details about Mrs. Gaskell, who was to join them shortly. She was a wonderful woman, Charlotte learned, the wife of a Unitarian minister (a Dissenter!—but after the shocks dealt by Miss Martineau, this was nothing), and the mother of four delightful daughters. She did much work among the poor of her husband's parish in Manchester, which had given rise to her deep sympathy for them. But Lady Kay-Shuttleworth saved the climax of the description to the end.

"You will ask whether, with four girls, she does not long for a son. Why, my dear, she had one—a sweet little lad, the idol of her heart. But alas, I must tell you that he died a few years ago, leaving her no less desolate than if he had been her one ewe lamb. How she recovered herself, and turned her loss into literature's gain, is her tale, if you can gain her confidence. So you see, my dear," concluded Charlotte's hostess, patting her hand somewhat sententiously, "she, too, has had her tragedy. No one in this life is so fortunate as to call forth wholehearted envy."

Charlotte said nothing, but she understood from this remark how an objective view of her own lot as compared to her fellow-authoress's might elicit the rather facile, head-wagging type of compassion in which Lady Kay-Shuttleworth specialized. "Nevertheless, I must beware of envy," thought Charlotte, "when I meet this woman. To have lost a child is terrible indeed; but surely no loss, even that, could cut as deep as mine, if one had the solace of a tender husband and four other children."

Their meeting took place in the long drawing-room of Briery Close. It commanded a peerless view out over lake, hills, and water-meadows; but just now it was dark outside, and the lamps were lit.

When Mrs. Gaskell walked in, still bonneted and cloaked, she was at first dazzled by the lamplight. Charlotte noticed her face—charming rather than pretty—enhanced by a warm look of eagerness; she rose at once and hurried to shake hands.

Mrs. Gaskell for her part had been frankly dying to meet this mysterious fellow-authoress, of whom their gossiping hostess had already told her the most extraordinary tales, and the first sight of the plain-faced little woman in her mourning black coming toward her aroused an instant, overwhelming compassion in her maternal heart.

"How *nice* to meet you at last!" she exclaimed. "This is really a thrilling moment for me—I've so looked forward to it!"

This enthusiastic greeting naturally pleased Charlotte. Later, when they were all sitting together, they kept glancing at each other over their sewing, exchanging little secret smiles at Sir James, who was holding forth at length about the desirability of artists putting aside pointless romanticism and "getting down to brass tacks."

"In the unfortunate absence of my good wife, I fear you'll have to entertain yourselves a good deal. But you shall not leave without having seen the glories of Westmoreland. I propose to take you driving as often as possible. Also I have a rowboat moored below. Do you row, ladies? Oh, but I forgot—you artists are too impractical for such things!"

Mrs. Gaskell laughed. "You mean to bring us down to earth with a vengeance, Sir James! Well, I am ready to try. And are we to drive the carriage too? I have always longed to, but my husband is so conservative! How splendid to find ourselves in such radical hands!"

There was little time to talk that evening; but next morning the two guests found themselves in the kitchen making their own breakfast, bumping heads over stove, kettle, and cups. Nothing could have promoted a speedier ripening of confidence between them; they laughed a good deal, searching for the bread knife and tea-caddy and getting in each other's way. To Mrs. Gaskell it seemed incredible that she was hobnobbing with this fabled creature, who (according to Lady Kay-Shuttleworth's prior account) lived in a virtual nun's-cell of penurious austerity with a mad old father, surrounded by the graves of her dead siblings, after a life of unredeemed gloom.

If Charlotte had struck up an instant affinity with Harriet Martineau, with whom she essentially had very little in common by way of opinions, how much easier was it for her to form a friendship with Elizabeth Gaskell! Here was a woman with no outrageous philosophical views, no inclination to mount crusades and wave banners or upset the natural order of things. She was that rare being—Charlotte had come only recently to realize just how rare—a happily married woman, securely rooted in a contentment of which Christianity and the love of husband and children were the prime constituents. She was, as a direct result, as soothing and reassuring to be with as Miss Martineau was challenging and disturbing.

They ate breakfast outdoors overlooking the lake, and talked about their favorite poets.

"It's so sad to think Wordsworth no longer walks these lovely hills," Charlotte said. "I wonder if we might visit his grave. For me it would be a pilgrimage."

"Well, for my part, his death, sad as it was, did not deprive us of the greatest contemporary poet. I would rather meet Lord Tennyson in the flesh than visit any man's tomb, believe me!"

"How can you claim him as greater than the divine Wordsworth?"

"Easily! Come, can you produce anything to compare with the felicities of 'The Lady of Shalott'?"

" 'The Lady of Shalott'!" echoed Charlotte scornfully. "Pooh! The great sequence of sonnets of 1802 shows what sterner stuff Wordsworth was made of. And his 'Ode to Duty'—"

"Oh, stop, stop!" cried Mrs. Gaskell half-laughingly putting her hands over her ears. "I won't hear such blasphemy! Tiresome, pompous stuff! I don't turn to poetry to be edified in that fashion, I leave that to my prayer-book! I require a poet to charm and delight me, to lift my spirits up on waves of lyricism, not to plunge me into gloomy reflections of how ill it went for England before I was born!"

"What, quarreling, ladies?" Sir James had appeared, sprucely dressed for an outing. "Ah, you artistic souls! Never at peace, even with each other. What's to be gained from arguing the merits of two men of letters, one of them dead? You should rather concern yourself with practical matters, from the contemplation of which some material benefits might accrue! Now," he went on, seating himself beside them and energetically pouring tea for himself into Charlotte's empty cup, "I am not without my artistic side—witness the fact that I can appreciate such as your good selves. Yet I would scorn to waste my time and brain upon such esoteric and unprofitable topics. You should employ your talents on the burning questions of the hour! You bohemians must learn the beauties of practicality and expediency!"

"Let me fetch you some fresh tea, Sir James," suggested Mrs. Gaskell, after exchanging a furtive smile with Charlotte.

"No! No time. We are going out at once in the carriage."

He ensconced his guests inside the closed conveyance, then mounted the box and took the reins himself. They sat snugly together, relieved of Sir James's hectoring presence, and prepared to enjoy the drive in each other's company.

Sir James drove relentlessly up hills and through woods, along lake-shores and past fields, all of an unmatchable beauty. But even when the tiring horses had struggled up to a peak from which a glorious panorama could have been savored, there was no stopping —down they plunged into another valley, while the ladies, huddled in the lurching interior, could only peer out of the windows, cut off from all real contact with the enchantments they passed.

"Oh, how I wish he would stop for just a moment, and let us out!" exclaimed Charlotte at last. "We are not enjoying nature, but watching a series of pictures flashing past."

"Look at that little dell, all lush and solitary—wouldn't you love to run there in bare feet, and lie in the grass, and explore the wood beyond?"

"Yes, yes! I'd rather stop all day in one such place than race all over Westmoreland as we are doing now. Look at the sky—it is going to rain after dinner," Charlotte added suddenly. "We should not go rowing today."

"Are you sure? It looks blue and clear enough to me."

"Those wispy clouds—do you see? They'll bunch together like sheep's-wool into big clumps, which will grow dingy and finally too heavy to hold their moisture. I know them."

"You have a wide view of the sky from the place where you live?"

"Yes, though it has a different aspect from this. Around Haworth the sky abuts moorland of a harsher kind, which has none of the Lakes' picturesqueness. God threw down our moors on a day when He was angry. You have no idea what a companion the sky becomes to anyone living alone—more than any inanimate object on earth, more than the moors themselves."

"You live entirely alone?" asked Mrs. Gaskell, torn between pity and curiosity.

"No. But without the companionship I once enjoyed, of those I loved best. They are all gone."

Mrs. Gaskell, with her delicate sensibilities, curbed her desire to know more for the moment. But later, when Lady Kay-Shuttleworth's indisposition had called her husband to her side and the ladies were left in each other's company, a companionable silence fell which Mrs. Gaskell felt able to break with a leading question. "Do you feel you could tell me a little about your life?"

Charlotte fixed her great honest eyes on her. "Do you ask as a person—or as a writer?"

Elizabeth Gaskell answered her look with one of matching honesty, and replied, "Both. I admit to great curiosity—but I had that before I met you. Now I have a personal interest in you, and sympathy, and—a strong desire to know you well. But if I seem intrusive, pray tell me nothing, for I respect reticence and would hate to breach it."

Charlotte began haltingly with her mother's death, and proceeded to the experiences of her childhood, dwelling on the clergy daughters' school ("I have often thought that the poor food I received there stunted my growth," she said half in jest, but Mrs. Gaskell was by then so involved that she took the remark quite literally). But Charlotte did not tell anything about the childhood writings. The imaginary worlds of Angria, Verdopolis, the Great Glass Town Confederacy, worlds created and inhabited by herself and her brother and sisters when they were children and even after, were somehow sacrosanct; to expose them would have been to tear open a secret room in her heart, to betray—even now— sacred trusts which no one, not even this sympathetic woman, must ever share.

Nor did she so much as mention the name of Héger.

This was no childhood sanctum, but the deepest chamber of all, the very tomb of her heart, where, for all she knew (she seldom looked into it now) Monsieur Héger might still be walled up alive. Thus when she described Brussels to Mrs. Gaskell she spoke only of the trials of living among papists, the difficulties she had had adjusting to the life of the school, but withal the great enlargement of her capacities she had gained from living in that beautiful foreign capital.

By the time she had reached, by installments, the griefs of recent years, two more days of the visit had passed, and she and her avid but incredulous listener were fast friends.

"Such a life as yours I have never heard of before," said Mrs.

Gaskell at last. What struck her most was the contrast between her own happy life and the lot of this no-less-deserving woman. She had a great urge to make up to her somehow for the discrepancy between their respective portions.

Reading some of this in the looks of her new friend, Charlotte said, "Don't pity me. I have compensations. And you have not lived without your griefs."

"You have heard?"

"About your little son . . . yes. Lady Kay-Shuttleworth told me."

"It was because of my despair at losing him that my husband urged me to try and write. But having known that grief myself, I find it all the harder to understand how you have stood up under all yours."

"God has supported me until now," said Charlotte quietly, and Mrs. Gaskell gazed at her in troubled admiration. Well, she thought, sighing heavily to relieve the sympathetic ache in her breast, however it was done, she has got through it. She has survived all those cruel losses. She has friends, she has fame—and best of all perhaps, she has faith. Surely I can console myself that the worst, for her, is over.

chapter 5 HEALTH AND MORBIDITY

$\mathcal{U}$nfortunately, Mrs. Gaskell was wrong.

The next few months—the worst months of the year always for Charlotte, whom the killing east winds of autumn had always afflicted in spirit as well as body—brought her as low as she had ever come. Letters alone—messages from the world outside her prison—kept alive some spark of hope and vigor; but the oppressive emptiness of the parsonage, and the company of the two old people who were all she had left, threatened to wear her down past recovery.

Seeing that no new novel was forthcoming, George Smith devised a way of keeping her busy—not to mention keeping the name of Bell before the public. He succeeded, after a great deal of frustration, in running to ground a certain Mr. Newby, a fellow-publisher whose quite unmerited good fortune it had been to publish—with a minimum of courtesy and efficiency—the novels of "Ellis" (Emily) and "Acton" (Anne). To his other malpractices, Newby had not scrupled to add dishonesty, for when *Jane Eyre*, under the Smith, Elder imprint, had had its wild success, he had tried to cash in by offering Anne's second novel to an American firm under the pretense that all the "Brothers Bell" were one person and that hence this was by the same hand as *Jane Eyre*.

Now George, after wearisome negotiations with this slippery gentleman, obtained the residual rights to *Wuthering Heights* (Emily's only novel) and Anne's two—*Agnes Grey* and *The Tenant of Wildfell Hall*. These George proposed to reissue, together with some of their poems, and approached Charlotte to edit these and write a preface, laying before the world at last the story of her sisters' lives and deaths.

This plan, born out of kind if not disinterested motives, brought Charlotte the most appalling anguish she had known.

She had been careful not to reread any of the work of Emily or Anne since their deaths, knowing what it would do to her—she felt it her duty to try always to subdue her sorrow, not to increase it. But now it became necessary to go through their desks and drawers, turning out their literary remains; this was hard enough, for nothing had been disturbed since they had died. But the worst was reading their poetry. And the worst of *that* was reading Anne's.

Two dreadful shocks awaited her in Anne's little desk. The first was the dawning realization that she had been in love with Willie Weightman. Such a thought had never once crossed Charlotte's mind, but now it was brought before her with a surge of that punishing guilt with which she was so familiar. She should have known it at the time—not to have seen the signs of it was a mark of the grossest insensitivity and unperceivingness on her part. It was some consolation, but only a very little, that Papa, to whom she carried the poems, had not known it either. So terribly did Charlotte need reasssurance that she even broached the subject with Tabby.

"Do you remember Mr. Weightman, Tabby?"

"Aye, I do that—the bonniest curate as ever we had."

"Did you ever notice that he was fond of Anne, particularly?"

"I'd not like to say. But she were main fond of 'im, that I do know."

"How? How do you know?" cried Charlotte. "I didn't!"

"Tha warn't at 'ome, Miss Charlotte, when it coom on strong, so don't blame thisen."

"And did she grieve for him much, would you say?"

"Oh, aye, she grieved. I noticed her a few times, standin' just there, where you are now near enough, by t'kitchen door, staring with those blue tender eyes at nowt. That were where she said 'er last goodbye to 'im."

"And she never said a single word, nor showed her sorrow by one tear!"

"She shed tears a-plenty, I expect. You'd not have seen 'em, though, even if you'd been at 'ome."

But it was when Charlotte came to the most recent poems that she found evidence of something even more unbearable. Anne *had* been afraid—desperately afraid—of death. Her poems, written after the doctor's verdict, proved it unmistakably.

That she had faced these two great tyrants—bereavement and death—with such apparent calm, argued a fortitude and unselfishness almost beyond belief. Charlotte, forcing herself to read and to apply all her insight to these poems which were all that were left of Anne, found them as poignant as a last message, or even a message direct from the dead. Charlotte "summoned" Anne's shade, and argued with it, asking why she had never told of her love and her fear, and claimed the comfort she was entitled to; but the imagined Anne only smiled and said, "It's all so long ago, I can't remember. I expect I didn't want to cause you pain."

When at last the moment came when Charlotte had to start putting the works in some sort of order for the publisher, she found that the best poems of both sisters were so personal that she could not endure to have them exposed to strangers—not even to George Smith and Mr. Williams. Of those Emily had left, which had not been published in the original book of all their poetry, most were about Gondal, a mythical world which Anne and Emily had created together, and these cried out so loudly of the enchanted years that Charlotte could scarcely clear her eyes of tears sufficiently to read them. Superimposed forever on the memory of those halcyon youthful days which had produced this rich harvest was the image of Emily, haggard and rigid, clinging to the table-edge, doing battle with her mortal ague—and, far worse, her face, become alien and frozen, turning upon Charlotte like a death's head when she tried to offer help. To her ghost, too, Charlotte perpetually cried out, "Why?" But the conflicting images blurred the remembered features, and Charlotte cried afresh because she could no longer see her clearly.

So much, then, for the poetry. And what of the Gondal prose— those stacks of essays, tales, and enchantments which were the joint product of her sisters' long, intimate, and exclusive partnership?

She destroyed them all.

Literally destroyed them. Not by tearing them up page by page; that would have been an act of violence which might have forced her, by its prolonged deliberateness, to examine her motives too closely. No. She gathered them together, wrapped them up as carefully as if for posting into neat, oblong parcels—seven of them, each large enough to be the manuscript of a novel. And then she consigned them to the fire, one by one.

As she watched them burn, the tears streamed down her cheeks. She told herself she was doing what Emily at least would have wanted. Had Emily not, on the last night of her life, wrought a similar destruction upon her own most recent output? Obviously in her feeble state such a major work of immolation would have been beyond her strength. Charlotte was only doing for her what Emily would have done for herself, rather than let any eyes pry into her heart's most secret places. But what she really burned was Gondal itself, that inner world belonging to its creators from which she and Branwell had been shut out.

This task done, she turned with a dragging sense of reluctance to *Wuthering Heights*. She was weary now, and depression was like an actual heavy weight which felt at times as if would bear her to the ground. She did her work by day to save her eyes, and the nights, empty of activity, were intolerable. She became almost ill through sleeplessness and a growing obsession with her grief. Rereading Emily's book would have been a trial for her even at her peak of strength; as it was she could not bear it.

To spare herself, she diluted the language, excising words and indeed whole passages which were too powerful for her to stomach in her present enfeebled state, telling herself she was acting to modify those elements of the work which had caused Emily's genius to be misunderstood.

So in the end Charlotte turned tyrant upon the work of her sisters, suppressing, cutting, even changing. Her excuse was that she would not sanction publication of anything which her sisters might not have wanted to expose. But, in fact, her motive was the terrible pain which distorted her judgment and entirely did away with any objectivity. Emily's outbursts of passion, and Anne's of love and dread, were for her ears alone—they were part of the precious, sacred thing that had existed between them and which death had almost, but not quite, destroyed. While she lived, it should be shielded, and thus its remnants preserved.

As for Anne's work, she left *Agnes Grey* alone, but she begged George Smith to refrain from reissuing *The Tenant of Wildfell Hall*. She found her initial dislike of the book had strengthened into a rooted detestation. She hated, as she always had, the character of Arthur Huntington, the drunken wastrel, for whom could Anne have taken for her model but their brother Branwell? How she could have brought herself to such an act of family betrayal, Charlotte did not know, and she had never reconciled the creator of this piece of grim realism with the sister they had all treated as a grown-up child. Charlotte wanted and strove to remember Anne as a quiet, reserved, pious—almost nunlike—girl; she fostered this soothing, doctored image by putting aside all but her religious poetry, ignoring the evidence—in her own memory, as well as on paper—of Anne's deep, strong character, her capacity for love, self-mastery, and rigorous clearsightedness. Charlotte could not bear to remember Anne the brave, the gay, the stubborn—the sister who had gone counter to Charlotte's wishes and exploited all that was sharpest and most cruel in her life to produce a book which she felt was marred by sordid violence and ugliness—and truth.

But when it came to the preface for the remaining collected works, Charlotte felt herself lifted, as if by God's own hand, above the stifling bog of anguish and confusion, and placed (albeit briefly) on some airy plateau. From it she could see her sisters clearly; the sorrow drew back like fog and revealed her true feelings about them, and she wrote as she had never thought she could write—simply, clearly, percipiently, and lovingly—of their characters, their talents, their lives, and their deaths. When it was done, she hurried to put it all together, wrap it, and take it personally to the post, feeling all the while as if some feverish swamp were sucking her down again into its thick, strangling morass. And when the parcel had gone, and she walked back to that tomb of a house again alone, the horror of loneliness closed once more over her head.

There followed three months of a misery so unflagging and acute that she became afraid for her own sanity; she even feared she might die of it. She could hardly eat or sleep. Days and nights were equally tormenting, but the worst were the hours of dusk and dawn: when the light was fading out of the sky and the long, companionless evening loomed ahead of her, and when morning came, like a slave-master, coldly demanding that she face another day.

She had hoped that, thrown back entirely upon her own mental resources, her creativity would be roused to aid her of necesssity. But it did not happen. It was not only the grief and solitude, but the utter lack of stimulus, that prevented it; her muse lay sleeping like the dead, and one of her most pervasive fears was that it would never wake again. Papa, who had recently made a gallant attempt to restrain his nagging inquiries about her health, substituted hints and urgings that she begin another novel, and the constant awareness of his desire that she do so distressed Charlotte further— as did the knowledge that in Cornhill, her friends at Smith, Elder were equally anxious for a new work.

At last she could stand it no longer. With a sense of defeat, she accepted an invitation from Harriet Martineau to visit her at Ambleside. Miss Martineau had a beautiful house which she had had built out of her own earnings—a house exactly calculated to suit her, and which she ran along the most unconventional lines.

"My dear Miss Brontë," she said on the day Charlotte arrived, "let me put you right at once as to the routine I follow. Visitors or no visitors, my work comes first. I rise earlier, I expect, than you will wish to, in order to get in my cold bath and my starlight walk before I settle to my desk after breakfast; but do *you* get up just when you like, and do whatever you please until we meet at lunch. At two o'clock I shall put my work aside, and devote myself wholeheartedly to you."

This suited Charlotte. In this house, free of all associations, she could sleep, and when she woke she would make a leisurely toilet and go down to the kitchen. There she found a little girl from the village, who cheerfully prepared a light breakfast for her no matter how late it was, brushing aside Charlotte's protestations.

"Bless you, Miss, I don't mind! Nothing's too much trouble for a friend of Miss Martineau's."

There were several young girls working about the place, and Charlotte soon realized they all adored the mistress of the house. Watching closely—for the relationship of mistress and servant was one which deeply interested her—Charlotte saw that Miss Martineau's secret was to treat each girl much as if she were related to her, talking to her, petting her, helping her with her work, and generally taking an entirely unpretending interest in all the girl's concerns. Charlotte had never in her life seen servants treated in quite that fashion. She herself loved Martha and Hannah (Tabby's position was unique) and they her, but there was not this degree of warmth and familiarity.

She spent her mornings in the drawing-room, while her energetic hostess worked away in her study for five or six hours without a break. At first, Charlotte simply sat gazing out at the wintry but still magnificent view, letting the fever in her mind and heart gradually quiet down, for her ghosts had not followed her here. She sewed a little, wrote letters, browsed through some books. But for the most part she did nothing at all, patiently waiting—and content to wait—until her hostess had time for her.

At two o'clock sharp, Miss Martineau would fling back the door of her study and come striding out, her trim, plain gown covered with an apron, her sleeves rolled up, and her hair tied back and swathed as if she had been doing manual instead of intellectual work. Her eruption into the drawing-room never failed to give Charlotte a slight shock—a sort of electrical charge of energy and dynamism radiated from her friend's person which went tingling through Charlotte, startling her out of her torpid meditations.

"And now, dear friend, how have you been keeping? Let us talk!"

Charlotte invariably asked, "How is your writing? Did you have a good day?"

And Harriet Martineau always exclaimed, "Of course I did! There are no bad days, only indolent ones!"

She was working on a history of the aftermath of the Peninsular Wars, and when Charlotte found this out she showed a lively interest and considerable knowledge of the subject which had been a passion with her and Branwell in childhood. Miss Martineau was astonished.

"I wouldn't have thought you to have been so fascinated by strife! One would think you had passed your youth in the thick of those battles."

Charlotte stared at her.

How could Miss Martineau guess that, in a sense, what she had said in jest was true? Charlotte and Branwell had been, in childhood, obsessed by these very wars, had read of them endlessly, and written their own idiosyncratic versions of them too. The Duke of Wellington had been Charlotte's hero, Bonaparte—till he fell from popular favor—Branwell's; and from these protracted adulations had grown a massive literature. Massive, that is, in wordage, but restricted physically to tiny papers and magazines, written in a minute script unreadable by adults without a magnifying glass but exactly tailored to a doll-sized world, a world of their own making in which they had, at times, immersed themselves so thoroughly that the real one seemed to disappear.

Charlotte's heart suddenly raced and clung to the memory of Branwell, who, for a moment, seemed to materialize and stand out clear of all the turbidity connected with his spoiled life—her darling soul-mate, co-editor of the little magazines. Watching her, Miss Martineau said suddenly, "I don't usually show my work to anyone unfinished, but since you are so familiar with all my protagonists, perhaps I may make an exception. I'll read you the introduction—tell me if it will do."

She left the room, and returned with some sheets of paper. Standing tall and easy as a man, with one elbow on the mantelpiece, she read aloud to Charlotte a passage in praise of the Duke of Wellington.

When she looked up at the end, she saw to her amazement that Charlotte had tears running down her cheeks. Anxiously putting up her ear-trumpet, Miss Martineau heard her exclaim, "Oh, I do thank you! We *are* of one mind. Oh, thank you for this justice to the man!"

Not knowing the echoes of the past which had produced this touching but exaggerated reaction, Miss Martineau merely said, "Well! I am glad you approve." Charlotte suddenly took her hand and pressed it. There is a touch of idolatry in the case, thought the older woman. But she was gratified, just the same.

Charlotte was not so inclined to confide in her present hostess as in Mrs. Gaskell. She admired her to the point of awe—her energy, discipline, and courage—yet that very awe militated against the cozy intimacy Charlotte had already entered into with her other new friend. Still, they had much to say to each other.

Charlotte was regaled by the hour with fascinating accounts, peppered with colorful expressions, of her hostess's foreign travels to Egypt, to Palestine, and, most exciting of all in a way, to America, where her passionate antislavery views had caused her to be pilloried and all but lynched.

One day the heavy December mists lifted and the sun shone down.

"Come, let me show you my estate!" said her hostess, and they put on their cloaks and pattens and went out through the French windows into the garden, Miss Martineau leaving a fragrant trail of cheroot smoke.

The brick-walled terrace just outside led down to a lawn, on which stood a stone sundial. "Have you heard about this? William Wordsworth approved the motto, hence it has become the most famous part of my little property."

Charlotte crouched and ran her fingers over the engraving, which read, "Come, Light, and visit me." She felt she was touching something of the poet himself, and looked up rapturously.

"Can you understand Mrs. Gaskell's preferring Lord Tennyson? *He* would have covered the whole sundial, and said not half so much."

"In his youth, Mr. Wordsworth certainly reintroduced us to the virtues of poetic simplicity. Yet I must side with Mrs. Gaskell in judging Tennyson the greater, ultimately. Perhaps because I came to know my other neighbor too well in his old age. Now come and see my farm."

The farm consisted of two cows, some chickens, and a thriving piggery, spotlessly clean.

"When I first began husbandry—largely to forestall the butcher, who was cheating me—all the local farmers jeered. First they said my beasts would starve, for I pastured one to the acre instead of one to three, as they did. Next, they averred I would pamper them to death, for they found out I supplemented their diet of grass with bought grain in winter. Now that I am self-supporting in milk, cream, eggs, butter, and pork products, all with the help of one man, the scoffers begin to sniff after my secrets. Now I've been asked to publish a pamphlet on my system, to enlighten those who have been muddling along for generations."

"You are very confident in all you do," said Charlotte as they strolled on.

"I am *now*—I have learned to be, for I see that what I believe in is usually proved right, more or less, by empirical testing. But when I was a child I had not one grain of self-esteem. I sometimes think the crisis of my going deaf aided me—I stopped listening in vain for the hoped-for words of praise that never came! Now I try to care nothing for praise or blame (and I've had plenty of both) but listen only to the inner voice. By the same token I try to learn from others instead of criticizing them. That's why I enjoy neither reading nor writing book-reviews, and scarcely ever do it."

"But you would give an opinion on a friend's book, if you were asked to?"

"Oh, that's different! But one must always allow that an author is more of an expert on his subject than oneself, and walk humbly."

"My books have no subject as such, unless it be the greatest subject of all."

"What is that?"

"Human relationships."

"Oh, Christ!" exclaimed Miss Martineau laconically. "When novelists talk about human relationships, they usually mean love. And love—that is, between man and woman—is a business I find so vastly overrated as to distort the purpose of life altogether. Believe me, dear Miss Brontë, there are enough women writers about—and men too—who can treat of nothing but human relationships. One of your keenness of mind should stretch herself beyond those narrow limits and apply her talent to the great topics of the day, as my friend Mrs. Stowe did in *Uncle Tom's Cabin.* I would rather see you guiding your sex to a realization that there is more to a woman's life than the quest for love."

Charlotte thought this over. *Mary Barton* had given her her first intimations that modern novelists might have didactic purposes. *Uncle Tom's Cabin* had impressed her even more, and humbled her, too, for she realized then that whatever her own gifts, she had never done any social good with them, for she could not handle the topics of the day, nor write a book with a moral, nor take up a philanthropic scheme. She felt it was useless to try.

"I believe," she said at last, "that Mrs. Stowe had felt the iron of slavery enter into her heart from childhood upward, long before she ever thought of writing books. One cannot and should not handle these great matters unless their bearings are known intimately, as a result of long study, and their evils genuinely felt. Apart from the minor evils—comparatively—of the oppressions heaped on the servant classes here, I have suffered and seen little of social wrongs; if I wrote about them, it would be a matter of getting up an indignation I did not truly feel, for reasons of business, so to speak—which would be to degrade them."

They had strolled slowly back to the terrace, and were now sitting there on a bench overlooking the lake. Miss Martineau reflected a little and then said, "It is hard for me to imagine isolation such as yours. My inclination is to urge you out of it, for your voice is needed; yet I should obey my own precepts, and, instead of interfering or criticizing, try to learn from your so-different experience. Nearly everything I have ever written has been socially based, and some think I have done it all to be useful to others; but you are right in this, that my real purpose has simply been to write what I felt, let others make of it what they would. If I did not feel as I do about economics and poverty and slavery, et cetera, no wish to benefit my fellow-men could make me so much as lift my pen. The need must come from within."

If this conversation disturbed Charlotte, another, held a day or so later, had an even more deep-rooted effect. Miss Martineau was correcting some proof-sheets over lunch, and Charlotte asked what they were.

"It's a book of letters which I exchanged with my friend Mr. Atkinson, a man of the greatest rationality and wisdom. Our views coincide on most subjects, but especially upon the social nature of man—the main theme of the letters—which of course includes our firm belief that Christianity is a decaying doctrine which must be replaced by a creed of rationalism. I don't doubt I shall be in for trouble when these letters appear. Although I've written in an atheistical strain before, I have never made my views so plain nor pressed them so far." She looked at Charlotte challengingly. "Are you shocked?"

Charlotte shook her head. "So long as you do not advocate the abandonment of a belief in those elements of religion which sustain so many—a future life, for instance, reunion with the dead—"

"But I do," said Miss Martineau.

"Would you rob us of our last comfort?" inquired Charlotte, so softly that Miss Martineau put forward her trumpet and asked, "Would I what?"

"Rob us of our last comfort," repeated Charlotte almost fiercely.

"May I speak freely, without hurting you?"

"Speak as you please. My hurt is my concern."

"Your comfort, dear Miss Brontë, should not depend upon belief in some vague palace in the skies in which your loved ones sit and wait for you. That is something you cannot be sure of, and in any case it is deferred. Your comfort is *here*. In your memories. In the knowledge that those marvelous women, your sisters, somehow produced masterpieces which will *live on*, and reach the minds and hearts of thousands. In the splendid fact that they lived, interacted with the world about them according to their separate destinies, and then gave place to those who are to follow them, as those before gave place to them. That is the only miracle we need —the beautiful, unchangeable law of existence. To worship this as rational beings, we don't need the impediment of fancies and extensions of our natural powers of observation—all that *is* may be absorbed through the senses, even by one like me who suffers under a double handicap (did you know I have no sense of smell as well as being hard of hearing?).

"For the rest—the suffering, sorrow, and injustice, the cruelties and stupidities, those elements of human life which cause believers so much bafflement—these are our tasks, and we are fitter to do them if we are not wasting our reasoning powers struggling to reconcile omnipotence and benevolence in a 'perfect' God. These ills are man's—his blunders, his responsibilities. You cannot imagine the sense of freedom which ensues when one breaks the last chain and accepts that no prayers but only constant endeavors can put these things right."

"If I had no belief in prayer, I should have nothing," said Charlotte.

"Nonsense!" cried Miss Martineau. "Listen. You think me cruel to take away your last hope, as you put it, and others will abuse me for trying to destroy people's faith with my book. I answer you as I will answer them—any of them I care enough for to bother answering. I see in you my very self, when I was young and before the chains were broken—your great gifts buried under a load of morbid grief so heavy you cannot throw it off, your nerves in shreds, your confidence shattered by a knowledge, deep down in your mind, that the God you trusted has proved other than you thought him." Charlotte started violently, and would have spoken, but Miss Martineau went on. "You cannot make sense of it! No more could I, and until I freed myself of it by the fighting powers of my intellect, I was as borne down as you by every disappointment and every loss. If I saw that prayer, the belief in an afterlife, faith in God's mercy and so on were helping you to fulfill your huge potential as a writer, as a human being, do you think I would dare to touch them? But none of them *work*. They are not working for you—are they? You are paralyzed with misery, and religion is not doing anything for you, though you think it is your only prop.

"Shall I tell you what must sustain you? Your belief in *man*. Your love for your sisters and brother, dead or alive. And, most of all, *your work*. It is all *within* you, the strength to do what you have a will to do, and what put it there is the inviolable law of nature that makes flowers grow out of the branch of a tree. Is it right that the tree should die of grief when the flowers of one season fall? No! It grows more, while its dead blossoms nourish the earth at its foot. Our dead must nor be permitted to poison our roots, Miss Brontë! They must feed us! That is the difference between health and morbidity, and you see that I am healthy, though I have lost loved ones too, and you are not. Because I see that, and because I respect and even love you, I must try to bring you into the warm, free, happy light of rational day where I stand, out of the darkness where you repine."

That evening they sat together in the drawing-room before a roaring fire, lovingly brought to a clear blaze by one of the little servant-girls whom Miss Martineau afterward obliged to stand up on a chair while she measured her for a Sunday frock she was making for her. When the girl had gone, and both women were bent to their sewing, Miss Martineau said, "You are quieter even than usual, dear Miss Brontë. I fear I've wounded you."

"Not mortally. But you have given me much to think of. I am troubled by what you said of our relative states of mental health. Do you not, in fairness, think that my contemptible nervous condition is to some extent the result of poor physical health, and that your almost incredible energy and ability to triumph over all obstacles is correspondingly due to your robustness?"

Miss Martineau laughed. "I am the last to underrate the blessings of a sound body as the domicile of a sound mind!—for I know very well what it means to have neither. Would you believe that I was once a physical and nervous wreck? Unable to work, unable even to get out of bed? I was thus for above five years, my dear, so I know all about it—too much to admire the Christian tenet that insists that illness and suffering are visited on us by God almost as marks of special favor! I long ago decided that disease and pain and early death are no more than the inevitable and natural results of our ignorance of nature's laws, the mastering of which is our entire business in this world. When we cease foisting the whole matter onto God, we shall learn to overcome that ignorance. Meanwhile, there are openings for those who are not too stultified by the Christian ethic of worshiping sorrow to put themselves to rights."

"I very much desire to put myself to rights, as you call it," Charlotte retorted with some spirit. "The doctors can do little more for me than they could for poor Anne, who obeyed them to her last hour in her desire to get well."

Seeing she had roused her visitor, Miss Martineau put aside her sewing, stood up, and came to sit on the footstool at Charlotte's feet. She took both her hands.

"Miss Brontë," she said, "forgive me. I am so convinced now by my doctrine that I proselytize with a lack of tact bordering on brutality. Listen. The doctors gave me up for incurable, until I was prevailed on to try mesmerism. It worked, and I was restored, not just to my former condition of uncertain health, but to what you see now."

Tears came into Charlotte's eyes. "You cannot imagine how I long to be like you!" she exclaimed. "Though I could never give up a belief in God and a future life, I would give anything to share your inexhaustible strength and spirits, your wholesome positive outlook! Oh, how I would like—" her voice broke, "how I would like to have no—bad—days!" Suddenly she clutched Miss Martineau's hands hard, her little fingers gripping like bird's claws. "This mesmerism you speak of! Would you try it on me?"

Disquieted, Miss Martineau stood up. "Why—I was the recipient of the treatment, not the practitioner."

"But you must know something of how it is done?"

"Yes, but ..."

Charlotte rose anxiously, holding her arm. Her eyes blazed. "Please try! I will submit myself to you."

Very reluctantly, Miss Martineau was persuaded. Had she had ambitions as a mesmerist, she would have been gratified by the speed with which she brought Charlotte under her influence by the simple act of stroking her forehead and speaking a few words in monotone. For a short time, Miss Martineau toyed with this new power; but an unwonted shrinking overcame her. She sensed how completely Charlotte was in thrall, how totally and readily she had yielded herself. The older woman recognized her as a subject almost too malleable, and knew herself unfitted to undertake any serious treatment. She clapped her hands and woke Charlotte up.

"Well? What suggestions did you make to me? Shall I be better?"

"I suggested nothing. I woke you at once."

Charlotte's face fell. "But why?"

"You must not put that vulnerable psyche of yours into another's hands."

"I want to be cured of my weakness, my grief!"

"There is no true cure for those but one, and you know it as well as I."

Charlotte gazed at her for a moment, then seemed to droop where she stood, as if she would sink to the ground under the old burden.

"Work," she said dully.

"Yes," said Miss Martineau. "Work."

chapter 6 MR. TAYLOR

*C*harlotte told Miss Martineau, before they parted, that she would prefer anything, even hiring herself out as a governess again, to writing before she had anything important to say.

"I have not accumulated, since I published *Shirley*, the material which would make it needful for me to speak again, and, till I do, may God give me grace to be dumb."

Miss Martineau put both hands on Charlotte's shoulders and fixed her compelling eyes on her.

"I respect your artistic scruples," she said, "but what you say is a mistake. You must not allow your muse to rule you—you must rule her, right ruthlessly. I have never spent a quarter of an hour at my desk, more or less, without the words beginning to flow from my pen, but that time must be spent commanding one's mind, not timidly waiting on its pleasure. Write, dear Miss Brontë! Something, anything, rather than rot in idleness and morbidity."

Such was Charlotte's admiration that she obeyed. One dull morning just after Christmas, she shut herself up in her room and "commanded her mind." She had little hope, but she forced herself, and after about an hour of intense concentration she began to write.

The seeds were there. It was a story conceived long ago, and even, in another form, already written: a plain little teacher in Brussels who falls in love with a professor. Now, so many years later, with the old anguish burned out, she felt safe in pouring her memories through the creative funnel, hoping they might emerge as art.

There was much she could now add. Her fresh impressions of London society, her relatively pain-free love for George Smith, and much more besides. So, she knew her location, she knew something of her plot and a good deal of her characters; and when the work began, she felt at first that perhaps Miss Martineau had been right—the block was broken and the stopped-up creative process might now flow freely.

But her work did not flow. Something was missing—some element, some character, or perhaps just inspiration. The words emerged grindingly, and each session at her desk left Charlotte dispirited and exhausted.

In this renewed depression, her letters from London increased (if possible) in importance. George's letters were the most precious of all those she received; she allowed herself a foolish, romantic dream or two over each. But the really unexpected thing was the gradual—almost insidious—change in her feelings about James Taylor.

She had always known that her love for George was a fantasy-thing, not to be taken seriously for a moment. But the little red-headed Scot was another matter. *He* was by no means too good-looking, polished, wealthy, or well-bred for her. At the same time he was intelligent and interesting; his correspondence with her showed they had a great deal in common and much to say to each

other—or, at least, to write. Charlotte sat very often over his sagacious and entertaining letters and struggled to reconcile their
writer with the little man whose physical presence had struck iron
into her soul.

"It is his mind I am kin to," she thought. "His person is alien to
me. Under such a handicap, have I the right to even play with the
notion of a union between us?" The very word "union" in connection with Mr. Taylor would, she knew, have made her shiver,
had he been nearby; yet after so many months of not seeing him,
this unpleasant effect of his presence had lost its potency.

One encouragement to her thoughts was the recollection that
Papa, on the occasion they had met, had actually taken a liking to
the little man. Knowing Charlotte had heard from him, he had
warmly inquired, "And what has Mr. Taylor to say for himself?
When will he honor us with another visit?" But if Charlotte tried
to read any portion of George's letters aloud, Papa would snort
loudly and wave her off with, "Oh, enough from that young coxcomb! I wish he would stick to business where you are concerned."

"Papa, that is not fair! One would think they were love-letters."

"Do not name it, Charlotte! Do not think of it. It is out of the
question."

On one such occasion, Charlotte asked, on a sudden impulse, "Is
your meaning that I am never to marry anyone, or is it just Mr.
Smith you object to?"

"Whom else have you in mind?" asked Patrick suspiciously.

Gathering her courage, Charlotte said, as carelessly as possible,
"Well! Mr. Taylor made some tentative overtures last time I was
in London."

Patrick stiffened, but he merely said, "And how did you receive
them?"

"I'm afraid they appealed to me so little—at that time—that I
turned them off rather vehemently."

"H'm. And now?"

Charlotte met his eyes, peering at her over his spectacles, and
there was a silence. At last she asked quietly, "Is it your wish that I
should live alone forever, Papa?"

Patrick peered at her for a moment longer, sighed heavily, and sank back into his favorite chair. He lit himself a clay pipe to gain time, and she waited, her heart thumping strangely. Finally he said, "I want nothing but what will be best for you, my dearest. Marriage is no light matter for a woman, especially one so delicate as you—"

"And so much past her youth," added Charlotte drily.

"We cannot ignore the facts of nature," said Patrick sharply.

"*I* am not ignoring them, Papa."

Patrick was silent. Of course he did not want her to live out her life in spinsterhood when he was gone—and surely, with his ever-precarious health, he could not live much longer. If only he could be assured that she would not marry *yet*. How old was she—thirty-four, thirty-five was it? Another few years, and they would both be out of danger—he of losing her, she of dying in childbirth. Could he but assure himself that the man she gave herself to would not be too passionate, selfish, greedy—with the wild blood of youth in his veins, as it had been in his own, alas! Only recently, in connection with Charlotte's prospects, had Patrick reflected upon that side of his own marriage. Much of his rooted dislike of the idea of a union between Charlotte and the dashing, handsome Smith was based on uneasy recollections of his own reckless young manhood.

At last he stirred himself and said, "Let us put it this way. Were you to find yourself a *suitable* lover, one who is worthy of you and at the same time one who would not make too many demands upon you—an older man, perhaps—"

"Does that rule out Mr. Taylor, Papa? He is not yet in his dotage."

"Charlotte, you are laughing at me! You know full well what I mean. I liked Mr. Taylor when I met him. He struck me as being neither rash nor impulsive, a steady, respectable sort of fellow. I do not say he is good enough for you, but perhaps, if there were a true affinity of spirit between you, I might be brought to consider it . . ."

"In that case, Papa, have I your leave to consider it myself?"

"Oh, if you must! But I would far prefer you to occupy your

mind with a new work, that would be more profitable and less dangerous."

The novel dried up completely when it was scarcely begun, and the new year brought no change and no real stimulus or hope.

In January, Miss Martineau's book of "atheist letters," as Charlotte called them, reached her, and she read them, torn between admiration, remembered happiness (she had more than enjoyed her visit to Ambleside), and horror. So much of what was in the letters seemed profoundly sensible and true, and yet the idea that one must give up all hope of and faith in a future life struck her—seeing it set down in print—as being so terrible that she wrote to Mr. Taylor, "The strangest thing is that we are called on to rejoice over this hopeless blank—to receive this bitter bereavement as great gain—to welcome this unutterable desolation as a state of pleasant freedom. Who *could* do this if he would? Who *would* do it if he could?"

And yet a seed was sown. She could not entirely dismiss anything emanating from Miss Martineau as either false or foolish. No longer was Charlotte as absolutely sure as she had once been that those she had loved and lost to death were still somewhere, waiting for her. During the long winter nights she fell again into her old ways, sitting by the fire with the dogs, Keeper and Flossy (now getting old and fat) snoring gently at her feet, straining her ears for the gusts of wind to bring her a voice to reassure her. When she had written the incident of Rochester's voice reaching Jane over many miles in *Jane Eyre*, she had based it upon truth, for she had, at school, once heard Branwell call her as she walked in the garden. But he had been alive—and Rochester had been alive. . . . Despairingly Charlotte took out the first volume of *Wuthering Heights* and read again, with nausea and tears, the harrowing scene with Cathy's ghost at the window, the little wrist sawn against the broken glass. Emily must have believed, to have written that, however cruel, however hideous it was. Charlotte ran up to the little study which had been Emily's, opened the window, and, kneeling upon the bed, called softly out into the storm,

"Emily! Emily! Please come—please come—" But there was only the sobbing wind, and the rain, and Charlotte's shame at her morbid weakness, strengthened now by the knowledge of how Mrs. Gaskell would pity it and Miss Martineau despise it.

In February, George wrote to her with a suggestion that made her heart leap for a moment, but then fall back to its usual dull beat. He was going for a trip down the Rhine with his sister in the spring, to visit the castles. Would Charlotte like to accompany them? She remembered Edinburgh, and for a moment the bright dream sprang up before her, as inspiring as Martin's engraving against the dreary wall opposite her. But it could not be, and she knew it. She wrote back refusing, on the grounds that she deserved no treats, no outings until she had written her book. There seemed no sign of that ever happening, and, sensing her anxiety, Mr. Williams wrote one of his most generous letters, telling her she must take her own time and not trouble herself about her publishers.

Charlotte carried this letter to Papa, whose importunings for a new book were becoming really burdensome.

"Very well, my dear. I shall say no more."

"When spring comes, this hateful depression that always plagues me in winter will pass. Then I shall be able to work," Charlotte told him, though she had no belief in what she said.

In truth all that was now keeping her going was James Taylor. His letters, and the magazines and books he regularly sent her, were slowly building up some quiet expectations in her heart; her own fears and longings were the cement that stuck the bricks of hope together into a structure strong enough to sustain her. This was no castle in the air such as she had created of the illusory materials supplied by George, but a plain square edifice with windows and doors and a chimney which she might, she persuaded herself, actually one day be able to enter and live in.

And then, in one of George's letters, he casually mentioned that James Taylor was leaving the London house and going to manage Smith, Elder's new branch *in India.*

The blow was far more painful than Charlotte had had any reason to expect. She was not in love with Mr. Taylor, not in the least, but she had come to rely upon him in her thoughts, and the idea of his leaving England for years was hardly worse than the fact that he had not bothered to tell her himself, but had left her to find out in this distressing way through George, who, she had for long suspected, did not get on well with him and had perhaps even engineered this move to get rid of him.

Charlotte found herself more angry than miserable, after the first shock. The next letter she wrote to Mr. Taylor was distinctly chilly. Her hand shook as she wrote it; she was convinced it was her last communication to him, and after dispatching it she prepared to tear down the little homely structure she had built around her heart during the winter to keep it warm.

However, its demolition was postponed.

The next day a letter arrived from Mr. Taylor himself from Scotland, where he was taking leave of his family. He told her his plans, and asked permission to call on her on his way south.

Charlotte's first thought was of the cold farewell note he would find waiting at his London office. Remorse gripped her. She must nullify its effect in advance! She ran to Patrick. "May I invite him, Papa?"

Patrick read the letter twice. Yes. This would do. The fellow would be five years in India. A betrothal of that space would almost certainly see himself in his grave, and a marriage *then* would be very timely, considering also that Charlotte would by that time be over forty and most unlikely to be put to the risk of bearing children. Besides, the little Scot, with his red hair, beaky face, and short stature would not be likely to arouse in Charlotte any passions which would make waiting difficult. Eminently suitable! Patrick smiled.

"You may, my dear. I shall be most happy to see Mr. Taylor."

He did not come for several days, and Charlotte did her best to plan calmly, soberly, objectively for the possibility that Mr. Taylor would declare himself during his visit.

"Could I? Could I?" It all came back to that. But she would not know until he stood before her; uneasy recollections made her doubtful; yet . . . to be engaged, to have an insurance against the terror of a perfectly empty future. . . . It was tempting!

He arrived one bright April morning, when spring was palpable in the air and Charlotte's senses were stirring from their winter lethargy. As she heard his carriage (uncharacteristic of this staunch son of Scotland to hire a private conveyance all the way from the station!) clatter to the gate, Charlotte found herself smoothing the unpretending planes of her hair and wetting her lips nervously. However, she forced herself to sit still and count five after the knock sounded, before rising sedately and calling to Tabby, "I will go."

She walked slowly to the door, opened it, and raised her eyes to her suitor.

It was nine months since she had seen him. His image had softened considerably in her mind under her new conception of his constancy and kindness, his pith and wit, as evinced by his correspondence. Now reality cruelly struck away that gentling effect. It cut off the extra foot she had added to his height, it rendered his darkened hair once more sandy, his eyes pale and pink-lidded, his skin sallow and freckled. She had told Ellen—and believed—that she knew she had no right to be exacting on the point of looks; yet for all his eager smile and outstretched hand, her soul shrank back within her. And when he possessed himself of her limp hand and pressed it to his moist, speckled lips, fixing her with those piercing eyes beside that nose—that nose!—her very veins ran ice.

The next few hours were an agony of embarrassment, aggravated by a sort of irritable disappointment. It was not only his person that repelled her; she would have been ashamed to admit that, for she believed she had long ago subdued her nature to the point where qualities of character far outweighed any physical disadvantages. But he was not—he was not a gentleman! By that word she did not mean polished, or courtly, or any nonsense of that sort—she roundly despised all that as a basis of judgment. But there was such a thing as being a natural gentleman, which involved something deeper than mere learned behavior: good breeding, in a word, would out, and in Mr. Taylor's case it simply was not there.

Looking for it, trying to see evidence of it, Charlotte found its lack jarring her nerves at every turn. He sat down fractionally before she did; turned his back sometimes upon her father, seeming blandly unaware that the old man could not hear him unless he directed his speech toward him. He trod on the ends of her sentences in his eagerness to make his own views known; his voice too was overloud and his turns of phrase, like his movements, graceless.

Yet it was not anything he actually did wrong which repelled her; he was not decidedly wanting in manners or deportment. It was an absence of the *inner* gentility. The soul of the man was somehow irredeemably second-rate. And thus when she strove to imagine herself joined to him, she knew that she would suffer humiliation in its true meaning. She could never love him as a wife should, for wifely love, to her, meant reverence, the true admiration of one soul for another. That was what she wanted, and she would not settle for less.

All day this interior struggle went on in Charlotte, while she shifted and maneuvered to keep Mr. Taylor at a distance and to prevent his being alone with her. To this latter end she had to recruit her father's help. After lunch she followed him into his retreat to summon him forth.

"I cannot have him, Papa."

"Why not, my dear? He seems to me—"

"It is not how he seems to you that matters, Papa. To me he seems impossible to be married to."

"You would not be called on to marry him for five years, my dear. Or even to see him."

"Am I to encourage his proposal, and accept it, on the strange grounds that I may then say farewell to him with relief?"

"But what is wrong with the poor fellow?"

"He is clever and pleasant enough, Papa. But he is lacking in some qualities of mind and manners that I find I cannot do without."

"I do not see it," said the old man flatly.

"Do you not, Papa? Why, Mr. Nicholls is more of a true gentleman! Besides, Mr. Taylor could never rule me."

"And Mr. Nicholls could, I suppose!" rejoined Patrick sarcastically. "I will hear next that you are in love with Mr. Nicholls!"

"Don't be foolish, Papa," said Charlotte with unwonted sharpness.

"Charlotte!"

"Pray don't let's quarrel. It is my life and my decision."

Patrick was, despite his martyred sigh as he rose to join them, not altogether displeased. At any rate he bid Mr. Taylor a hearty goodbye when the time came for him to take his leave, standing on the doorstep and exhorting him to be true to himself, to his country, and to God. Then he remained standing there while Charlotte followed her luckless suitor to the gate and watched while Mr. Taylor turned and pushed a book into Charlotte's hand.

"Keep this for my sake," he said. "I shall hope to hear from you in India. Will you write?"

"Of course," said Charlotte—warmly, now he was going.

"Your letters have been and will be a greater refreshment than you can think or I can tell."

Charlotte said nothing, convinced she would die of embarrassment if this awkward scene went on much longer.

"I had much to say to you, had you allowed me. I do not ask in what way I have offended you—"

"Mr. Taylor, believe me, I deeply appreciate your many kindnesses—the magazines—particularly your letters—"

He waved this away with his freckled hand. "Pooh! All that is nothing. I had much to offer you. I had wished to make up to you for all your losses in life, and I could have done it, too—"

You? Never! thought Charlotte almost fiercely. The idea of this hard-bitten, peppery little man on one side of the scale against Emily, Anne, and Branwell on the other made her angry. It certainly enabled her to say goodbye to him without one quiver of regret.

But regret, of a sort, overcame her when it was too late. When he was gone—far gone, already on his way to India—a strange sadness began to temper the relief with which she had seen him withdraw. He had been—she had no doubts about this—her one and only chance of marrying, and she had let him go. Again she began to think perhaps she should have struggled harder against the pride in her (was it that?) which had caused her to reject a man so provenly devoted, so worthy, against whom there was really nothing tangible. Loneliness, whose threatening shadow had dwindled in the light of the expectations she had entertained last winter, reared itself again before her; she sank under it into such a state of enfeeblement that she could not retain the strong personal aversion which had caused her instinctive recoil from James Taylor. The further he went from her in time and space, the harder it was for her to reconcile herself to her refusal of him. She had bade farewell to her last slim hope of domestic happiness; now she realized, belatedly, that the slimmest hope is better than nothing.

chapter 7 SUMMER VISIT

*I*t was not until the summer that Charlotte began to rally from this confusing loss. And then only because she went against every resolution she had determined on, and allowed herself another trip to London.

Ellen urged some new clothes upon her. "Come out of mourning, Charlotte. It is time."

But when Charlotte returned from her shopping trip to Leeds, she had nothing to show Papa but a new bonnet and some yards of black silk.

"Oh, why all black? Could you not have found something more cheerful?"

"Well . . . there were some beautiful silks in sweet pale colors . . . but they were five shillings a yard, so I turned my back on them."

"Charlotte, my darling! Would you have liked them, and had not the means? I would have lent you a sovereign, had I known!"

A pang shot through her of pure regret for the lavenders and apple-greens and palest yellows that had been tumbled out on the counter before her in all their shimmering glory. But seeing Papa's disappointment, she timidly brought out the bonnet from its box.

"It looked so grave and quiet there among all the splendors, but when I had it alone and looked again its lining seemed altogether too gay."

"Try it on for me."

She tied the ribbons and tilted her head. A lining of pink set off the dove-tint of the little modest thing. Patrick clapped his hands like a child and kissed her.

"My little rose-bud daughter! You will catch every eye." Then he grew sober, and drew her to his side. "Charlotte?"

"Papa?"

"Tabby, you know, has a strange instinct about you. She says, and Martha has hinted the same thing, that you will come back from London betrothed."

Charlotte stifled a sigh. "Oh, Papa! Pray do not encourage her. *You* do not believe such nonsense, I hope?"

He looked at her piteously. "If you marry and leave me, I shall give up housekeeping and go into lodgings."

Charlotte laughed. "And Tabby will be sent to the workhouse, and it will serve her right!"

She had been due to leave on May 29th, but George wrote to her to come a day earlier in order to see the second in a series of lectures Mr. Thackeray was giving on English humorists. When the time came, she would have been glad enough to wait, even at the cost of missing the occasion; the mounds of sewing she had done to get her wardrobe ready, together with her irrepressible excitement at the thought of London (and George), had brought on her customary headache and sickness, which the long train journey did nothing to improve.

She was excessively tired and drawn when she reached Euston Station. George was there, with his mother, despite the late hour. Looking up into his handsome face in the lamp light beside the carriage, her gloved hand in his warm one, Charlotte's tired heart swooned. Something in her face, thin and haggard as it was, moved him strongly and he bent and, for the first time, kissed her cheek. "I'm so happy you've come!"

"I had no right—I've achieved nothing."

"Foolish little Puritan," he said affectionately. "We must feed you on a diet of hedonism—mustn't we, Mama?"

Mrs. Smith, leaning from the carriage window, said, "It is likely to prove too strong for such an austere little stomach." She had seen the kiss and had not liked it; nevertheless, she kissed Charlotte herself as she climbed in wearily, and Charlotte, who had been tormented with guilt-feelings all the way, began to feel so warmly welcome that her conscience thawed somewhat.

As they bowled along the dark streets to Gloucester Terrace, George rallied her with assurances that all her friends were eagerly awaiting her. "Thackeray's lecture is the first item on your program. The cream of society always attends—they are great events; I can't go, I am working all the hours God sends, but Mama will take you."

"You will promise not to introduce me to anyone, won't you?" asked Charlotte anxiously.

Mrs. Smith patted her hand. "Assuredly, if it is your wish. I cannot answer for Mr. Thackeray, however."

"He will not even notice me," said Charlotte.

She was wrong. No sooner had she arrived in the sumptuous ballroom at St. James's where the lectures were held, and taken her first dazzled glance at the jeweled and splendidly dressed "cream of society" swirling like multicolored waters beneath the painted and gilded ceiling, than the Titan himself spotted her. He came straight at her, breasting the crowd like some great ship. He greeted her graciously enough, but with sufficient flamboyance to draw every eye in the vicinity, and then conducted her to a well-preserved elderly lady who was seated on one of the long sofas which served as benches for the audience.

"Mother, you must allow me to introduce you to Jane Eyre."

Conversation stopped three deep in the crowd around them,

and all heads turned. Charlotte flushed a deep red and then turned pale. Her hand went out automatically and was stiffly shaken by Mrs. Thackeray's. She straightened, and without looking at Mr. Thackeray, took Mrs. Smith's arm and let herself be led into an inconspicuous corner.

Seeing how upset she was, Mrs. Smith murmured soothingly, "Never mind, my dear, never mind! It is only his naughty way."

Charlotte's head was bent and her hands clenched in her lap. "How could he! How could he!" she got out between clenched teeth. She was trembling with rage. "Are they all staring still?"

"Why, there are a few heads turned this way, but they will soon turn back when he gets up to speak."

Somebody leaned over their chair-backs from behind. "Permit me," said a deep voice, "as a Yorkshireman, to introduce myself."

Charlotte looked around. It was a face she knew from portraits. "You are Lord Carlisle," she said flatly.

"And may I, by the same token, claim acquaintance with our most eminent novelist?" said another voice. So it went on, with one after another admirer until, mercifully, the lecture began.

Angry as Mr. Thackeray had made her, Charlotte soon forgot personal animosity in objective admiration. He addressed this dazzling elite as if he had been holding forth to a few friends by his own fireside. His subject this time was Congreve and Addison, and his trenchant appreciation—and occasional barbed criticism—of these his dead rivals kept his audience in his palm throughout, and gained him prolonged applause at the end. Charlotte felt she had not only been splendidly entertained but also instructed, a combination calculated to please her and mitigate her wrath; yet her admiration sharply declined once more when, immediately the lecture was over, Thackeray stepped down from the platform and, brushing aside (though not rudely) the crowd of high-ranking congratulators pressing round him, made his way straight to her.

"Well! What did you think of it?"

Charlotte felt ashamed for him. What naivety, what lack of self-command, to ask outright like that for praise! She did not reflect for a moment that it might be his way of flattering her. She had had plenty of kind words about the lecture in her head a moment earlier, when she had not thought there would be opportunity to say them; yet now, when he stood before her, so vulnerable somehow despite his eminence, she could hardly get out a couple of words, and he turned away looking as disappointed as a schoolboy.

Mrs. Smith, meanwhile, had noticed something else which disquieted her beyond measure. Behind them, in the aisle between the seats, the audience was forming itself into two lines, and since every eye was upon Charlotte it was all too obvious that this signal honor was not for the lecturer. As Charlotte turned to leave, she saw for the first time what was happening, and stopped cold. Perspiration started out on her forehead and her face turned ashen; as Mrs. Smith gently drew Charlotte's hand through her arm, she felt it to be cold and rigid as that of a corpse.

"Come, my dear, quickly! Do not think about it!" she urged under her breath, and, holding Charlotte firmly, stepped resolutely forward.

They walked the gauntlet of staring eyes, flashing quizzing glasses, murmured words; Charlotte was in a daze. She had never been nearer to fainting in her life; only her realization of the unspeakable embarrassment such a thing would cause to Mrs. Smith kept her moving forward to the end of the lines—and of the ordeal.

In the refuge of the waiting carriage, Charlotte sank back, trembling in every limb. "Oh, heavens—heavens!" she kept murmuring.

"You poor, poor thing! I was afraid to speak one word of sympathy or encouragement to you, lest you should faint away! Your fortitude was splendid—I am so sorry it occurred."

Charlotte opened her eyes. "If I were a man," she said, "I would challenge that gifted monster to a duel for what he has done to me tonight."

The "gifted monster" himself had no idea that he had done anything amiss; he had the golden rule as his justification, for had *he* been used so, he would have been delighted, extrovert and insatiable drinker of plaudits as he was. So it was without a qualm that he knocked on the Smiths' door at the visiting hour next day, and was shown into the drawing-room where Miss Brontë sat at her needlework.

Her glittering eye as she lifted her face to him, however, took him aback and gave him some warning that he had wandered into a hornets' nest.

"Well, Mr. Thackeray! I am surprised you dare to call on me. Have you come to offer the most abject apologies?"

He started back with his hand on his breast. "I—? Not the least in the world! I have come as your admirer and friend to welcome you to London."

Charlotte rose. "You did that last night, in your own peculiar fashion, and your welcome was such that I would have been glad to return forthwith to a place where the very publicans and coal-heavers have more tact. Do you not realize that not every author is as eager for fame and adulation as you seem to be? That some of us prefer to live quietly, and modestly, and retiringly, and not in the meaningless glare of publicity and ignorant mass acclaim? That you, sir, are all too dependent upon these things, and upon a certain class of people whose attention to their own appearance and comforts generally precludes much deep appreciation of literature, is all too painfully obvious. But I am of a different temper, and you, as a gentleman, should have deferred to that in your behavior toward me."

Mr. Thackeray was staggered. "But what have I done?"

"*How could* you introduce me to your mother as Jane Eyre? I am *not* Jane Eyre, and besides, you know that I use a *nom de plume*, which should tell you that I do not want to be known at all!"

"It was a manner of speaking, no more! Don't you know we all call you that, affectionately and respectfully?"

George, entering at that moment, saw Charlotte standing close up to Mr. Thackeray upon the hearthrug, her head thrown back and her face white, and heard her say, "No, sir! If *you* had come to our part of the country in Yorkshire, what would you have thought of me if I had introduced you to my father, before a mixed company of strangers, as 'Mr. Warrington'?"

"You mean 'Arthur Pendennis.'"

"No, I *don't* mean 'Arthur Pendennis'—I mean 'Mr. Warrington,' and Mr. Warrington would not have behaved as you behaved to me yesterday."

George saw that his male caller was getting the worst of it—it amused him mightily but he felt he should intervene. "Pray let me act the peacemaker, since you make war upon my hearthrug," he said. "Mr. Thackeray, sir—a glass of wine will often soothe the wounded, and, my dear Charlotte, allow me to tempt you to one of my sister's caraway biscuits."

They all sat down. Mr. Thackeray was more bewildered than angry. He could not help seeing some justice in Charlotte's attack, but his motives had been entirely good; he felt his only fault was in not appreciating the basic differences between her temperament and his.

"Who ever heard of an author who did not wish to be famous!" he muttered into his wine. "You are a rare bird indeed, Miss Brontë. You must pardon me, for I am used to the common kind of sparrow-writer, who delights in company and relishes the public gaze, if only because it helps sales. Mr. Smith will be on my side on that, I am sure."

"But you do not write for money, surely!" exclaimed Charlotte.

"Do I not! I assure you I write for nothing else, nor is anything else worth the effort!"

Charlotte stared at him. "I don't believe you," she said at last. "That is just your detestable cynicism. No man writes as you do who has no awareness of his responsibilities, whose primary satisfaction does not come from the fulfillment of his talent."

"I acknowledge my talent, as you're pleased to call my flair for storytelling, as a means to make myself thoroughly happy and comfortable, to give me *entrée* to places I wish to go and amusing people I wish to meet, to enable me to travel and give parties and indulge my daughters and in general enjoy myself to the hilt.

Your life, Miss Brontë, may be filled with higher satisfactions; but mine is as I have told you, for we live in this world, not the next. Why should the devil have all the best tunes? Eh, ma'am? Answer me that!"

As before, Mr. Thackeray talked to George Smith, standing in the street beside his carriage.

"What an intriguing creature! I have a theory about her. That scorching rage that burns within her—depend on it, Smith, she has passed through the fires of some kind of unhappy love-experience. Her books are suffused, *in*fused with passion quite at odds with her Quakerish appearance and Mother Superior airs. Inside that spinsterish exterior bubbles a cauldron which never quite goes off the boil. Beware! A woman who has loved and lost is peculiarly vulnerable to simple kindness and affection."

George found this analysis troubling, echoing as it did a number of pithy lectures he had had on the same subject from his mother.

"My dear boy, it is not only the discrepancy in age and fortune I object to, for she is a great artist and a dear, sweet creature, which would compensate for much. But she has depths you could not match. She would devour you with her love. Besides, when I see how nervous she is, how plagued by spells of sickness and headaches, I cannot be blamed for not wanting to see you tied to an invalid."

His uneasiness about the relationship caused George to try to cool his manner to Charlotte. He thought this might be the wisest and kindest course. But Charlotte, noticing at once, and knowing something of the reasons, was hurt. She was not enjoying or bene-fiting from this trip as from the last. Several times she suggested going home early, but perversely George would not hear of it. A romance between them might be out of the question; but that did not mean that he wanted to drive her back to her solitary life a moment before time. Instead he tried to force pleasure and diver-sion on her.

She was obliged to make five trips to the Great Exhibition, which was the current rage of London—indeed, of the civilized world. She was only moderately impressed. The great Crystal Palace in Hyde Park housed most of the scientific and cultural wonders of the modern age, as well as being packed all day long with throngs of eager visitors. Though she recognized it as a feast for the eyes (and the brain, if of a scientific bent), it meant little to her heart and spirit. She would hurry from it to a gallery to nourish her soul on treasures of art and beauty.

She would totter home exhausted from these day-long excursions to lie on her bed and be ministered to by Mrs. Smith, who, whatever her personal qualms, was always the soul of kind consideration as a hostess.

In the evenings Charlotte's program included several trips to the theater. One night George took her to see Rachel, the great French tragedienne. Charlotte was shattered.

"Is she not wonderful?" George asked her afterward.

"Wonderful somehow suggests something divine. From the feelings she aroused in me, I would judge her inspiration to be of Beelzebub! Yet I must see her again. I must write about her."

George pricked up his ears. Williams had made him promise not to nag her, but this opening was irresistible. "You mean you'll introduce her into the—er—new book?"

Charlotte gave a little shudder, and changed the subject. "What did you think of the performance?"

"Oh, splendid! A little ornate, perhaps—too full of overblown emotion—but that's the French for you."

"I noticed you watched it quite impassively."

"*You* looked perfectly horror-stricken!"

"Our reactions typify our incompatibilities," remarked Charlotte quietly.

That night she lay awake, her headache a sullen throb, and gave way to sadness. Now the visit was turning sour. The sorrow inherent in her love for George, which she had always held at arm's length, now invaded her, and she cried, not passionately, but weakly and miserably. If only Ellen would not keep writing her those ingenuous letters, telling her how lucky she was, how happy and enviable her situation. Didn't she realize how assiduously

Charlotte had to reject feelings of pleasure? She did not deserve them, and, besides, too much unmerited pleasure now would inevitably have to be paid for by a double measure of a reaction she called "the weird" on her return to her real life. It was always so. Even during the summer months she had come to dread the winter. Its shadow was flung back upon her, and, lying now beneath its chill, she wept more angrily. It was unfair of fate to poison the happiness of the present with a foreknowledge of the future's misery.

One last time Charlotte's departure was put off.

"This year I shall have but one day's holiday," said George, "and on it I shall take my family out to Richmond. You are to come with us." This impulsive insistence ran counter to his resolves; but the truth was that he was increasingly loath to part with her.

The day of the outing was sunny and glorious. The Smith ladies were all gaily dressed and carried flowerlike parasols. Charlotte sported her new bonnet and George admired it. At each juncture in their journey he offered her his arm. Mrs. Smith did not like it; Charlotte did not like Mrs. Smith's not liking it. But they all privately thought, "Never mind! It is the last day."

After luncheon, eaten overlooking the sparkling Thames, George led Charlotte along the towing path for a stroll.

"Well, Charlotte, so you are off home tomorrow. Will nothing detain you?"

"Three times I've said I was going, and three times you've prevailed on me to stay. Truly my conscience must be on holiday too. Even now I am not going straight home. Mrs. Gaskell has invited me to spend a few days with her in Manchester on the way."

"Good! You'll like that. She is a charming creature." He was obscurely relieved that he need not, quite yet, begin to fret about her. He glanced at her in her little pink-lined bonnet, her elfin hand so trustfully resting on his arm, and felt a great longing to rescue her from that appalling life. Yet it was true, what Mama had said. He would drown in the tumult of her love, and, besides— those teeth! That complexion! He sighed gustily and gazed across the river, deeply dissatisfied by the shallowness of his own heart.

For her part, Charlotte was equally observant of him. He had changed greatly; she thought she could detect a change even in the month she had been living in his house. The fine bloom of youth was gone; there were lines of strain and grim determination on his face, a touch of gray in his hair and beard. His waistline was not as trim as it had used to be—only last night his mother had teased him about it, warning him that if he grew into a "John Bull" she would disown him. Charlotte, making an automatic mental note of her exact phrases—she planned to use her in her next book, if she should ever write it—was pained to see how, through his answering raillery, George had been pricked by his mama's remarks. He cared for his looks, for his disappearing youth. She pitied him. To have beauty and to be threatened with its loss must be terrible.

"You are working too hard, George," she said suddenly. "One day's holiday a year is not enough. You will harm your health."

He sighed again and turned back to her. "Have I a choice? If I do not struggle now with all my might, my father's firm—my firm—will collapse under its load of debt."

"But how did matters come to a point where you are obliged to work sometimes until three in the morning, and can allow yourself so little relaxation?"

He gazed at her. Here indeed was a woman with whom one could share one's troubles, who would not merely understand and sympathize—the role of woman as comprehended by his mother and sisters—but participate fully, give aid in the form of sensible advice. More!—he could well imagine this little elf at his side joining him in his office, rolling up her sleeves and turning to, lifting part of the sheer physical burden of work from his shoulders, not as a secretary might, but as a true partner.

But no. How could he confine her genius within the cramped bounds of his need? It would not be fitting. And others would not understand. A wife's place was in the drawing-room, the morning-room—the nursery. Mama was right. It would never do.

He sighed once more. He would not, after all, confide in her the awful secret of Elder, his father's partner, whom he, George, had once thought the world of, but who had turned out to be—under his bewitching veneer of worldly charm—a systematic embezzler. Instead he palmed her off with the sort of vague generalizations which satisfied most women.

"Things went wrong before I took over the firm. . . . We lost a lot of money. . . . Really, Charlotte, it was only with *Jane Eyre* that we began to recoup. What we need are a few more authors of your caliber."

"Mrs. Gaskell? Mr. Thackeray?"

"Now we deal in dreams. They both have publishers."

Charlotte said nothing, but her eyes narrowed behind her spectacles. His ambitious heart leaped. Might she—would she . . . ? But he would not demean himself to ask her.

Charlotte turned suddenly, as if someone had tapped her on the shoulder. Mrs. Smith was looking at her burningly from her bench a hundred yards away.

"George, we must go back to the others."

But he lingered.

"It will be hard to say goodbye tomorrow. I'm afraid I am going to miss you more than usual."

"You will work too hard to think of me."

"And you? Will you miss me?"

For a moment they looked at each other, and each was aware of the other's discrepant love. But then Charlotte said lightly, "Not the slightest in the world! Out of sight, out of mind!"

And he laughed, took her arm again, and they walked back to Mama.

chapter 8 THE PALE BLANK

*I*n the household of the Gaskells, in Manchester, Charlotte found an atmosphere of harmony and warmth tangible enough to feed her wilting spirits.

She could relax with her hostess as with no one else except Ellen, and here there was an extra element to nourish her—a parity of intellect. Of course there were plenty of divergencies of opinion to keep the conversation lively; Mr. Gaskell was a Unitarian minister—a Dissenter—and Charlotte felt bound to argue theology. But it was a comfort to do so from the same side (so to speak) of the gulf dividing them both from Miss Martineau's terrifying atheistic doctrine.

"It is so confusing," Mrs. Gaskell said, exactly expressing Charlotte's own feelings, "to like and admire a person whose views on fundamentals one so strongly disapproves of."

Miss Martineau's views led them on to the woman question. Here they found much to agree about. Mrs. Gaskell was at work on a new novel on a very charged subject—the story of a young girl, a poor seamstress, seduced at sixteen by a high-born young man who deserts her at the behest of his mama. After bearing a son, the heroine, Ruth, is saved from dereliction and death by a kindly clergyman (a Dissenter, of course!) who takes her into his own family and rehabilitates her.

"You have no idea, Miss Brontë, how many similar cases I have seen in the course of my social work in the slums of our city. Similar, I mean, of course, in their origins—not, alas, in their outcome, for there are all too few, if any, respectable people who would take such a girl up and try to save her. They all seem to think permanent disgrace, if not complete downfall and even death itself in one grim form or another, is no more than such a girl deserves, no matter how little at fault the poor thing was to begin with. The woman is *always* blamed in these cases, no matter what their age or circumstances. I aim to show in my book that such a girl can have a character not only worth saving but which will, given help, rouse up and prove finer and stronger and, ultimately, more worthy perhaps than many who have never stumbled."

She spoke so warmly and earnestly that Charlotte was swayed from a private inclination to believe that a girl seduced was indeed hard to redeem. She, too, had known such cases personally, in the parish around Haworth, had even visited them and tried to comfort them; but she secretly felt that, in their situation, she would be beyond comfort, of any earthly kind at least. Now she began to see that she had been too rigid, too censorious in her outlook, for Mrs. Gaskell went on to tell her of specific cases of girls brought to grief, essentially by a society which condemned them unheard, not through their own wickedness or even weakness; many had given themselves initially through misguided love, through hunger, or through simple ignorance.

"Society has much to answer for," said Charlotte musingly. "Of course it is wrong that a girl should be driven onto the streets for one mistake. But I for my part am more preoccupied with the plight of—well, may I call them 'respectable' girls and women— those who have not and never would stumble as you put it, but who are nevertheless made miserable their whole lives long by being driven by society into other forms of servitude—less degraded, no doubt, but no more free, no more independent, no more fulfilling of their talents than the life we have been speaking of."

"You mean governessing?"

"And marriage."

"Goodness!" exclaimed Mrs. Gaskell, starting back with a smile. "Am I in servitude? I don't feel it!"

"Then you are not. And you are very fortunate. You manage to combine your work for your husband and family with a career of which you can be proud, and in which you are self-sufficient. But you must know you are a rarity among our sex. To most girls, even if they are wealthy, marriage is the only avenue open to them—the only type of fulfillment, the only way to achieve status in society. For this she must sell herself as surely as must a street-woman. If she can find love and a true compatibility of tastes and talent; if her husband can bring himself to regard her as a person in her own right and not a mere adjunct to himself, then she is blessed indeed, as you are. But I dare say that if the truth were known there are as few like you in England—happy *and* fulfilled, unsolitary *and* unsuppressed, partnered, yet free to pursue a path of their very own—as are girls like your Ruth, who find the right kind of saviors and can reach the twin goals of happiness and self-fulfillment that each one of us is seeking."

"I am sorry to see you such a cynic about marriage, Miss Brontë!"

"Most of the happy ones I see are so only because of the willingness of the wife to submit herself in all important things to her husband's will."

"Would *you* then *not* be willing—?" inquired Mrs. Gaskell with a twinkle.

Charlotte was silent. She had refused two proposals in her life:

one from Ellen's brother Henry, and one from another clergyman after a single meeting. So in a way she had proof that she would not be willing to forego her selfhood for the security and companionship of marriage. Yet still she could not be sure.

"What I am saying," she answered (or rather, avoided answering) at last, "is that it is quite wrong that a woman should be forced to choose between spinsterhood, which is to say loneliness and dependency and an entire absence of status, and wedlock, which may well be a form of slavery in which even her person is not her own." She sat up straighter than usual and willed herself not to blush at this bold statement, but Mrs. Gaskell took no particular note of it. She was brooding herself now, her chin on her hand, and suddenly burst out:

"Of course, I must kill Ruth in the end."

"What? Ruth—your Ruth? But why?" asked Charlotte.

"Oh, they will quite cast me out otherwise," she said moodily. "They may do anyway."

"Who, the critics?"

"Yes. And the readers. I am a minister's wife, don't forget. I cannot afford to allow her to go quite free."

"But you say she is at the point of death when her rescuer finds her! Is not that punishment enough for her sin?"

"Not for that sin. Not in our times. I must rest content to show she is not wholly bad . . . that she is in fact a good woman, a *good mother*. Do you know what courage it will take for me to publish a book which says *that* much? So die she must in the end, there's no help for it, or I shall be pilloried and my family with me."

In the evenings, when Mr. Gaskell was sometimes free to sit with them, they got on to politics. A very novel subject was then being discussed (jokingly in most cases) in the salons—that of a petition, presented earlier that year by the very Earl of Carlisle who had introduced himself to Charlotte at Thackeray's lecture, calling for the enfranchisement of women. It was Miss Martineau who had first told Charlotte about it. Needless to say she had been exuberantly "for"—and Mrs. Gaskell agreed; but Charlotte was not so sure. Again, it was not women's *fault* that they were not ready to have the vote; but voting was a matter of independence of mind. Women, if given the vote now, in the present climate, would invariably vote on their husbands' or fathers' instructions, and if they did have minds and opinions of their own on the subject it would cause great dissension in the home, which, in the end, would only make their lot harder.

"First set them free of men by giving them the right to earn their own living in a variety of spheres," she said. "*Then* we will see about votes."

"Do you really think, Miss Brontë, that women could compete successfully with men in the professions?" inquired Mr. Gaskell seriously. "I myself feel that only the exceptional ones are fitted for such things as law and medicine, for example. Such special cases make bad law."

"If there is a natural unfitness in women for men's employment there is no need to make laws on the subject," said Charlotte. "Leave all careers open. Let them try. Those who ought to succeed will succeed, or, at least, will have a fair chance. The incapable will fall back into their right place."

Mr. Gaskell looked at her admiringly. "There is a touch of ruthlessness in you, Miss Brontë, which gives your conversation a most cutting edge," he remarked.

"If you mean to imply that I have a masculine turn of mind, I shall take instant offense," said Charlotte. "That is what some critics have said about my books, and I shall deny it to my last breath. That ruthlessness, that cutting edge is nothing more than common sense, a quality we women have long been known to excel in." Mr. and Mrs. Gaskell laughed and exchanged looks. They both liked her more and more; she felt this, and responded to it as she never failed to respond to affection.

They were not alone in liking her. Their children felt the same. There were four daughters in the family, of all of whom Charlotte grew very fond. There was one in particular, the youngest, Julia. She was a tiny, dainty creature, not quite five, and yet, in her delicious precocity of language and manners, not really infantine at all. This unaffected adult quality reminded Charlotte poignantly of her dead eldest sister, Maria; and this association deepened Julia's appeal.

With her usual lack of confidence she made no overtures to the child. But the attraction was mutual. Julia made her own approaches; and soon Mrs. Gaskell was touched to notice the two earnestly engaged with each other. Before the visit ended, it was clear that a rapport had been established strong enough to make it hard for them to part.

In a word the short trip to Manchester benefited Charlotte to a greater extent than the six weeks she had spent in London, and she returned to Haworth in improved health and spirits, ready at last to pick up her novel and get down to serious work on it.

The theme of the book was loneliness, and the thesis was how loneliness may be borne. Charlotte used the writing of it not only to exorcise finally the moribund demon of her love for Monsieur Héger, but as a means of coming to terms with the overbearing dilemma of her own solitude. The necessity of learning to live with it—and live, furthermore, creatively, bravely, and faithfully —preoccupied her during the entire time she worked on the text, which she dredged out of the very stuff of her heart and life.

She called the book *Villette*, after the town (really Brussels) where her tale was set. As she strove to make it perfect in every detail, she did not know how to regard the torturous labor involved in the evolution of her heroine, Lucy. Her deep-grained Puritanism told her that reward should be proportionate to effort; yet the lesson of her first two books bewildered her. It did not seem right that *Jane Eyre*, which had come so easily, should have achieved greater success than *Shirley*, which had cost her such pains. Now here was her heroine, Lucy, who lived inside her and did not want to come out; Charlotte fought to have her way, and dragged her reluctantly forth—herself, yet not herself.

Monsieur Héger she "used" almost from life. She dared do this now because to her he was no longer alive in the flesh. It never occurred to her that in fact he, and Madame Héger, might read the book and recognize their characters.

The problem of George and his mother was different. George was writing to her regularly and warmly—the glaring realization that he would be the first to read the book and could scarcely fail to recognize himself in "Dr. John" and his mother in "Mrs. Bretton" constantly inhibited Charlotte and made his truthful portrayal more difficult.

On top of this, the structure and plot of this book were the most complex she had yet attempted. The effort it all cost her suggested to her that this would be her best work to date, as indeed by all the laws of maturity and progression it had to be. Yet how could she get even a hint of confirmation? The craving for companionship at the day's end, the hunger for someone to read to, discuss with and criticize, gnawed at her, all but destroying the satisfaction of writing steadily again.

Thus her longing for her sisters Emily and Anne, which time had begun to blunt at least a little, returned to her full force. The exhaustion of the work itself, her sense of bereavement, together with their ally—the cruel Haworth winter—triumphed at last over Charlotte. She fell ill.

Influenza gripped her, filling her with burning aches and pains. Bending over her desk made them worse and forced her to stop writing. A continual low fever kept her weak and depressed; she lost her appetite and could not sleep without falling prey to ghastly dreams. But the worst thing was that her lungs became congested, and when she heard the echoes of her own labored breaths she became terribly frightened.

Patrick, far more afraid than she, sent for Ellen, who hurried over from Brookroyd.

"I am desperate! Tabby and Martha are both under the doctor, but *she* will not see him. I cannot go through this again, Miss Ellen. If it were the same disease—!" The old man wrung his hands. "Where did this scourge in my children's blood come from? My health is disastrous, but my lungs are sound! My poor wife died of a growth. Yet they, poor helpless creatures, have succumbed to it one by one, five of them, as if cursed from birth! I had hoped and prayed my last darling might be spared. . . . Yet now, if she will not seek help, it could be as it was with my sweet brave Emily, who refused all succor and forced us to watch her fight death's approach all unaided and uncomforted." He blew his nose and wiped his eyes repeatedly before he could go on. "She may listen to you. She loves you as a friend. Parents set up a strange resistance sometimes. . . . Help us, my dear girl, if you can, or my heart will break."

When Ellen taxed Charlotte, she took her hand and drew her down on the sofa where she was lying. "I'm afraid of the truth," she confessed. "What if it *were* my lungs? I would rather not know. I am not like Anne to face death so bravely."

"Would you do to your Papa what poor Emily did to you?" asked Ellen quietly.

So Charlotte braced herself and the doctor was sent for.

"It is the liver which is at the root of all your troubles," he pronounced. "Your lungs are sound."

Charlotte was cured, for the time, by simple relief. Whoever heard of the liver killing anyone? Before long she had joined Ellen in caring for their other invalids.

Ellen shared her bed, as Emily had used to. The nights were no longer cold and lonely. It was so pleasant to have someone to talk to again that Charlotte let her tongue run on and on in the dark.

"It is hard, Ellen, to live this secluded life, and stick to it firmly, where so many temptations are offered! George invited me for Christmas, dear Mrs. Gaskell begs me to go to Manchester, Mr. Thackeray assured me that half the duchesses in London would welcome me with open arms if I were to make myself accessible. Yet if I only contemplate a treat or a holiday while my book is unfinished I feel guilty."

"You are too hard on yourself, Charlotte."

"No. If every time I got depressed I fled from my private battlefield, it would never do."

"Then you should invite more people here."

"That I can only do with my closest friends. You know Miss Wooler, our old teacher, was here in October. I think she expected to find me changed into a frivolous butterfly! Yet after narrowly observing my unchanged mode of life for ten days, she declared herself more proud of my adherence to duty than she ever felt of my 'worldly success,' as she calls it. We have not always drawn well together, Miss Wooler and I; yet now I think we are true friends at last."

"And what of that other 'true friend,' Mr. Taylor? Do you hear from him?"

Charlotte sighed. "He has written to me from Bombay. Each of his pleasant letters obliges me to remind myself that in marriage the only paper component is the certificate—the others have a third dimension! No. If Mr. Taylor be the only husband fate has to offer me, single I will remain."

They talked about Mary. Her cousin Ellen Taylor had gone out to Australia to join her, and they had opened a shop together, so there was much food for conversation, the tone of which was half-wondering, half-envious. And yet, whence the envy they could not fathom, for neither of them could conceive of selling miscellaneous goods from a wooden cabin in the middle of nowhere, under threat of earthquakes, native uprisings, wild winds, and strange diseases. It was not Mary's specific situation they envied, but her robust happiness, though each woman knew that she herself could not achieve an equivalent satisfaction within a life which held no love.

"Do you think she will ever marry?" asked Ellen wistfully.

"No, not now. Practical though she is, she would disdain to marry for anything but love. On the whole I think she prefers the companionship of clever, industrious, like-minded women to any but the most exceptional men—and I doubt there's a man in all that wilderness who would measure up to her."

Ellen was silent. *She* would not be so hard to please, and yet somehow she was still single.

"In her letter to me about *Shirley*," said Charlotte, "Mary accuses me roundly of being a coward and a traitor, for seeming to apologize for my working women. She believes with all her heart that it is not only the right but the duty of every woman to work. She says one who does so is by that alone better than one who does not. She says that not to work is almost a crime, leading to all kinds of degradation."

Degradation! Yes, thought Ellen soberly yet with some bitterness, there is truth in that. She felt degraded very often in her idleness, her—unneededness. As a spinster she had no assured place in the world, no occupation, no satisfaction. Things were not easy for her at home—most of her brothers and sisters were married. The family fortunes had dwindled, properties had been sold off to pay debts. Now Ellen and her mother had to share their home with married relatives, and often felt like mere obligated appendages. Mary, in a letter, had put it bluntly, "You seem almost turned out of doors by the new arrangement."

Of course, her situation was not tragic like Charlotte's; she should not grumble. Yet she couldn't help thinking sometimes that her lot was harder. It was not easy for her to contemplate the exciting possibilities and triumphs in Charlotte's life without envy —or even, occasionally, suppressed irritation. For Charlotte to keep claiming she had no chance of marriage, for instance, seemed the merest humbug, while right on her own doorstep poor, good Mr. Nicholls was all too evidently ill with love for her.

But as Ellen lay in the dark at her friend's side, warmth of feeling of the purest kind ousted, for the moment, every other sensation. Where would she, Ellen, be without this friendship? *What* would she be, indeed? Nothing and nobody! For years and years Charlotte and all connected with her had been the focus of her existence. Through Charlotte, Ellen had lived a life of vicarious enchantment. Without her she must have lived the only kind of life that, by herself, she deserved—one of unrelieved genteel and parochial dullness.

When Ellen left, Charlotte had something of a relapse, but she kept on her feet to nurse the sick servants and attend Papa in his inevitable winter bronchitis. One dark rainy morning she went down to make up the fire and brew tea for all her invalids, and found yet another.

Keeper, Emily's dog, listless for some days, now lay in his basket, and as she bent to stroke him she saw that his eyes were glazed. He lay there all day. By nightfall he was so obviously dying that Charlotte did not like to leave him. For Emily's sake she sat up with him all night, rocking herself in Tabby's old chair.

In the morning, Mr. Nicholls, having failed to get an answer to his knock, came around to the back, and found Charlotte sitting on the kitchen floor in tears with the big brindled head in her lap. As he quietly came in, she started, and turned up to him a face so pathetic in its weariness and sorrow that he felt the strength leave his body with the pain of seeing it. He crouched beside her and touched the cold carcass gently.

"People kept hinting we should have him put down," she whispered.

"It is much better that he died a natural death," Mr. Nicholls replied. "Miss Emily—" She moved her head sharply and he stopped. "He was a grand dog."

Charlotte stood up with his help, but she could not seem to move away. Mr. Nicholls longed to offer to make her some tea, but he feared to trespass across the bounds he knew she had set for him, which fell far short of such an intimacy.

Suddenly she gave a sob. "I don't know what to do—with him."

He straightened. Here he might fairly help—there was no one else, and despite his anguish at her sorrow, his soul leaped up. "Leave him now, Miss Brontë. I will do what is needful."

He was glad when she left the kitchen. It was hard enough to be near her when she was not in need of comfort, all but impossible when she was.

All writing was in abeyance during the winter, due to Charlotte's own and others' ill-health. George Smith, in London, grew more and more worried by the lack of progress; in January he very nearly came up to Yorkshire to spur Charlotte on himself—but she had gone to Brookroyd, in despair, and by the time she came home, Mr. Williams's more patient policy had prevailed in Cornhill.

"When spring comes, Miss Brontë will be better. Meanwhile it is kinder to leave her in peace."

"I wonder if that fellow Taylor is still disturbing her with his wretched, impertinent suit," muttered George.

"No letters have passed through this office for months," said Mr. Williams. "You must allow me to say, Smith, that you never did our colleague justice. He was a man of the highest principle, the most temperate disposition. I wrote as much to Miss Brontë when she inquired as to my opinion of him."

"The devil you did, Williams! So you've given him a good reference, have you? Well, much good it will do him. She told me herself, when they were first acquainted, that she couldn't bear him—we used to joke about him together."

"A woman may come to reverse first impressions," said Mr. Williams quietly. "I infer that recently she thinks more warmly of him. For her sake it was perhaps a pity you dispatched him so far out of your way."

"I don't regret it for a moment!" George said shortly. "The fellow was hard as nails, as unfeeling as a brick. What use would he have been to a woman of feeling and sensibility?"

Mr. Williams shook his head thoughtfully. He was fond of his young superior, and in business matters greatly admired him. But he did not think the role of dog in the manger suited him.

Mr. Williams's faith in a change in the weather was misplaced. Spring came, and *Villette* lay half-finished while Charlotte struggled with the yearning for Emily and Anne which seemed to sap all her strength. Harriet Martineau's doctrine tormented her. Could it be true? Was it possible that she must not only live without her sisters but die without the hope of finding them? Even the possibility of this black, blank, friendless eternity crushed her.

Her conscience was also perpetually at work. It left her no peace about her unfinished manuscript, but nothing it could inflict on her did any good. By the beginning of June she was so despairing that she decided, after all her staunch refusals of invitations, to take a trip. But to avoid any hint of real pleasure or relief from her battle to accept loneliness, she determined to go alone to the

East Coast to look at Anne's grave, where the stone would now be in place.

She went first to Filey, where she and Ellen had stayed before. The season had not yet begun, and the weather was terrible— storms and bitter winds made it impossible to go out at first. Charlotte sat in her modest sitting room and wrote a few letters and looked at *Villette* with a sense of futility. There was no one to talk to here, no one at all; the rooms were bleak and cold, the view of the sea desolate. Charlotte set her teeth. *Get used to it!* she kept repeating fiercely to herself. *This is just the beginning.*

When the storms blew away, she traveled to Scarborough and climbed the hill to the cemetery. Hollow-hearted, she stood at the foot of the grave and stared at the stone. There were no fewer than five mistakes in the engraving—even the name was spelled wrong! She struggled to feel somehow closer to Anne; all she could really feel was irritation with the blundering stonemason. She laid some flowers on the mound, tried to talk to Anne and failed, and walked down the hill again to seek out the sexton. When she had arranged for the refacing of the stone she went back to Filey, feeling that the real object of her holiday had been accomplished and that she should now go home.

However, the weather improved, and she decided to stay on and try what the sea air could do for her health. Her headaches, nausea, and other aches and pains had followed her here; she determined to shake them off.

Every day she would set out, across the tops of the cliffs or down on the sands when tides allowed, and walk and walk. She became aware that her motives were confused; she was punishing herself, or at least taxing her strength to its limits in an effort to drive away the demons of solitude. She allowed herself only occasionally to stand and look at the sea which she loved so much. For the most part she stared down at her feet, appearing and disappearing beneath her sand-bordered skirt monotonously hour after hour. Her face grew "almost as sunburnt and weather-beaten as a fisherman" she wrote to Miss Wooler, adding sadly, "No spirit moves me."

One sunny day the urge came on her to shock her torpid system as violently as possible. She hired a bathing-wagon and a costume and let one of the burly bathing-women thrust her, gasping, into the icy water. Toweling herself dry in the brine-smelling wagon after this ordeal, she looked down at her shivering body. How thin—how painfully thin she was! There was scarcely a bit of healthy flesh about her anywhere. Yet as she rubbed, she began to glow, and, back in her warm clothes, she strode along the beautiful empty sands feeling better. That evening she delighted her kind landlady by eating an excellent tea.

One Sunday she went to a tiny chapel she had heard of, instead of the regular church. It was green with age and hardly bigger than twice the length and breadth of the parsonage hall, with a little choir-gallery over the altar. The service was strange to Charlotte, but she kept her countenance until the choir rose to sing an anthem, and, to her astonishment, they turned their backs on the small congregation! At the same moment, the congregation turned *their* backs, so that priest and choir faced one way, people the other, all singing devoutly. For the first time since her arrival at Filey, Charlotte felt a surge of laughter rise in her throat, and laying down her hymn-book, she buried her mouth and nose in her hands. The face of Arthur Nicholls flashed into her mind, and she thought, "How Mr. Nicholls would laugh outright if he were here." It was long since she had heard him laugh. The notion cheered her immoderately, and she walked home after the ludicrous service feeling quite happy.

But it was just an interlude. Utter misery claimed her again that night, and the face of the friendly curate was replaced in her mind by that of "the little man," James Taylor. She did not welcome thoughts of him, nor encourage them; yet they came, despite her. It was months since she had heard from him. Would he resume correspondence with her—was there yet, despite everything, something to look forward to, some little light in the dark tunnel of the future?

She had told Papa not to forward post, for those close to her knew where she was and other letters could wait. Might there, lying on the table in the parlor at this very moment, be a letter from Bombay? She was angry with herself for wanting it, yet in the blank that was her life any scrap of hope must insidiously recur.

So she returned to Haworth willingly, even hopefully. And there in a neat pile were the month's letters, which she shuffled through with an eagerness which shamed her. But from India there was nothing. And she laid the rest down unread and went up to her room. There she sat down at her table. For once she did not weep, but sat staring at the church tower, thinking deeply.

What was happening to her? What was she allowing to happen?

Her grief for her sisters and for Branwell was real and true. That she allowed herself, though her common sense informed her coldly that it was continuing too long and too destructively. But what of this other matter?

Was she, who had known the true nature of love, however unreturned, to be duped and chivied by this pallid substitute? Was she to go on allowing a weak, wan, confused, and contradictory hope of escape from loneliness, based upon a man as inferior to her ideal as a dwarf to a titan, to vitiate her strength and, worse than all, corrode her self-esteem?

Even her love for George was a plaything, a child's comforter, and thus a despicable symptom of weakness in its way, for she knew how this essentially trivial emotion compared with the all-encompassing, all-consuming passion she was capable of, when such passion was inspired by a man truly worthy of her, as Monsieur Héger, for all his ultimate cruelty in rejecting her love, had been.

At that moment Charlotte forgot all humility. She forgot her plain face, her stunted body, her lack of grace and charm. She saw herself as if in a mirror which reflected mind and heart, intellect and emotional capacity; and in that mirror Charlotte saw herself as a woman worthy of a great love.

In the same moment, she knew it would never be hers—never, that is, requited and complete. To have experienced it once, one-sidedly, as she had, was to have already passed the climax of her emotional life. She had come down from those heights, her soul scorched but tempered in the white-heat of a great vitalizing fire;

now she was at the foot of the mountain—the pain had died away and that towering pinnacle was behind her. All that lay ahead was an endless plain, across which she had to journey indefinitely. And to clamber pathetically up little molehills she passed on the way, in a craven effort to gain the view she had glimpsed from her former eminence, was an insult—an insult to the sublime quality of her one true love-experience, an insult to herself.

"No. No," she thought fiercely. "I must accept my destiny. God ordains all these things, and He has blessed me with a vision of love which must serve to illuminate the quiet road my real life is fated to follow. By the light not of Monsieur Héger, but of what I felt for him, I must travel; and I must not diminish that vision with little petty loves unworthy of the name. I must accept my lot, and my lot is loneliness. God has set it upon my back as a cross and I shall not lay it down by means of ignoble dreams and insectlike struggles to escape. I shall bear it because it must be borne; and the pale blank that lies before me I shall face, and hold my inner groans within my heart, not seeking relief in words or claiming it in tears if I can help it. For I have had what I have had. Ellen has not had love; Mary has not; even the great Miss Martineau has not had a love like mine. I do not believe even Mrs. Gaskell's contentment springs from the same fountain as the one from which I was allowed to drink. I will not envy her! Nor shall I ever again chide my master in my mind. I shall cherish and revere what he caused in me, and when I write of him there will not be one touch of bitterness or disillusion or anger or disappointment in my treatment of him, for I am free of them all. My love for him was all my portion, for all my life—am I to poison the well which will water my barren way and make my work bear fruit? My return for what I had will be that I shall tell the truth about love, as I know it, in all its moods and all its disguises. And that shall be my answer to God for my talent, my pain and my brief, exalted happiness."

PART II The Years of Grace
1852–1855

chapter **1 THE LAST THING LOOKED FOR**

It took a little time longer for Charlotte wholly to accept, absorb, and digest these conclusions: to face and acquiesce to spinsterhood. For two months more, her muse lay still. But it was awake; it stared her in the face whenever she turned toward it. It waited, poised, till she should submit absolutely to her fate. Then it rose up and took possession of her.

But in the meantime, Patrick had a stroke.

Had Charlotte wished to begin writing during that time, she would not have been free to do so. The stroke was mild; but at Patrick's age any degree of apoplexy was very dangerous. He lay in bed, partly paralyzed, and she nursed him day and night, her mind in turmoil. If he died, her last link with the past would be broken. She would have to leave her home and remake her life. The idea filled her with panic, with incipient and terrifying grief, and with a wild elation. To be alone—quite alone—to have not even Papa! Unimaginable horror . . . and yet. . . . To be free!

It was a trauma that shook loose the final bonds that had held inspiration inert. In September, when her father was on the mend, she began to write.

She still had her nursing duties, and often she sat writing in his bedroom while he slept, scribbling on small bits of paper held close to her eyes against a piece of board. At night, downstairs, she would copy the day's production, correcting, polishing, and amending as she went.

Papa was fretful, wanting her with him whenever he was awake. His temper, never very stable, was irritated by his new helplessness. The focus of this irritation was, of all people, his sound and reliable curate, Mr. Nicholls.

Every morning since Emily's illness, Mr. Nicholls had made a habit of calling at the parsonage. This was ostensibly to take the day's instructions from Mr. Brontë; but he invariably inquired if there were any little task he might do for Charlotte, such as carrying letters to the post, walking Anne's Flossy (now sadly dull without Keeper), or even carrying in coals or other heavy duties. He was unfailingly friendly and kind to old Tabby and he always had a cheerful word for Martha. Charlotte had long ago come to rely upon these brief morning calls as a routine break in her day; and if at times she had dim misgivings about the root cause of these faithful attentions, she did not allow herself to think about them.

Now the "morning knock," as Tabby called it, suddenly got on Patrick's nerves.

"There's that fool fellow again! What does he keep coming for, day after day? I told him yesterday all that was needful for a week. Why doesn't he get on with it and not come troubling the house with his rat-tat like a tradesman? Tabby's too lame to be shuffling off to the front door every minute."

"I will go, Papa."

"You will sit *down*, Charlotte! I don't like you jumping about, it unnerves me. Call down from the window that I've no need of him. Tell him to come back on Friday."

Charlotte had no recourse but to obey. Mr. Nicholls's face, turned up to her, became stricken. He walked away without a word.

"He has been very helpful, Papa. We shouldn't reject his kindness."

Patrick made an impatient gesture. "Phah! Fellow's always hanging around here, like some lost dog. His long face and heavy sighs bring on my indigestion. Keeps muttering about leaving here and going abroad as a missionary. Well, the aboriginal cannibal that eats him will lose all his teeth, great soft gloomy thing that he's grown into. Grumbling about his health all the time when he should be reflecting on those like myself, who really suffer . . .'"

"I have never heard him grumble, Papa."

"Oh, so you take his side, do you? No, he takes good care to see that you see only his best, such as it is."

"Papa, why have you turned against him?" asked Charlotte, refusing to understand the strange imputations her father was making.

"Because the fellow's falling off—falling off week by week. Less and less use to man or beast! Let him take himself off to Australia and welcome, so he stops clear of here!"

The effect of all this was to draw Charlotte's attention willy-nilly toward Mr. Nicholls. Meeting him by chance next day in the village, gratitude for past favors obliged her to speak kindly to him, explaining that in his present condition her father could not help being occasionally irritable. The face which had turned pale the day before now flushed, and the dark eyes kindled.

"Say no more, Miss Brontë. So long as I know I have done nothing to offend *you*."

Charlotte nodded and walked away from him, shrinking inwardly with sudden acute misgiving. Could it be that—? No, she would not imagine it! All such matters were finished with. Suddenly she turned and called him back. Something in the glad way he hurried to her seriously alarmed her.

"Just the same, Mr. Nicholls," she said firmly, "it would be better if you refrained from calling more than once a week hence-forth."

"I thought—if I came around to the back—"

"No. I would rather you didn't. Nothing must be done just now which might affect my father's blood-pressure."

"Just as you wish, Miss Brontë."

And he turned and walked away, his back very stiff and his hands clenched. Charlotte noted it with dismay. Then she hurried on, pushing the curate rigorously from her thoughts.

The work proceeded. Two volumes were finished. Before they went off, Papa, who had never in all the years interfered or asked to read a word until a finished book was put in his hands, now begged Charlotte to read to him. Day after day she read, till, near the end of the last volume which she was still at work on, he burst out, "Charlotte, you will let them be happy, won't you? You'll restore them to each other?"

He knew he was breaking unspoken laws; yet when Charlotte sat silent, he persisted, "It is so real—so true, my darling . . . I know it is true, Charlotte—yes," he added decisively, in answer to her sharp glance. "But I say nothing of that. Only give them to each other! You will, won't you?"

"I can't, Papa."

"Charlotte! Why not? What is to happen?"

"I'll read it to you when it is finished."

"You mean, it is already decided? What—no, don't read, I can-not bear it—does he die?"

She nodded, her head down.

"How? How?"

"At sea, Papa. He dies in a storm on the way home."

At that, Patrick astonished her by growing frantic. He buffetted his bed with his fists. "*No—no—no!* You can't! I won't have it! Why should it end thus? Do they not deserve each other? Is God so cruel—*even in books?*" And then, as she did not speak, he said with an air of discovery, "But for them, you are God. You can be merci-ful. You can save him. Please, Charlotte. Please, my darling! I want her to be *happy! Why* can she not be happy?"

At last Charlotte looked at him. She moved to the bed and sat on it, taking his clenched hand in hers and gently unknotting the fingers.

"I will tell you why, Papa. Because it would not be true. Lucy has a dark star to live under, and dark stars do not light up at the end. I have assigned her *more* joy, not less, than her fate really entitles her to. Her professor loves her. But marry her he cannot. She must live out her life alone."

There was a long silence. Then the old man drew his hand away.

"Then read me no more," he said bitterly. "'I have had my fill of sorrow."

In Cornhill, there was equivalent dismay.

George, when he had read the first two volumes, had blanched. Of course he had known, more or less, what Charlotte felt for him: his own feelings had been sufficiently tender, and her behavior sufficiently discreet, for an unembarrassed understanding to have prevailed. But to see it all exposed—to see his mama so piercingly delineated! "To the very life," he muttered. "Even to quoting some of her pet expressions verbatim—heavens! What will she say?" It all took some adjusting to, before he could begin to get down to criticizing the novel with any detachment. And he was tired, desperately tired. He was overworking, and the continual strain was telling on him, mentally and physically.

Mr. Williams was far too tactful to comment on his recognition of his colleague in *Villette*'s pages. His criticisms were based strictly upon objective considerations.

"She doesn't give enough of the early history of Lucy's life to explain her susceptible, morbid nature. I fear her weaknesses will not endear her to a public still obsessed with conventional romantic heroines."

"What worries me far more," said George, "is how people will take the double love-interest. Hardly is she out of love with the doctor than she is in love again with 'Paul Emanuel.' Damn me if they don't overlap! Unconventional women we have had from this pen before; but a girl in love with two men at once!"

"You realize by the same token, that young 'Dr. John,' having had a weakness for 'Miss Fanshawe,' is obviously destined to fall in love in the last volume with the delectable 'Paulina'?"

"Delectable!" snorted George. "She is an odd and fascinating little minx, but *I* would never fall in love with her." His older colleague smiled into his beard at this innocent gaffe. "Anyway, surely hero usually marries heroine in even Miss Brontë's novels?"

But it was when the final volume arrived that George grew seriously alarmed. The book was broken-backed. The interest switched abruptly from his own character to that of the crusty little Belgian professor. And then, a tragic ending! No, it would not do. It stuck in the throat, after all the waiting and hoping. Brilliant as he acknowledged it to be in terms of writing, as a story it did not satisfy.

And yet . . . and yet. . . .

The book was a great achievement, greater, in its way, than either of the others. He had not been able to put it down. He could not decide about it, and was for once so agitated—almost angry—that he refused at first to let even Mr. Williams see the last volume. "It must be altered," he said. "She must alter it!"

"She won't. Let me see it, my dear fellow."

"Not yet, not yet!" exclaimed George irritably.

He kept it a week. Charlotte would be getting anxious. On that Friday, he sent off a routine acknowledgment, with a money-order. When it came to the amount, he hesitated. The firm had paid £500 for the copyright of each of the other books. She was an established author now, and they had profited greatly by her— indirectly also, for due to her example Thackeray, Mrs. Gaskell, and other famous authors had come over to them. He had meant to give her more this time. But his confusion, his disappointment with this long-awaited book brought out in him a narrow streak of niggardliness which lurked in his normally generous nature.

"Let her have what she had before," he thought. "For the present. If she agrees to make changes, I can always reconsider."

The communication reached Charlotte at Brookroyd, where she was taking a little holiday after the completion of her labors. Miss Wooler was visiting too, and the whole party was seated around the breakfast table when Charlotte, opening her post, suddenly jumped up with a little cry and rushed from the room.

Miss Wooler and Ellen hurried after her and found her crying bitterly in her room, clutching the scant contents of the envelope.

"Charlotte—dearest! What is it? Don't they like it?"

"How am I to know?" cried Charlotte. "I must assume not! Look at this! Not a word, not so much as a line! Only the money, and that in itself is an indication of dissatisfaction. It is the same as before. How am I to tell Papa, who confidently expected £750 this time? And I confess I looked for no less myself. But that's not the worst. To think they would send it like this—so insultingly—oh, I can't bear it! I'll go to London myself, this very day, and ask them what's the matter!"

"Don't be hasty, darling! Perhaps it was just a clerk's error. Do wait a few days, Charlotte! I'm sure there will be a proper letter tomorrow."

And so there was, for by then characteristic kindness and a sense of proportion had been restored to George. His long letter, by contrast with Charlotte's fevered imaginings, gave an overall judgment which was very favorable. It contained strong criticism of the last volume, but no more than she had expected. Soothed and relieved, she put her disappointment about the money aside.

"And will you make the alterations he wants?" Ellen ventured to ask.

"No. Although I agree with most of what he says."

Ellen looked at her quizzically.

"Because I *cannot* change what is once written. It is as if he asked me to change some element of the real past. 'Would you please make it that you never traveled to Brussels?' 'Would you kindly alter the date of your birth?' There are a million things I would like to 'rewrite' in my own story, but I cannot, however much more harmonious and fitting such changes would make it to some future biographer. It's the same with Lucy. She just *is*, and all that happened to her happened."

So Charlotte had to tell her irate Papa that she had been bilked of the extra £250, which put him so out of temper with the world at large that for days no one could cope with his vagaries at all. It was only when Charlotte summoned courage to call him strongly to order on the grounds that the Season of Good Will was approaching, and that he was now quite well enough to spread a little Christmas cheer among his parishioners, that he began grumblingly to pull himself together.

Mr. Nicholls had stayed well away for some time, but now, at Charlotte's insistence, he was invited for tea.

"He has proved an excellent deputy during your illness, Papa," Charlotte said. "Now you are better, we must get back on the old footing. Monday is and has ever been the day the curates come to tea. I shall bake some biscuits."

When Monday afternoon came, Charlotte served tea in the parlor. Mr. Nicholls seemed out of sorts. He was pale and nervous; twice his trembling hand, too large anyway for the delicate teacup, spilled tea upon his waistcoat, and as for the biscuits, Charlotte might have saved herself the trouble for all he ate of them. Each time she proffered the plate he looked at her strangely, shifted his eyes from hers as soon as they had met, and shook his head with a spastic jerk. At last Charlotte felt constrained to ask, "Are you quite well, Mr. Nicholls? You look rather feverish."

He muttered something inaudible.

"I beg your pardon?"

"I remarked that I have not been—well—for some time," he repeated, so loudly that Patrick gave an exaggerated start.

As soon as politeness allowed, Charlotte excused herself and went into the dining-room, leaving the men alone. She sat by the fire writing letters until, at about eight o'clock, she heard the parlor door close. Mr. Nicholls was leaving. Although not attending, Charlotte's ear expected the clash of the front-door closing behind him; and she was suddenly and painfully alerted by the fact that it did not come.

Instead came a light tap on the dining-room door.

In a flash, she knew what was coming. All the tiny indications, like little pieces of a puzzle, fell together in her mind; insight and intuition shone upon the picture with a brief, sharp glare. She jumped to her feet, as if seeking some escape, her heart pounding under her ribs. The knock was repeated.

"Come in."

In he came, and stood just inside the door, which he silently shut behind him, and stared—or rather glared—at her with eyes glazed and breath coming short.

"Miss Brontë, I must speak to you!" he almost gasped.

Oh, God! she thought wildly. She compressed her lips. They looked intently at each other.

"Do you know what I want to say?"

She half-shook her head, but her frightened look said the opposite.

"You do not wish to hear it. I know that. In all these dreary months—all the years—I have been here, seeing you constantly, I have waited for one sign that you would welcome my love. Indeed, I well know that I would spare us both pain if I could keep silent forever. But I have borne as much as I can. You can never, *never* know what it has meant to me to watch you, through all your great trials and sorrows, unable to give you comfort, unable to offer you my strength or so much as my hand to steady you—" His voice— finest thing about him she had often thought, deep, rich and warm —broke, and he put one hand up to cover his eyes, the other backward against the door as if he felt himself tottering.

"Mr. Nicholls—"

"No—I must speak now, whatever comes of it—forgive my weakness—I love you so dearly—"

"Please, oh, please! Say no more!" whispered Charlotte, seized by such a hot wave of pity for the man's obvious suffering that she could not stand apart from him. She hurried to him and took his arm.

He drew himself up, and looked down into her face. There were tears in his eyes, but the big hand that took hold of hers was steady.

"Give me hope."

He spoke with such intensity, such longing and yet such dignity in the midst of his vulnerability, that she was moved almost to tears herself.

"Mr. Nicholls, have you—did you speak to Papa?"

"I did not dare."

"Please leave me now. I will speak to him. You shall have your answer tomorrow."

She half-put, half-led him from the room, pressed his surtout and hat into his limp hands, and somehow got him out of the house. Then, without giving herself a moment to reflect or recover, or to lose her composure even further, she went directly into the parlor.

"Papa!"

"Yes, my dear?"

"Mr. Nicholls—Mr. Nicholls has—" She faltered as she saw his face change.

"Mr. Nicholls has—what?"

"He has—declared himself."

The old man turned first as white as paper, then his face flushed a threatening, choleric red. Putting both his wrinkled hands on his desk, he levered himself slowly upright, and Charlotte found herself cowering back against the door as if she saw some wild beast loom up before her.

"He—has—dared! That whelp! That—spawn of the Irish bogs! That hundred-a-year nobody has dared to speak for *you?*" His aged voice, still powerful enough, rose to something like a screech.

"Papa—!" gasped Charlotte, but her protest was drowned by his succeeding roar.

"I will thrash him! I will make his miserable name a byword for impudence and scoundrelly self-aggrandizement throughout the Church of England! He would have *my daughter!* A penniless curate, without portion or prospects, dares to aspire to the foremost authoress of our time! I shall banish him! I shall—"

"Papa, don't, don't work yourself up so! You will have a seizure! I shall refuse him—decidedly, definitely—tomorrow. Tonight, if you will! Only, for heaven's sake, calm yourself!"

Patrick, exhausted by his own fury, sank down again in his

chair. His temple-veins throbbed less violently, but his bloodshot eyes still glared and his hands shook.

"You will refuse him? No, Charlotte, by God, that you shall not! For you shan't set eyes on him again if I can help it! Give me paper and pen and see how *I* shall deal with his insolent proposals!"

With trembling violence he wrote, and Charlotte, in growing anger, read over his shoulder the curt and cruel note of utter repudiation and scornful rebuke that emerged from that wavering nib. "It's as well I do not love the poor man," she thought, "or such epithets would transport me beyond all patience." As it was, she was appalled to think of the effect such a letter must have upon a man in such a vulnerable state as Mr. Nicholls.

She delayed sending it as long as she dared, to give him a day or two to recover himself. When at last duty (and Papa's continual interrogation) forced her to send it around to the Browns', where Mr. Nicholls lodged, she accompanied it with a short letter of her own.

> Dear Sir,
>   While you must never expect me to reciprocate the feeling you have expressed, yet at the same time I wish to disclaim participation in sentiments calculated to give you pain.
>   Pray try to maintain courage and spirits.
>   Believe me, very sincerely your friend,
>   C. BRONTË

Martha took the letters, and returned with two brief notes, one directed to Charlotte. It thanked her for her gentleness to him, which had helped to mitigate the expected blow of her refusal. He regretted that he had so outraged Mr. Brontë's feelings, and hoped he would not inflict them too severely upon the one for whose welfare both he and the writer cared more, surely, than for their own lives. He added that he was going away, and that the other note was to tender Mr. Brontë his resignation.

Looking up, with a strangely sick heart from reading this, Charlotte found Martha still in the room watching her.

"What is it, Martha?"

"Just wanted to tell you, as 'e's gone, Miss Charlotte. And a good riddance, I say—for 'e's fair worried wits out of our mam, refusin' food and niver speakin' a word to a soul these two weeks. Me father says it's you 'e's after, Miss, and that 'e deserves shootin' for 'is presumption! And I think t'same road, for I can see 'e's upset you sommat cruel, and parson's like to go into another apoplexy all on account of our lodger!"

chapter 2 VILLETTE

*C*harlotte's next trip to the capital
was primarily a business one. The proof-sheets were coming in
steadily, and there was much to discuss in connection with them.

Mrs. Smith was as courteous as ever; but Charlotte felt that
something had gone out of her courtesy, some essential warmth. It
was as if Charlotte had caused the older woman too much anxiety,
robbed her too much of peace of mind. Besides, there was the
character of "Mrs. Bretton," which was modeled after her. She
never mentioned it, but Charlotte was made to feel that offense
had quietly been taken.

As to George, she was shocked when she saw how he had
changed. His fine boyish handsomeness and trim physique had
been further impaired by the strain of overwork. He no longer
looked young. Yet his energy and vitality were as strong as always,

and Charlotte had much ado to stand up to his persistent demands for changes in Volume III.

"The ending at least must be softened!" he decreed at last, when he had met defeat on all but a few minor points. "This you shall not refuse me! It is too abrupt, too harsh, too shocking. It does not follow naturally, it is not prepared for, it is entirely gratuitous misery-making on your part and springs—I must say this, Charlotte —from a morbid streak in your own character which I would fain see you try hard to conquer. Now then. If as you say you cannot see your way to giving your readers the happy ending they will crave—and, may I add, *deserve*, after all you've subjected them to, you must at least veil Monsieur Paul Emanuel's death—give those with no taste for sudden tragedy an option of some kind. Give us at least an enigma."

"I cannot change what happened!"

George, weary and out of patience, threw back his chair and stood up. "Then I will not publish it!" he all but shouted. "There now. Take it to Newby! You must bend in this, Charlotte. I insist that you bend!"

So Charlotte bent, and veiled, and enigmatized. But "Monsieur Emanuel" was drowned just the same. And "Lucy Snowe" was left with her school, and her library, and her plants, and the rest of her life to be lived—independent, self-respecting, hard-working. And alone.

There was an irony in all this for Charlotte. Only a few months before, she had read the manuscript of Mrs. Gaskell's *Ruth*. It was a brave book, and Charlotte had deeply admired everything about it—except the ending, where she felt her friend had lost her courage, and yielding to convention, given "Ruth" society's idea of her just deserts. "Why should she die? Why must we close up the book weeping?" Charlotte had written. Now here she was, killing her own hero for no greater crime than that he would have made her heroine happier than Charlotte thought she was fated to be.

Mrs. Gaskell wrote to her while she was in London, asking, in the name of friendship, that she delay the publication of *Villette* to avoid clashing with the appearance of *Ruth*. This gave her a little extra time in London after all her work was done. And because George was so busy, and Mrs. Smith so distrait, Charlotte found herself freer than on any previous occasion to do and see the sorts of things she chose for herself.

No Crystal Palaces or operas or theaters drew her. Instead she took herself to where she believed the real life of London could be seen—to the places where, she felt, Harriet Martineau would have taken her—or, indeed, Mrs. Gaskell, who, through welfare work, knew a great deal about the dark side of life and society. She visited two prisons, Newgate and Pentonville, and was appalled, not least because she was forestalled when she tried to talk to the prisoners. The warders, assuming her to be one with the society ladies who visited such places for "interest" (that is to say, amusement), felt it their duty to prevent her "touching pitch." One poor girl, who had killed her illegitimate child ("There but for the grace of God goes 'Ruth'!" thought Charlotte), was quite roughly pulled away when Charlotte took her hand and tried to speak a kind word to her. Looking into the haggard, suffering, sin-ridden faces and the God-abandoned eyes of the prisoners, Charlotte asked herself whether after all she might not one day be capable of writing the kind of book she had told George she could never write—a book with a philanthropic purpose, a social message. Was it not a kind of abrogation of duty to write mere tales when there were such lives as these, crying out, one and all, for a spokesman to plead understanding for them? Mrs. Gaskell spoke out for them; Miss Martineau lived to do so. Why not Charlotte?

She felt this even more strongly in the foundling hospitals she visited, looking at the poor unloved, unwanted children who sat or stood around, torpid in their misery, the look in their eyes a hopeless blank.

Emotionally wrung dry by these experiences, she relieved her mind by asking to be taken to the City of London. Here she could revel in an aspect of life she admired most—the fascinatingly exact organization of a mighty human endeavor. She enjoyed the controlled bustle, the feeling that each of the hundreds of hurrying figures had his appointed place in the vast business complexes of bank, Exchange, brokers' offices, or Law Court. Here she could feel that human energy was under control, harnessed for the common good, and that its highest abilities were being fulfilled, not corrupted and perverted as in the other institutions she had been to. The men whom George had appointed to show her the City were impressed with the interest and appreciation she showed for its workings. "Extraordinary for a woman!" said one of them, to her annoyance.

Mrs. Smith and her daughters also annoyed her by seeming to bear out the prevalent male opinion that the female mind could not generally rise above trumpery subjects, for they all expressed amazement at her "gloomy" tastes and kept trying to cheer her up with parties and dinners. But she refused them all. Looking around at their family circle, she felt in some strange way that she was saying goodbye to them. She sensed that an era, that of her friendship with the Smiths and their like, was over. Even Mr. Williams was not as attentive as he used to be, and this did sadden her.

"Those boxes of books you send have sustained me through more hard times than you will ever know," she told him once. "Yet each time one arrives, I feel it should be the last. I never want it to become a burden, I would rather you stopped it at once."

"Not at all, not at all," Mr. Williams replied. But he did not look at her, and Charlotte thought with a pang, "He is tired of it, it has become a nuisance. I do not write enough books to deserve continuous attentions. I should relieve him, tell him to send no more." But she couldn't. The boxes of books were too precious, and she suspected that from now on—Papa so out of temper, Mr. Nicholls going—she would need them more than ever.

She tried not to think of Mr. Nicholls, for whenever he came into her mind, she saw him as she had seen him in the dining-room that night, shaking, overcome. And since—wretched, sullen, deprived (by her!—it was terrible!) of appetite and zest for life. He had written to Patrick just after Christmas, asking if he might retract his resignation, and Papa, though still seething with rage, had agreed (in consideration, Charlotte suspected, of the horrors of finding and adjusting to a new curate), provided Mr. Nicholls promised not to "broach the obnoxious subject" ever again. He had evaded this issue, but was nevertheless reinstated, though he and Papa were not on speaking terms. Charlotte dreaded to think of the atmosphere she must return to, and, when the time approached, she wrote begging Ellen to meet her at Keighley and come home with her.

Ruth came out in the middle of January and was greeted in the salons at least with an outburst of shocked protest. What! A minister's wife (albeit a Dissenter) pleading the cause of a fallen woman, and, far worse, excusing a minister of religion who helps her disguise the fact, lies to his parishioners about her status, and generally aids and abets her in her sin! Charlotte, angry and indignant on her friend's behalf, shrank from her own oncoming fate. She herself saw nothing to take exception to in her own novel, but, then, neither had she in *Jane Eyre*, nor in *Ruth* either. She had learned to her cost that her ideas of propriety and society's were widely different. It was Miss Martineau who had explained this to her, and it was to her that Charlotte now turned.

She sent Miss Martineau an advance copy of *Villette*, begging for her honest comments. She meant every word when she wrote, "I kneel to Truth. Let her smite me on the one cheek—good! The tears may spring to the eyes; but courage! There is the other side; hit again, right sharply." But her underlying motive was to arm herself. If Miss Martineau saw nothing wrong in her novel, Charlotte felt she would be immune to any abuse hurled at her by ordinary critics; and she felt confident of her friend's verdict. When it came, it was not so much a blow on the cheek as a lance through the vitals.

Charlotte returned to Haworth immediately the book was published, and the reviews reached her there. Ellen would sit with her each morning after the post had come, sharing the joy of the good reviews (which were by far the majority) and bemoaning with her any that were less than good. But one day Charlotte came upon one in the *Daily News*, the shock of which was so cruel that she broke down and buried her face in her hands with a little cry.

Ellen took the paper and read the notice through carefully, then looked up, bewildered. "What is so bad about this? It is full of praise, in the main. It's only the part about your attack on the Catholics—"

Charlotte raised a stricken face. "You know who wrote it? Harriet Martineau! I am certain. Oh, how is it possible she could write so of my work in a public journal—she, who told me she dislikes reviewing—and not even signed! It is infamous of her!"

"But Charlotte, dear, it's by no means unfavorable! Listen—"

"I won't hear any of it—don't inflict it on me! I know her. Her strictures on the all-pervading painfulness of the book, the affliction on the reader of subjective misery—saying there is no one 'serenely and cheerfully good' in the whole book—what a calumny! And worst of all, this part—this—" she snatched the paper back and found the place with a shaking finger, "about love. 'All the female characters, in all their thoughts and lives, are full of one thing . . . so incessant is the writer's tendency to describe the need of being loved. . . . Lucy entertains a double love'—A lie, a lie— and this! Oh, it is she all right! With her great independent soul, her indifference to what every normal woman cares for. 'There are substantial, heartfelt interests for women of all ages, quite apart from love: there is an absence of introspection, an unconsciousness, a repose in women's lives of which we find no admission in this book . . . readers will reject the assumption that events and characters are to be regarded through the medium of one passion only.' " Charlotte looked up wildly. "How could she! How could she show me myself through her eyes! She sees me as weak, lovesick, obsessed. *But I know what love is!* If one need be ashamed of such a feeling, there is nothing fine and noble on earth!" She burst into tears, but as Ellen rose to comfort her, she shook her off. "No! It is not pain, it is anger! The gulf between us is too great, Nell—I have done with her, and I shall tell her so!"

"You had better wait till you have confirmation she wrote it," said Ellen practically. "You have loved and admired her so, it would be a pity to rupture your friendship on a suspicion."

But suspicion was confirmed a day or two later, when a letter arrived from Miss Martineau carrying an almost identical message about the book. "I do not like the love," she wrote bluntly, "either the kind or the degree of it."

"She knows nothing of it, that is why," said Charlotte. "With all her intellect and all her intrepidity, she has a barren heart. I will not see her again."

"Well. Miss Wooler at least will be relieved to hear that," said Ellen prosaically. "She always thoroughly disapproved of her, and of your friendship with her."

"Only a few weeks ago, she wrote advising me to break it off," said Charlotte dully. "I refused . . . I said I would not be a fair-weather friend, or abandon her for her doctrines. Yet now it is over just the same. Oh, how could she wound me like this? We were so wrong about each other!"

Despite this unpleasantness, which gnawed at Charlotte's heart for a long time, the winter passed tolerably. Her health was much better now the book was out of her system, and its success so pleased Patrick that he was quite his old self and even contrived to tolerate Mr. Nicholls's brooding presence about the parish with only occasional sarcasm and acidity. Still, there was no question of his attitude to the "obnoxious subject" softening in any way.

If Charlotte dared to defend the curate, the old man would flush angrily. "I warn you, Charlotte! I'll not hear good spoken of him."

"Then do not you speak ill of him, Papa. I have refused him. He is to leave, when he gets a new curacy. Let that content you, without abusing him more."

Patrick muttered, "Such a match would be a degradation. If ever you do marry, I expect you to do a great deal better than *that* presumptuous young bigot!"

"Better in what way, Papa? I hope you are not speaking of worldly goods. Such considerations are surely beneath both of us."

Patrick snorted and waved her out of the room.

Martha exploited the dramatic potential of the situation to the full. "Eh, Miss Brontë! Didsta see how that Mr. Nicholls looked after ye? A most darkling, flaysome look, as if he'd like to kill summat—*or summ'n*—"

"That will do, Martha!"

Charlotte was angry because it was true. And he did more than look. Once he followed her home after evening service, up the dark lane. She hastened her steps, not out of fear, but to escape from his yearning misery which she could feel. She was oppressed by his behavior, by his giving Papa genuine cause for derision and complaint. Somehow, despite her lack of love for him, she didn't like to see him put himself at a disadvantage.

This he very notably did on an occasion of unusual pomp at the parsonage: the visit of the Bishop of Ripon. Ellen, in a letter before the event, mocked Charlotte gently for the elaborateness of the preparations, but Charlotte retorted, "It is very well to talk of receiving a bishop without trouble, but you *must* prepare for him." Extra hands were employed in the kitchen; the entire lower floor was spring-cleaned; the local shops were ransacked by Martha for the most splendid tea and supper they could provide. All the local tribe of curates was invited to both meals. In short, everything that could be done to make a suitable impression was done. And in the end the effect was all but ruined—by Mr. Nicholls.

Normally he was able to control his moroseness in company, and at those times Patrick spoke to him with something approximating to civility. It was only in their few but necessary private encounters that they displayed their antipathy in all its raw unseemliness. But on this of all occasions, when everyone else was on his best behavior, the smoldering volcano belched forth some all-too-visible sparks of acrimony.

Charlotte thought their visitor a most charming bishop—"the most benignant little gentleman that ever put on lawn sleeves; yet stately, too." His cherubic face was all aglow with condescension and good will. At first, all went well. Martha's tea, complete with custard tarts, bakewells, a splendid seedcake, cold meats, three kinds of bread, and golden hillocks of butter-rolls topped with parsley, was thoroughly approved, and the bishop ate heartily. Conversation seldom flagged when the curates were about, and Mr. Nicholls's sullen silence passed unremarked. True, Charlotte, anxiously aware of the tensions, thought she noticed the bishop throw one or two puzzled glances at the scowling, bearded face of the resident curate—the only person present who did not appear to be smiling at him with eager deference.

After tea, Mr. Nicholls's duty was to accompany Patrick and his guest on a tour to see the church and the National School, where religious instruction was given to the local children. On impulse Charlotte elected to go with them. She sensed trouble brewing: her father's requests to Mr. Nicholls had taken on the tone of sharp commands, which she felt could not but provoke him, and she thought, "If I am there, he may more easily contain himself."

But, alas, her presence only exacerbated his black mood. Outside the school Patrick, not bothering to turn, put out his hand and snapped his fingers imperiously for the keys. The curate stood stolidly, his eyes on the ground, until Patrick was forced to turn and say irritably, "Come *along*, Nicholls—don't keep His Reverence waiting all day in the wind!"

The heavy dark face had lifted and the eyes, usually so bland and calm, darted a look of hatred which would have shriveled a lesser man than his employer. The bishop started visibly and Charlotte's heart pounded with premonitory dread.

"The keys, sir, are with you," said Mr. Nicholls in tones of ice.

"With me? Nonsense, Nicholls! You always have them! If you have been remiss enough to leave them in your lodgings, be man enough to admit it and run and fetch them instead of standing there like a—like—" Patrick choked back the epithet, but he was plainly furious.

"Sir. You have the keys. I handed them to you yesterday at your request. They are in your pocket at this moment."

The two men glared at each other like mastiffs. Charlotte half-expected to hear growls issuing from their throats. As for the bishop, he looked seriously alarmed, and hastened to step between them.

"Gentlemen, pray don't trouble about me! To be frank I have seen so many schools that I am very ready to forgo this one in favor of a longer look at your delightful church . . ."

Patrick opened his mouth to fling more angry words at Mr.

Nicholls. But he didn't stay to hear them. Without a glance at the bishop he turned on his heel and strode away up the hill, leaving them standing there gaping after him.

Charlotte thought her father would burst. "Young ingrate! Unmitigated incivility and insolence!" he spluttered. "I can hardly express—allow me to offer—the most abject apologies for my curate—his rudeness is unsupportable—"

"My dear Mr. Brontë, don't upset yourself. It is quite plain the poor young fellow is laboring under some deep distress of mind. I'm confident that such is not his customary behavior. Pray excuse him! I do, with all my heart. After all, we ourselves were young men once, were we not?" he added, startling Charlotte with an almost sly little twinkle in her direction.

Mr. Nicholls was barely in evidence for the rest of the visit, but after it had ended—with many protestations of gratification from the bishop—he voluntarily submitted himself to Patrick's anger for half an hour in the study. Charlotte, listening to the monologue of abuse, felt less pity than usual. She was very angry with him herself, even after she had found the missing keys in her father's pocket.

One admirer Mr. Nicholls still had—Flossy. When his walking-companion ceased to come for him, the spaniel would seek him out at his lodgings and drag him out onto the moors. It struck Charlotte to the heart to see the poor man trudging over the brow of the hill in the gloomy twilight, hunched up and desolate, knowing that no friendly fireside awaited him—for he shunned all his old friends—only a return to his dreary, lonely rooms, and the sour looks of the Browns, with whom he lodged. They, along with other former admirers, had turned against him now as completely as if he had ruined Charlotte, instead of respectably offering his hand. It was not fair, she thought—he had not deserved this!

"They don't understand the nature of his feelings. He is one who attaches himself to very few, whose sensations are close and deep, like an underground stream, running strong, but in a narrow channel." She sighed, a thing she seemed to do many times a day, for her heart was like a stone. She pitied him inexpressibly, yet since she could not love him she felt helpless to offer him any support in his extremity, which would only exacerbate his feelings.

Sometimes, as the future stretched before her as blank as ever, she could not help wondering if she had thrown away "the purest gem" (as she wrote to Ellen), a genuine attachment. But in his present mood, Mr. Nicholls was not an attractive prospect. It best behooved her to remain passive, but her heart ached for him just the same.

chapter **3 COMMUNICATIONS**

A short visit to Mrs. Gaskell in the spring cheered her up. She made new friends there, Catherine and Emily Winkworth, whose charming singing voices quickly overcame Charlotte's painful initial shyness during the evening party at which they met.

Charolotte and Mrs. Gaskell talked a great deal, chiefly about their books, as often as they could snatch half an hour alone together in that lively household. Mrs. Gaskell, though she tried to restrain herself for fear of upsetting Charlotte, was in a pitiable state of distress about the reception of *Ruth*.

"I meant so well!" she said. "One would suppose, from the way some of even my closest acquaintance regard the book, that it was an open invitation to vice. Perhaps I *was* wrong to let my kind old vicar tell lies for her, but when people ask if my husband would have done the same, I am obliged to answer that I hope so, and then they are more profoundly shocked than ever! Many put it down to the depravity inherent in Unitarianism, and that makes me feel I have betrayed my own sect by my outspokenness. Orthodox ministers' wives have been kind enough to let me know their husbands have ceremoniously burned the book, and would as soon read the veriest heresy in their family circle as read my *Ruth*. Oh, Miss Brontë, it is hard to bear. I am all one black bruise, and I sometimes wish I had never written a line!"

Charlotte was indignant. "You have written a book you can be proud of. There is not a word or syllable in it which could offend any true Christian—I swear it. They are all canting bigots and humbugs, the very same as those who tried to stone Mary Magdalene. Pray don't let them make you regret!"

Mrs. Gaskell, near to tears, put her hand out to Charlotte, who clasped it warmly. "You are so sweet," she said impulsively. "Thank you."

Charlotte had thought of telling her friend about Mr. Nicholls, but with her hostess so preoccupied, she decided not to. Instead, she tried to forget all about him, in the pleasure of seeing the Gaskell daughters again, and renewing her friendship with Julia in particular. As she was leaving for home, Julia sidled up to her and put a fresh flower into her hand. "It's a wild one," she said, adding oddly, "Like you, Miss Brontë."

"I shall prize it," said Charlotte solemnly. The whole visit had revived her. She would be able to face Haworth now with a stauncher heart—especially as Mr. Nicholls had secured another curacy (somewhere in Yorkshire—he had told no one where) and she would soon be relieved of the sight of his unhappiness.

He was to leave in May. Everyone, not only Charlotte, was glad. His distress had upset the whole village. But not all loyalty for his past service to the parish was forgotten, and a subscription was taken up to buy him a watch. Word of this pleased Charlotte strangely. Perhaps, after all, he could leave without too much unpleasantness.

The last Sunday of his curacy was Whitsun. Mr. Nicholls had to take the morning service. Though he was much subdued, all went well until the end, when those who wished to take communion came up to the rails, and he suddenly saw that Charlotte was among them.

Though he did not know it, every eye—at least every woman's eye—was upon him. They all knew he was perishing with love of "t'parson's Charlotte," that he had been sent off for asking for her (and quite right too! Their very own celebrity—the notion!). Yet now, as he slowly approached her along the altar rail, they all held their breaths with something akin to compassion. When he reached her, his love and grief laid such a mighty hold on him that he could not move or speak. His knees buckled; he all but let the chalice fall. One of the communicants, an old man of the village, rose and murmured a few strong words to him, which rallied him a little; making a visible effort to master himself, which caused several of the women present to break into sobs and certainly brought tears to Charlotte's eyes, he managed to stumble and whisper through the rest of the service. As Charlotte hurried out of church, with deeply bent head, when the ordeal was over, the looks she got spoke volumes—if not about their attitude to *this* ill-fated romance, then about romance in general and the need of it even in a dour Yorkshire village.

The little ceremony in which Mr. Nicholls's testimonial was presented to him was the warmer for this—to Charlotte—infinitely painful incident. Many handkerchiefs were seen; fellow-curates from the district came and shook hands with their departing colleague; even John Brown looked less implacable, and as for Martha and her sisters, for long poor Mr. Nicholls's most scornful detractors, they wept with the best while the valedictory words were said and the watch handed over. Mr. Nicholls's rejoinder was the briefest possible, but that was only to be expected and nobody was offended.

He was to leave early the next morning.

Charlotte was in her room when she heard him coming up the path to hand over his keys to Mr. Brontë, and take his leave. The dining-room was in the throes of redecoration, so she had a good excuse for not being downstairs. She heard Martha let him in, and heard his knock on the parlor door, followed by a few words from each man, the iciness of which seemed to permeate the floorboards of Charlotte's room. She knew it would be only the simplest courtesy to go and bid him goodbye; yet she would not, not before Papa—it would be too painful. But when she heard him leave, she waited for the secondary sound of the garden gate, and, not hearing it, hurried, against her will, to the window.

There he stood in the dusk by the gate, stooped and motionless, with an air about him as if his feet had refused to carry him further without some sign or word from her. Unable to stop herself she flew downstairs and out into the gathering darkness.

For a moment she stood on the steps, wondering if she were doing right, if it would not be kinder and more honest just to let him go. But then she saw that he was sobbing.

Impossible to endure! She ran to him and touched his arm.

"Oh, my Charlotte—" he said brokenly.

"No, Mr. Nicholls, you mustn't—"

"Charlotte—once I will say it—I thank God you came—I could not have moved a step further without a word of goodbye from you."

"That's what I have come to give you. Only that."

"I ask no more."

She gave him her hand. They looked into each other's eyes. His were half-blinded with tears. Devoted love for her seemed to flow out of his big, bearded, sorrowing face and it moved her despite herself.

"I have borne up but poorly these last months. I ask your pardon."

"I have pitied you sincerely."

"Had I but known that—I might have behaved better—"

"I feared to mislead you."

"Yes—I see—that is like you—"

They were silent for a moment. Then she pressed his hand and took hers away. "Goodbye, Mr. Nicholls. I wish you happiness."

He half-smiled and shook his head. "Goodbye, Miss Brontë."
He passed through the gate and walked out of sight down the lane. By next morning, he was gone.

"I heard about his performance in church last Sunday," said Patrick contemptuously. "Unmanly driveler!"

"I will ask you, Papa," said Charlotte sharply, "to say no more."

The old man spread his hands and smiled, a smile that angered Charlotte by having something of spiteful triumph in it. "Of course, my dear! Out of sight, out of mind—and a good riddance, I promise you!"

However, Patrick had reckoned without the inevitable concomitant of his enemy's removal. Another curate had been found to replace Mr. Nicholls, a Mr. de Renzi. Foreign by name and foreign by nature was this reverend young gentleman to his aged employer. One of the quirks of Patrick's age was an increasing distrust of strangers, and this particular one had neither the manner nor the personality to overcome this prejudice. He could do nothing right, and the worst of it was that Patrick had to keep his displeasure bottled up: clearly it was impossible for him to relieve his irritation by complaining to Charlotte, or she might begin to suspect he was regretting the loss of his assistant.

Charlotte knew him too well to be long deceived, however. She soon saw that the luckless new curate was out of favor, and not only with her father—the parishioners also "took agin" his " 'igh-fallutin' " airs and graces, his thin voice, his prancing gait, his tolerant smiles at local ways. Nor was he half the worker Mr. Nicholls had been. Rheumatics or none, duty had come first with the former curate; the slightest head cold served as an excuse to take Mr. de Renzi's name off the work-roster of the parish, and Mrs. Brown, who had so bitterly complained of Mr. Nicholls's taciturnity and poor response to her victuals, now loudly bewailed his loss, protesting that Mr. de Renzi was eating her out of house and home and talking so much "other folks can't slip a word in edgeways."

So it came about that Mr. Nicholls began to be sorely missed.

Charlotte did not exactly miss him; but she very often thought of him, and worried for him, which was just as bad. She supposed she would never hear of him again, unless it should be at second hand, through Mr. Grant or Mr. Sowden or others of his fellow-clerics in the neighborhood, and for this she was sorry, for how could she help having an interest in one who had loved her with so deep a constancy? Well, but at least he had given up his original plan of going to Australia. His new parish was in Yorkshire—but where, exactly? She allowed herself to wonder.

Meanwhile she felt the need of change and distraction. Cornhill had every reason to be satisfied with the progress of *Villette*, and for once Charlotte's conscience was at peace. So, when opportunities came to get away from the still-sour atmosphere at home, she grasped them. All but one. When Miss Martineau wrote in July and asked when she was coming to Ambleside for a visit, Charlotte fulfilled her determination to end their friendship. Miss Martineau was baffled and angry. Had not Charlotte implored her to be honest? She did not understand how deeply her words had cut—right to the quick of Charlotte's self-esteem. It was a wound—inflicted by one whom Charlotte had so much admired—that nothing seemed to heal, nor ever would, and Charlotte would not face her. Instead, she went to Scotland with friends.

On her return home, Charlotte found Patrick very low-spirited and testy.

"Thank heaven you are back, Charlotte! Matters are going from bad to worse here. Martha is ill; Tabby is too deaf to hear the simplest request, and too lame to act on it if she did; and as for Mr. de Renzi—!" He silenced himself, but the truth was out; he threw Charlotte a sly, almost guilty look.

"Is he not giving you satisfaction, Papa?"

"Oh. . . . He could be worse, I suppose. But he is unreliable—unreliable! I hate that of all things in a curate—that, and pretentions. If he is so clever and cultivated, why does he not find a more salubrious post?"

Charlotte dropped the subject. In truth she did not know whether she felt loyally sorry, or disloyally glad, at this turn of events. She still burned inwardly at the injustice done and the contumely heaped upon Mr. Nicholls by her father, and it aggravated her sorely to hear how neutrally, even civilly, he referred to his ex-curate to outsiders, while to herself he still employed the most spiteful sarcasm.

Quite a pile of letters awaited her, including one from Miss Wooler, inviting her to stay on the coast with her, and another from Mrs. Gaskell, appointing a date only a few days ahead for her long-promised visit to the parsonage. Charlotte was delighted, and wrote a confirmatory note even before she had read the rest of her post.

At the bottom of the pile was a letter directed in an unfamiliar hand, and postmarked Kirk Smeaton, a village near Pontefract. Charlotte thought it might be from some would-be novelist, announcing the arrival of another of the pathetic manuscripts with which she was these days often bombarded, and she tore it open with indifference. But the writing within was not unfamiliar at all.

It was Mr. Nicholls's hand.

She clutched at it in a sudden nervous spasm, and looked instinctively over her shoulder. She should not read it! If Papa knew— Yet she must. Hurrying her eyes over the words in guilty haste, she learned that Kirk Smeaton was indeed the parish of Mr. Nicholls's new appointment, that he was settled in there now, that it suited him "as well as he could be suited anywhere, longing as he did to be in but one spot on all the globe"; in short he begged her for a line, however brief, to give him courage to behave and be better in his new situation than he had, latterly, in the old.

Charlotte read the letter through once, crumpled it quickly, and threw it, with a tense, jerky motion, into the fire.

Mrs. Gaskell arrived on a leaden-gray day in September. They had mutually delayed her visit throughout the summer so that she might see the purple heather in full bloom across the moors, a spectacle Charlotte had often described to her as one of the loveliest in nature. Unfortunately the first heavy thunderstorm of autumn, only a day or so before, had killed every bloom, and the plants lay blighted and brown as when Charlotte had carried one last sprig to Emily on her death-day.

That disappointment, however, did not prevent Mrs. Gaskell reveling in every moment of the four-day visit. She found the house (quite recently embellished with its first new coat of paint in many years) everything a country parsonage should be, and approved thoroughly of the perfect order and daintiness of all its appointments. Charlotte saw to it that fires burned all day in every room Mrs. Gaskell was to use, and her guest—continually on the lookout for things to praise in the modest household—became rhapsodical about the dancing light of the flames flickering on the pretty new walls. The dining-room was now predominantly crimson, a color Charlotte had chosen for its warmth; the wallpaper was rose-speckled. Against this background her portrait looked its best in its oval gilt frame.

Mrs. Gaskell stopped before it. "Oh! So you have sat for Mr. Richmond, too!" she exclaimed. "So have I, but I must say he has made you a regular beauty, whereas I look like an old dowager in mine!"

"Papa and Tabby both said he made me look too old."

"Whose idea was it that you have your likeness sketched?"

"George's—Mr. Smith's. It was a present from him for *Shirley*."

"Indeed! Well, now I have gone over to him, who knows? Perhaps he may make me a gift of a portrait by one of the Pre-Raphaelites!"

"I am so glad you have joined Smith, Elder," said Charlotte quietly. "You will not regret the change, I am sure. George—Mr. Smith—is such a gentlemanly person."

Mrs. Gaskell took instant note of the muted sadness in her voice and glanced at her. Charlotte had spoken of George as if he had recently died. Being so happily married herself, it was Mrs. Gaskell's constant preoccupation to see those she cared for similarly established. Her deep pity for Charlotte led her into a greater-than-usual concern to spy out romances. She saw at once that there was nothing to hope for as far as their young publisher was concerned.

But something must be done. She was more convinced of it now than ever; for here in the parsonage she saw something worse even than solitude—she saw what she took to be an uncongenial companion.

"I hope, by the by, that my being here will not inconvenience Mr. Brontë?"

"I have not seen him so cheerful for a long time as he was in anticipating your visit."

He was indeed very gracious to her, in an old-fashioned way. But Mrs. Gaskell was not entirely at ease about her host. Her quick perceptions registered early something badly amiss between the old man and his daughter. Charlotte behaved very dutifully toward him; yet there seemed, for the moment at least, to be little love lost between them. The smallest blunder on her part—the placing of his cup of tea too far from his hand, a little slowness in responding to his call—brought forth a look from him which, intercepted, made Mrs. Gaskell shudder. *Selfish old man!* she could not help thinking, for Mr. Brontë struck her as quite despotic in his expectations from Charlotte and even in his treatment of her; and Mrs. Gaskell noticed that Charlotte resented it.

On the third morning, when Charlotte had completed her chores (with some help from her guest), they wrapped themselves up and went walking on the moors. The heather might be dead, but there was a great deal of wild beauty still to see, and much associated romance and tragedy to savor. Everywhere they walked, Charlotte had stories to tell, about Emily in particular, but also about Anne and Branwell, and, stretching memory even further, her eldest sisters, Maria and Elizabeth, too. It seemed to Mrs. Gaskell that every hollow and height, every boulder and twist in the beck (now tumbling in its first autumn spate) was invisibly labeled with remembered incidents from Charlotte's childhood and youth. Long she listened, with her heart's ear as well as her head's, and very often she wanted to weep at the pity of those brilliant and beloved lives cut short.

It was a rough autumn. The rain clouds overhung the moors constantly, and sometimes emptied themselves on the walkers.

They had to take shelter at a little farmstead four miles or more from Haworth. It stood high above the strange deep fold between the hills which harbored the beck—a square, uncompromising, black stone building isolated from its neighbors and exposed to every gust. The owners looked as dour as their home when they first cautiously opened the door; but, seeing Charlotte, the weather-beaten faces broke into smiles and the two women were invited to sit by the fire and dry themselves and take "a cuppa tay" to warm them. After tea it was still drizzling and the woman insisted they borrow an umbrella, saying she would pick it up at church the coming Sunday.

As they walked away down the hill, Mrs. Gaskell, glancing back, remarked with a shiver, "It is like I imagined Wuthering Heights."

"That is what Ellen says. But Emily never discussed the originals of her people, or her places. It's my opinion they were all created from within."

"Do *you* write from life?"

Charlotte was silent for a while. "In some cases, of course. For instance, 'Shirley' was Emily."

Mrs. Gaskell could not help looking very surprised. She had formed an impression of Emily as reserved to a fault, surly, taciturn . . . as unlike the lively, sparkling "Shirley" as could be. "Really?"

"No one knew Emily, outside the family. If she had been happy, if she had been rich and free—she would have shown a different face to the world, I assure you."

"And 'Caroline Helstone'?"

"She began as a loving portrait of my friend Ellen. Toward the end I saw her as Anne."

"How interesting! And . . . in *Villette?*"

Charlotte confessed about George and his mother.

"And the . . . Belgian characters?"

Charlotte glanced at her as they trudged along. "You are asking, of course, about 'Paul Emanuel.' "

"That most fascinating of nonheroes! Who, that dared, could resist asking?"

"He was—real."

"May I ask one more thing? Was he married?"

"Yes."

"To . . . 'Madame Beck'?"

"Yes."

"I see."

They walked on, and talked of other things. But Mrs. Gaskell's understanding of and curiosity about Charlotte had deepened.

Next morning, sifting through the post after breakfast, Charlotte abruptly froze.

"What is it, dear Miss Brontë?"

Charlotte, in her confusion, looked up at her. It was a strange look, as if of appeal.

"It is a letter I—must not read," she whispered, and glanced at the door of the parlor.

She turned at once into the dining-room. The fire was burning brightly. To Mrs. Gaskell's astonishment, she saw Charlotte, after the briefest hesitation, throw the envelope unopened into the fire.

"My dear!" she could not help exclaiming. "*I* could not do that, not with Pandora's box! Oh, I cannot restrain myself—*do*, if you please, tell me how you could overcome a woman's nature enough to burn it unread!"

Charlotte stood with her back turned, watching the letter burn away. Then she looked around. "It was from a man my father has forbidden me to see or hear from," she said quietly.

"A lover? Oh, forgive my curiosity! Do not answer if you would rather not!"

"He loves *me*. I—I do not reciprocate."

"You do not—or your Papa does not?"

"Both," said Charlotte, after a brief struggle to express the situation more accurately. Then she hurried around the table to Mrs. Gaskell and grasped her hands. "Pray don't tell anyone!"

"Never! I am dumb. What is he like?"

"I will tell you a little of him. . . . Not that there is the least point, as I shall not see him again."

They sat down, and Mrs. Gaskell leaned forward eagerly.

"He is a Puseyite," Charlotte began, "and, I must say, an extreme specimen. Were he to walk in now, and see me hobnobbing with a Unitarian, his face would set itself in lines of frigid disapproval—like this." Charlotte, as well as she could, imitated what she thought of as Mr. Nicholls's "Dissenters' frown." Mrs. Gaskell burst out laughing, but stopped when she saw Charlotte could not join in. "Yes," she went on with a strange air of determination. "He is very narrow-minded about such things. As to intellectual matters, they are a closed book to him. Never could I have shared with him even a fraction of my inner life. So what would have been the use? However much a man may love, and even be worthy of love, if he cannot unite on a mental and spiritual level with his wife, they had far better remain apart. Don't you agree?"

"On the face of it, yes. Yet I feel you are giving me a one-sided view . . . that you are, so to say, deliberately souring the grapes."

Charlotte looked startled.

"There must be another side to him?" pressed her friend.

Charlotte opened her mouth almost eagerly, then pulled herself up. "I see no sense in reviewing his good—his many good qualities, now he is gone," she said firmly.

"'You are quite right," said Mrs. Gaskell regretfully, "I suppose."

They sat in silence for some time and suddenly Mrs. Gaskell could bear it no longer. "Miss Brontë, may I speak?"

Startled at the urgency in her friend's tone, Charlotte looked up, as if alarmed. She is afraid I will trouble her somehow, Mrs. Gaskell surmised. Once one is sunk into such deathly tranquillity, even a kindly disturbance can be unwelcome. But Charlotte said, "Go on."

"Is your life not a—forgive me, I beg—a kind of slavery?"

Charlotte's face stiffened. "I do not feel it so."

"Perhaps that is because you are so certain you are doing the only thing possible."

"So I am."

"It is neither in accordance with Christian nor with social morality that you should lay down your whole life upon any man's altar, no matter who that man may be."

"Nor how great his sufferings have been? Nor how much he has deserved of me?"

"His sufferings are no fault of yours. They are the responsibility of Providence, and Providence must answer for them. As to his deserts, of course I don't presume to measure those, but has he really done more for you than any father must do? Has he not, perhaps, exacted more than his due already? We who are parents know this truth, Miss Brontë: that to have children for any other reason than our own fulfillment and pleasure—to have them, for instance, as an insurance against a lonely old age—is a kind of perversion. We may not demand lifelong payment in return for giving our children life."

Charlotte stared at her.

"I would not say anything of this," went on her friend, "however I might feel it pitiful to see you living this immured existence when you should be out in the world, enjoying your fame and gathering material for more fine books. But when it comes to a matter of such importance as love, and possibly marriage, then I feel it is my duty as your friend—and a woman older than you—to tell you that no one, no, *no one at all*, Miss Brontë, has the right to interfere between you and anyone you even might come to care for. Sacrifice for a beloved parent is very fine, up to a point; but the sacrifice becomes self-immolation and blasphemy when it is carried so far."

She sank back in her chair, and Charlotte continued for some minutes to stare at her unblinkingly. After a long time she rose. "I would rather not discuss it anymore just now," she said. But Mrs. Gaskell could tell she was not angry, only disturbed. And she was not sorry to have disturbed her.

That night, after prayers (which were held, as they had been held all through Charlotte's life, with the servants in the parlor) and a brief, noncommittal talk by the fire after the rest of the household had retired, Mrs. Gaskell had a strong intuition that Charlotte wanted to be by herself. She yawned and declared she was sleepy. Charlotte came upstairs with her and saw her to her room; but a little while after, Mrs. Gaskell heard her quietly going downstairs again.

Creeping onto the landing, she thought she could hear a soft, continuous whisper of steps, on and on and yet not getting appreciably louder or softer. Curiosity at last got the better of her, and she tiptoed down.

The dining-room door was slightly open. There was a candle on the table. Without entering, Mrs. Gaskell could see Charlotte's shadow, crossing and recrossing the light of the candle as she walked around and around the table.

After a long time, Mrs. Gaskell put out her hand and pushed open the door. Charlotte stopped walking, but without alarm. Their eyes met, and Charlotte said, "Come in. I knew someone was out there. I thought it was a ghost."

Mrs. Gaskell came in. "And weren't you afraid?"

"No. If this house were as full of ghosts as I would like, there would be one for every room."

"Do you do this every night?"

"The pacing? Yes. I could not sleep without it."

"May I walk with you?"

Charlotte looked up at her, and now there were tears. "If you really care to."

"I do."

Gently she drew the thin little hand through her arm and they walked together.

"I have been thinking of what you said," said Charlotte.

"Good. And?"

"And I still do not see any alternative to my present way of life."

"Why, of course there is an alternative! You must escape. Oh, not for good, but you must have a place to run to. Now, I know several comfortable and respectable lodging houses in London where you could stay incognito, entertain if you pleased, be alone and write if you did not please, and the same with visiting. You would not be dependent upon the Smiths or the Kay-Shuttleworths or anyone else; you could come back here when you liked; and you would be free."

"Free . . ."

"No, I know. You will never be wholly free while your father lives. But you would be free to meet Mr. Nicholls if you liked. And so you should be."

"Deceive Papa? ... "

"It is *he* who makes some subterfuge necessary. You would do all openly if he were not so obstinate."

"But you speak as if I loved Mr. Nicholls. I assure you, I don't!"

"How can you know whether you do, or could? You have never seen him except under the shadow of your father."

"That is true."

Twice more they circled the table. Then Charlotte stopped. "I will take the addresses of the lodging houses," she said decisively.

"Good!" said Mrs. Gaskell, and gave her a kiss.

chapter 4 PERSISTENCE

$\mathcal{I}$t seemed that Mr. Nicholls was not to be put off—not by refusal, nor by distance, nor by silence.

In October, Charlotte went off for a week to stay with Miss Wooler in Hornsea, on the coast. When she returned, there was the familiar post mark, and the unfamiliar hand (always different —Mr. Nicholls was showing an unsuspected streak of low cunning). Again, Charlotte threw it on the fire without opening it; but this time Martha had just put fresh coal on the embers and the letter lay there in the smoke for too long. Just as its corners were beginning to curl, Charlotte snatched it out.

The reason she did so was *not*, she assured herself, out of compassion for the sender, as such, but because she had suddenly wondered—looking at the doomed thing, smoldering on the coals —whether Monsieur Héger had so heartlessly flung away her impassioned pleas. Had her letters to him, so carefully wrought, each word weighed and inscribed as if in her heart's blood, ended thus? All she had craved was his friendship, knowing love to be impossible. And indeed, reading Mr. Nicholls's letter—so simply worded, so guileless, not like hers—she found this much in common with herself during that dark time of her loving madness—that all he asked was a line, a little, little message, to help him through the misery of his loneliness.

Oh, it was hard to refuse him! He even used the same metaphor as she had: "crumbs from the rich man's table." It awakened echoes in her emotions that almost deafened her inner ear. A line —a line would not hurt—he would not mistake it: he knew, as she had known, that more than friendship could never be. It was as if she saw him again before her, as if he pleaded with her; she felt his suffering in her own soul.

Yet Papa had forbidden it, and Papa trusted her. No matter how shamefully he had behaved, how wrong and even worldly were his motives, he was her father—he had only her in the world. A letter, the shortest possible, to Mr. Nicholls would be a betrayal which she could never confess to. No. The dark oppressive tidal wave of guilt rose threateningly before her, her familiar monster-companion. She could not face it.

The third letter went into the fire: she jabbed it in with the poker, and she felt its demise as if her flesh were scorched. "Please God, let it be the last," she prayed silently.

But at the end of the month came another, and a week later, a fifth. She read them now, her resolution defeated by his persistence; a strange sense of helplessness was overtaking her, as if she were being worn down. His pleas reached her, like a physical pull through the envelope, and though she burned each letter after she had read it, she could not do so before.

He was making a strong effort to involve her in his life at Kirk Smeaton, an effort to write about day-to-day events as well as his love. His letters were hard to reconcile with the man; no narrowness, no bigotry appeared in them; he took a warm interest in his new parishioners, despite his heartache, and his superior had praised his diligence: "He says diligence is my forte. Did he but guess how I turn the word in my mind, till it can be applied to the one for whose happiness I would most *diligently* exert myself if she would but allow me." She strove to suppress the dreaming part of her which she had thought she had killed forever after the fiasco of James Taylor; yet it lived still, and tormented her now with strong images of all the simple, normal delights which she had so sternly rejected.

Meanwhile, she could not get on well with her father at all. Whether it was his increasing shortness of temper and general crabbedness, or whether it was a deep-seated resentment in Charlotte that he had denied her the chance to find out what she might really want, she found she had little patience and less affection for him. The time had come to "escape." So she pretended that she had business in London, and arranged to take rooms in Bloomsbury Square, one of Mrs. Gaskell's addresses. She did not plan to let anyone at Smith, Elder know she was coming, nor to contact them; she had *entrées* to various potential new friends, specifically through the Winkworth sisters, whom she had met in Manchester, and her plan was simply to have a holiday and meet new people, quietly, at her own pace, and perhaps see some more real sights which might give her impetus to begin another novel.

Patrick, when she announced her trip to him, was distinctly against it.

"Why are you forever rushing here and there?" he asked peevishly. "You are becoming like a bluebottle, Charlotte, never still! I want you near me; I shan't live long to trouble you, that's certain, and meanwhile is it too much to beg a little of your time? I do not intrude on your life, do I? I only ask that you breakfast with me, and take tea with me in the evenings, and help me a trifle with my work, and read to me occasionally when my spirits are low—as, alas, they too often are now, with all I have to put up with. That wretched curate of mine is worse than useless. I am sure any would answer better than he."

"Even Mr. Nicholls, Papa?" asked Charlotte in an impulse of boldness.

He looked at her, his watery eyes sharpening to a sudden needlepoint of suspicion. "Have I not forbidden you to mention him, Charlotte? Are you trying to drive me into an apoplexy? I do not want to hear of the young coxcomb!"

"I mentioned him only as a curate, Papa. You must own he was a better one than Mr. de Renzi."

"Presumptuous idiot!"

"But a hard and conscientious worker. The parish misses him sadly."

"And you? You miss him too, I suppose! Well, confess! Do you or don't you?"

"I cannot help regretting his sufferings on my account. I would be heartless indeed if I could."

"Serve him right for ever having let himself glance at you."

She was due to go to London on November 25th. On the 23rd, a sixth letter arrived from Mr. Nicholls, and this time the pressure of her pity for him had so accumulated that she could stand it no longer.

"I am going away," she thought. "I shall stay away for some weeks. I shall strive to put him wholly from me, and return to my former sense of my duty and my destiny. In the meantime I will write him the line he begs for. It will be the final contact between us."

With a sense of a long, hard tension being released, she wrote him a brief letter, holding out no hope at all, and advising him (rather overbearingly, she knew) to submit to his lot with what courage he could, as she had. She hinted that they were both destined to live alone, and might take a little comfort in knowing that this fate was shared. She signed it formally "C. Brontë" and carried it to the post before she could change her mind.

The moment it had gone, guilt set in. In vain she tried to stifle it. In vain she set her teeth and repeated under her breath Mrs. Gaskell's remarks—true, all of them true!—about her entitlements as a free agent. She enlarged upon her friend's hints about her father—his obstinacy, his parsimony, his despotic hold over her. She went back into the past in search of ammunition for her war, remembering far back to the days of adolescence when he would not give her an allowance of her own, nor lend her and her sisters money to start their school. Freedom to *work*, to be drudges, he had always allowed them, but help in achieving any kind of true independence—that had come from within themselves. And except in rare instances he had never freely opened his arms and set them on the wing if it meant that they might eventually leave him.

But even as these thoughts tormented her, an awareness of her disloyalty overwhelmed her. Deceitful, disloyal, angry, and unfilial in her thoughts. . . . What sins was she not guilty of, against this old man who had lost so much, and been as good a father as possible according to his lights?

For each uncharitable memory that she had stored up against him, she found she had a parallel one, recalling his goodness and his love. He *had* given them freedom, in childhood—freedom to read whatever they liked, to stretch their minds, freedom from bigotry and needless restrictions. How many hours had they all spent in the little study above the hall, inhabiting their imaginary worlds, untrammeled by supervision or the consciousness of wrong-doing? (But then, he was quite glad to have them out of the way while he pursued his own muse. Perhaps he was not so much consciously giving them freedom as selfishly neglecting them!) He had sacrificed a great deal for Branwell. During the long, agonizing months of Branwell's decline, Papa had cared for him when none of the rest of them had the strength. (Yet was not Branwell's plight mostly Papa's own fault? Had not indulgence and careless-ness in childhood weakened the boy's character, did not Papa owe him all that in the end, when it was too late, he tried to repay?)

So the arguments went on day and night for two days after she had written to Mr. Nicholls. And at last she was exhausted, and threw herself down in her chair, thinking, "The whole thing is an absurdity. I am a grown woman, near to middle-age! May I not write a blameless letter, out of Christian charity, to a poor sufferer, without paying for it with hours of anguish? Tomorrow I shall be gone to London, I shall be away from Papa and from all of it, and I shall put it all quite from me!"

She sat still for a long time. Eight o'clock struck on the landing. It was time for prayers. She roused herself, smoothed her hair, and walked across the passage, tapping on the parlor door.

Tabby shuffled out of the kitchen. "Time for prayers," said the old woman, as she always did.

Patrick was not in a pleasant humor. He had been in a bad mood ever since Charlotte had announced that she was going to London. Now he scowled at her, and the prayers he said came out in a growl quite at odds with their plea for blessing and grace from on high.

"Why's Parson in such a fret?" whispered Tabby as they bent their heads together. But being deaf herself, her whisper was louder than she had meant and Patrick heard her.

"Tabby! Return to the kitchen, and henceforward keep your remarks to yourself!" he shouted.

"Papa!"

"Leave me to run the house, Charlotte! I shall have to do so alone from now on in any case."

Tabby was clambering up off her knees with Charlotte's help, dabbing her eyes. "I didn't mean owt," she muttered. "Is 'e tryin' to kill uz all off, wi' 'is frets and rages? 'As 'e not lost enow? But 'e'll not listen, 'e'll not learn. Ye can't teach an old dog nowt," she flung at him from the door. "Tha'lt 'urt uz and 'urt uz till uz is all dead, and then per'aps some sense'll get in through that white noddle o' thine!"

With that she hobbled off, banging the door behind her.

Charlotte stood looking at her father. She was surprised to see that he looked quite crushed by Tabby's strictures; his shoulders, usually so erect, stooped now, and his head hung down. "Even my own servant abuses me," he said miserably.

"Papa."

"Well?"

"I know you are not trying to hurt me, but Tabby was right in one thing." His head came up, his tear-filled eyes sharpened. "You have injured me."

"I? How?"

"You have subjected me too much to your will."

He stared at her, waiting.

"Look at me. I am no longer young, and I was never pretty. When you die I shall be left quite alone—alone, Papa, as you are afraid to be for even the few weeks I shall be in London. Yet you have taken from me the one chance I had of happiness."

His face darkened and he opened his mouth to speak, but some reckless strength, of the kind that came to her only in moments of crisis, now had Charlotte in its power and she went on, hardly knowing what she was doing. "I am going to tell you something because I cannot bear not to tell you, and that is part of the injury you have done me, because I have no need to feel guilty at it. I have written to Mr. Nicholls."

"You have dared—"

"You see, Papa? Why should I have to dare to write a perfectly innocent letter to a man who, like Jacob, has served seven years for me? It was not a love letter, but a letter to a sufferer, and yet I had to *dare* to write it! And now here I am, confessing it to you as if it were a crime! *That* is what you have done to me, Papa. You have stolen part of my soul. I am no longer—no, I never was—free. And Tabby is right! You will kill me in the end if you will not give me my freedom!"

The old man slumped into his chair and put his head in his hands. Charlotte stood before him, pale and apparently calm though she trembled from head to foot. At last he looked at her. "Would you give yourself to a *curate?*"

"My mother did."

"Charlotte!"

"I am not saying I shall marry him. Only that *if* I marry at all it must be to him."

"Never! I shall *never* agree to a union which would bring into my house that worthless, puffed-up, deceiving scoundrel! You shall not write to him again—you shall swear to it before you leave this room!"

Quietly she answered, "It is not given to everyone to be loved with the depth and constancy with which Mr. Nicholls loves me,

Papa. Worthless you may think him, but I doubt whether a worthless man is capable of the devotion he has shown. You sent him away; good. You did what you thought right. But I am thirty-seven years old, and I thought it right to send him that letter. If I think it right I may send others."

"You will kill me if you do!"

"I trust not, Papa. I will displease you, that's true, and I am sorry for it, but I must do as I think best."

For a full minute they stared at each other. Then the old man broke down and wept. "Charlotte . . . Charlotte . . ."

She hurried around the desk to comfort him. "There now, Papa, there now! Don't distress yourself. All will be well."

He clutched her hand, his tears coming fast. "Detestable brute . . . he will steal you from me . . ."

"No, Papa! Believe me, I would never leave you."

He looked up at her pathetically. "Never?"

"No. Whatever happens I shall not leave this house. I promise."

"Then you will not go to London tomorrow?"

She stifled a sigh. There must be compromise. "Very well, Papa, since you ask it, I won't."

"And you will not write to him anymore?"

She withdrew from him, but he clutched her back. "All right, all right!" he cried hastily. "Do as you please. Much good may it do him! Only don't go away from me, my dearest!"

So Charlotte canceled her visit. And in the next day's post there was an answer to her letter, one which seemed to ring with new strength. Mr. Nicholls wrote that he was so comforted, just by knowing that she was well, and having her letter in his hands, that he craved a little more . . . just a little more. . . .

chapter
5 BETTER
ACQUAINTANCE

*C*hristmas in the parsonage that year was as far from being the season of good will and joy as it could be. And no sooner was it over than Patrick came stamping into the house one dark snowy day in a thundering black mood.

At first he would not talk to Charlotte or anyone else. But after he had had his frugal supper alone, he sent Martha to fetch her from across the passage.

"Papa?"

"You know all about it, I suppose."

Charlotte stood indecisively in the doorway. Useless to feign ignorance. What attitude to take was the puzzle.

"You mean Mr. Nicholls's proposed visit to Oxenhope. Yes, I know of it."

He fixed her with an eye like the Ancient Mariner's, at once dim with age and glittering with passion.

"Charlotte, I want the truth."

"You shall have it, Papa," Charlotte answered instantly.

"Are you in regular correspondence with him?"

"I have had seven letters from him, Papa—and written two."

"And he is coming to Oxenhope for one reason only—to renew acquaintance with you."

"He is also visiting his friends the Grants . . ."

Patrick made a sound expressive of ridicule and waved this aside. "I know what he is at. I know him! Indeed he need not think he is hoodwinking *me* by his deceitful proceedings—not for a moment!" Yet in his mutterings there was a lack of his earlier conviction and determination. "Charlotte! You know the man is a falsifier?"

"No, Papa."

"I say yes! All that fiction about his rich connections in Ireland —trying to impress me with his family background—I little guessed his purpose *then*, but I know it now!"

Charlotte stood silent, waiting. More was coming, and she knew it—of a different tenor. All this was face-saving for the change of direction which was to follow, and every nerve she had stood alert to catch the nuance that would serve the end she now had firmly in view.

"Well?" he barked suddenly. "Are you not going to ask my permission to meet him? For receive him under my roof I will never do, and so I tell you! If you're to see him, it shall be out-doors. This weather should cool his ardor!"

Charlotte's blood leaped to her face and her hands clenched in her deep pockets. "Do I have your permission to improve acquaintance with him, Papa?"

"If I refuse it he will contrive to meet you clandestinely, so what choice have I? Only I demand that you be open and honest with me, Charlotte, and not join ranks with that underhand, furtive, falsehearted—" He caught her eye and fell silent. She turned swiftly to go.

"Charlotte?" His voice was suddenly soft and querulous—old—beseeching. She turned back and went to him.

"You gave your promise never to leave me."

"Yes, Papa. Never fear that."

"Mind! My approval you shall not have!" he added, with a flash of his old fire. But he was defeated and he had already begun to know it. And when he saw her a week later, in cloak and bonnet, passing his window on her way to a rendezvous on the Oxenhope path, all he could do was clench his fists and curse George de Renzi, whose total unsuitability had so weakened his resolve.

Charlotte walked swiftly along the track. The snow deadened sound but brightened what came to the eye: the shining white of the hills under the lowering sky made a contrast symbolic of Charlotte's strange blinding excitement under the dark menace of something more than her father's displeasure.

She would not think yet of her confusion. All she wanted was to see him again, to demolish the double-image so similar to that she had had of James Taylor—the correspondent and the man. Perhaps, perhaps when Mr. Nicholls again stood before her, he too would seem repellent, his love untenable. That would resolve everything. She almost hoped it might be so, and restore to her her image of herself as austerely independent in her determination to accept a single life.

Suddenly she looked up from the slush beneath her feet and saw him. He stood, tall and almost silhouetted against the white hillside and the deep gray sky, motionless, portentous. She stood still for a moment, looking up at him. She shivered. Then each walked slowly toward the other until they met. He took off his hat.

"Miss Brontë."

"Mr. Nicholls."

He took her hand and pressed it, gazing down at her. His bulk stood between her and the harsh, snow-scented wind that crept down from the height behind him. She felt almost warm in his shelter, and then, sensing the danger of such a feeling, said quickly, "Let us walk a little."

He tried to put her hand through his arm, but she drew it primly away. They walked side by side toward Oxenhope.

"It is good of you to come."

"Papa agreed to it," she said hastily, and had to stifle something like amusement to see that he looked disappointed. Clearly he had hoped this was a secret meeting, and she was touched by his hoping so.

"Is he still as set against me as ever?"

"Yes. But he is still more set against your successor. Next to him, my father cannot help seeing you in a warmer light."

"I have one fault which I trust my successor has not."

She glanced at him and then bent her head to let her bonnet-brim hide her smile.

"*That* fault is peculiar to yourself alone," she murmured.

"I must tell you I am unrepentant in it."

"Let us talk of something else. How do you get on at Kirk Smeaton?"

"As well as I could in the antipodes or anywhere else where you were not."

"I said 'something else,' Mr. Nicholls."

"Miss Brontë—for me, there is nothing else."

All these avowals were spoken in a wholly serious, unflirtatious way. It was so strange. . . . Charlotte heard these words, spoken in deadly earnest, and she could neither believe nor disbelieve them.

"We had best be turning back."

"Are you cold, my dear?" he asked with such a sudden access of tenderness that she felt obliged to turn to him.

"Mr. Nicholls, you may not speak so to me—"

"Yet? Very well, I will try not to. But when you show yourself, even to the slightest degree, in need of comfort, protection, aid— even to the extent of a shiver or a sad look—my blood fires up in my veins and words and actions become imperative which I know to be imprudent and presumptuous. Yet, why? For you know my heart, and I have the impossible delight of seeing you at my side notwithstanding. May I not, now, entertain some faint hope?"

Charlotte stopped, closing her eyes tightly for a moment to get her feelings under control. "You must not assume too much. Pray don't."

"I am patient. Only remember—for me, nothing will change. Come. It is getting dark. I will take you home."

"Not all the way!"

He smiled a trifle grimly. "Not this time. But I will watch you down the last steps. And when you are safe and warm, think of me, standing awhile looking down at the place where you rest, warm too because I have seen you, no matter for wind or snow."

Wordlessly, Charlotte looked at him and he met her eyes fully, boldly, hopefully. She did not know what she felt; but it was not repulsion.

He was in the neighborhood for ten days. He saw a good deal of Charlotte, and, despite her repeated plea that he should not press his suit too hard, he was too much in love to resist taking full advantage of what he was convinced was a change in the wind.

Toward the end of his stay, she became frightened at the speed at which matters were moving, at the inconsistency of her attitude, the confusion of her emotions. One day she decided she would not keep their rendezvous. She stayed at home, hoping, as it were, to get her breath back, to regain her perspective, which his ardor had decidedly begun to distort.

It never occurred to her for a moment that he would dare to come to the parsonage in quest of her. When she heard his step, and immediately his knock (greeted by joyous barks from Flossy), she leaped to her feet in utter dismay and—almost—terror, for he must have walked straight past the window of Papa's study. She hurried to the door of the room, and as she opened it, Patrick opened the one opposite, and the two stood staring at each other while Mr. Nicholls firmly knocked again.

"He means to be admitted," said Patrick finally. His voice shook. "You had better let him in, before he knocks the door down. But if the young puppy dares to come anywhere near this room, old as I am I shall show him something he will not forget. I still carry my pistol, you know."

He went back into the parlor and slammed the door.

Charlotte hurried to admit the caller. Flossy jumped all over him, and he bent to pat him.

"Mr. Nicholls! How could you!"

He looked up at Charlotte's pale face and his eyes twinkled.

"Have you perhaps a cup of tea to offer me? I have walked twice my normal distance today."

He departed back to his post at last, leaving Charlotte to contemplate the wreckage of her—and her Papa's—resolutions; different as they were and made from different motives, Mr. Nicholls's steady, indefatigable audacity had conquered them.

Alone again, Charlotte struggled to return to the equilibrium she had won for herself before the completion of *Villette*. That seemed to her now her soul's high-water mark, as that summer in Brussels at the Pensionnat Héger had been her heart's. It would, she felt, still have been better, more noble—and far safer—to have stayed upon her frozen pinnacle of resolve; for now she was once again in the warm, languorous valley, where all the cozy, normal, ordinary things were possible—courtship, marriage, even children . . . in short, a life like Mrs. Gaskell's. And what was wrong with that? Was it not what she had longed for all her life?

No! It was very far from what she had desired. She had not wanted an ordinary love, even of the degree of constancy now offered her. She had wanted something a great deal more. Sitting alone night after night through the long winter, Charlotte let her mind go back through the sequence of "lovers" she had created for herself, from Byron, through the glorious Duke of Wellington, the forbidden delights of Zamorna, and on to the mature versions of "Rochester," "Robert Moore," and "Paul Emanuel." Could she, who had lived, truly lived, a whole inner life with such gods of love as these, be now contemplating a mere mortal such as Arthur Bell Nicholls?

Was she now to compromise, was all that suffering and stiffening of sinews to have been for nothing? It was as if she had taken her final vows as a postulant, thinking she had a vocation, and then discovered that a weak place within herself rendered the whole long ordeal null and void.

In the still dark hours, she forced herself to face what she was considering. Ignoring altogether her father's belittling taunts (which continued, though more feebly), what *was* this man? Not merely the opposite of a brilliant match. No hero, no titan; no intellectual mate for her at all; unable to follow her even one step into the deep, turbulent, mysterious regions of her mind or her past. A country curate, devout but narrow; a swallower of whole doctrine, not a questioner, not even one who had wrestled for his faith.

And yet—good. Kind. Faithful. Flawed, as she was—though not in the same way. His imperfections of temper inclined her to him, more than his fine qualities, more than his integrity or his piety. In moods when she *wanted* to love him, she reverted in her mind to last summer, when he had been surly and ill-natured, refusing food and being uncivil to the bishop. For *that* she warmed to him, because then, with his tall, bearded "blackness" (and blackness of soul), there was a trace—just a shadow to be perceived in him—of "Rochester" and "Monsieur Emanuel." . . .

To aggravate matters, she quarreled with Ellen.

Ellen saw clearly how things were shaping, and she felt a horrible sinking of the heart. To be a spinster was bad enough when your oldest friend was one too. Despite all the arch hints Ellen had let fall throughout the years, the sudden real prospect of a married Charlotte was unbearable, not least because marriage—especially to a man like Mr. Nicholls—would inevitably take her away from Ellen, robbing her not merely of her friend, but of the fundamental interest of her life.

She therefore did a sharp about-face and roundly advised Charlotte against letting herself be drawn further into an entanglement which could only end in her "being inconsistent with her life and goals." This touched Charlotte on the raw. She stopped writing to Ellen and they both suffered for it. But Charlotte was aware that she was no longer, as she had been once, entirely dependent on Ellen for friendship. Yet when she caught herself thinking this, she felt disloyal, and heart-hungry for the old untrammeled intimacy which was a casualty—temporary, she hoped—of this unresolved situation with Mr. Nicholls.

As to her father, it was obvious that the massive obstacle that had once lain in the path of her lover was slowly, imperceptibly melting away. It was hard to know how, or measure its diminution. The taunts gradually lost their sting, became mere querulousness, almost reflexes; they no longer had power to anger or even touch Charlotte, whose inner wrestlings with her personal problem continued without regard to them. It was as if she saw winter melting into spring in her father's attitude as clearly and inevitably as it was doing outside the parsonage windows. One day might wax frosty or stormy; it had only to be borne with patience, and the next would be milder, for the season was turning and summer *must* come. It was a matter of time.

And then it was April, and Mr. Nicholls got leave to pay another visit to the Grants in Oxenhope. Charlotte was not even surprised when Patrick said one morning over breakfast, without preamble and with only the faintest overtones of displeasure: "I have decided that my wisest course is to receive Mr. Nicholls and let us talk about this whole matter. I had hoped it would not come to this, and I still hope that I shall not be forced to give my consent to a proceeding of which I so deeply disapprove; yet you are of an age when I cannot justifiably oppose your wishes without alienating you, Charlotte, and as you are all I have left, and moreover have given me your promise not to desert me. . . ."

So Mr. Nicholls received the formal invitation which would, three months before, have been totally unthinkable—to come to tea at the parsonage as Charlotte's acknowledged suitor.

All day, prior to his arrival, Patrick was steeling himself for the encounter. Yet when he at length entered the dining-room (where Martha, whose own views had undergone a total about-face, had laid a tea which would have done no discredit to a visiting archbishop), one would not have guessed from his manner that this was not the most ordinary meeting of parson and ex-curate, who had parted company in rather regrettable circumstances but were now each hoping to restore the old arrangement. The old man even offered his hand, which was shaken, if not with cordiality, at least without ill-will, and Patrick, after a few minutes' awkwardness, found himself describing his most recent symptoms to Mr. Nicholls, who favored him with his usual earnest attentive sympathy. (Mr. de Renzi was so infuriatingly healthy, he had no time at all for medical matters.)

Charlotte sat sewing modestly and dispensing tea while these essential preliminaries were got out of the way. When Martha, trying not to simper, had cleared the table, Charlotte folded her work and said, "Now Papa, there are things we should discuss."

"You had better leave us, Charlotte," said Patrick.

"Mr. Nicholls wishes me to stay, Papa."

The old man looked sharply at the younger. So it had begun!— the transfer of authority. His heart misgave, and he all but fell into one of his stubborn rages; but in fact, the sight of his old colleague sitting at his table, looking so four-square and solid, the antithesis of the flighty and detestable Mr. de Renzi, caused Patrick to curb himself. If he opposed this union, anything might happen. Nicholls might elope with her, take her away altogether. Better capitulation, however humiliating, than any such outcome.

He sighed deeply. "Very well. It most nearly concerns you, after all.... Well, sir—what have you to propose?"

What Mr. Nicholls had to propose was generous indeed. He might have had a living of his own and £200 a year; yet he was ready to return to Haworth in his former subservient position in order to marry Charlotte without taking her away from her father. Unjust as he had been in the past, Patrick could hardly help realizing how much arduous and underpaid labor his own poor health would lay upon this man, and feel a dawning of reluctant appreciation for the sacrifice he was willing to make.

But he had to put up one last objection. "And where do you propose to live?"

"Why, here, sir, if that is agreeable to you. Then you will have your daughter near you, as she has ever been, and your life will be changed as little as possible."

"That's all very well! But certain clarifications are better made now than left to cause trouble later. I tell you frankly you cannot share my study. *Some* privacy must be left to me."

"I have thought of that, Papa," said Charlotte quickly. "There is the little storeroom next door to this. I shall have it converted into a study for Mr. Nicholls. It can be made very pleasant. I think green would be a good color, if Mr. Nicholls approves—?"

"I would greatly approve if you would now call me by my Christian name."

She looked at him, startled. He stood up, his back to the fire, and looked down at them both. "May I take it, Mr. Brontë, that we have your consent?"

Slowly the old man nodded.

"Thank you, sir! Charlotte!" He put out his hand. She took it and he drew her up to stand beside him. "We are engaged." And there before her father, he kissed her lips for the first time.

chapter 6 DOUBTS

*N*ow the thing was agreed to. It was going to come about.

Beforehand, Charlotte had naively imagined that when it was once settled, her soul would be at peace about it. She had always tried to believe that if God guided her in one way, that must be the right direction for her. Unfortunately this faith proved an inadequate barrier to the doubts and fears that beset her the moment she found herself on the straight road to marriage.

Mr. Nicholls was now in charge, and he brooked no delay. The wedding was set for June, only two months away, little enough time for all her preparations. Sewing, shopping, decorating the little room, notifying friends—all these activities should have left no time for inner questioning. But it was not so.

Even while she was writing to her closest friends—Ellen, Mrs.

Gaskell, Miss Wooler—to announce her engagement, she was aware of a current of forlorn apology running through each letter when it should have been filled with joy.

But *she* was not filled with joy. Why not, oh, why not? She thought of "Jane Eyre" engaged to "Mr. Rochester," "Caroline Helstone" to "Robert Moore," even poor morbid, nerve-wracked, insecure "Lucy." . . . Creating them, she had felt what she should be feeling now, and was miserably aware of the discrepancy. Even her play-love for George Smith had had more of sparkle and breathlessness in it than this strange, joyless sobriety.

George meanwhile had met and married a society girl, just as Charlotte had predicted. In her letter to him, Charlotte longed to match his evident happiness with the prospect of her own; yet this letter like the others fell irresistibly into a more and more muted tone, until she found herself writing, "My expectations are very subdued—very different, I dare say, to what yours were before you were married. Care and Fear stand so close to Hope, I sometimes scarcely can see her for the shadows they cast. . . ."

I am ungrateful! she thought. What more than Arthur do I merit? An upright man, a man of principle, a soundly loving heart. . . . And in whom else could she have found one who would so have put her mind at rest about the future of her old father? He, ironically, was the happier of the two of them about it now it was settled, and it was a great consolation to her to have Arthur's word that he would stay on as curate for as long as Papa lived. But the very word "consolation" distressed her. This was not what love should need!

Endlessly, as she directed the paperhangers in the storeroom and sewed and made out wedding lists, the anxious analyses went on and on in her head. She was lost, somehow—lost to direction, to judgment, even to a sense of her true self and her needs.

In May she visited Mrs. Gaskell in Manchester.

Mrs. Gaskell was in great excitement about the marriage. But at the same time she was doubtful about it, not from Charlotte's point of view so much as her own. "If I am not mistaken," she said to Catherine Winkworth before Charlotte came, "we had best make the most of her while we have her. Mark my words, he will do his best to keep her from the contamination of overmuch contact with us heretics; he dreads the influence of Dissent, not understanding, it would seem, the nature of a writer who must participate in life in its broadest sense. . . . Well! We must wish her joy, but also prepare to do covert battle with her husband. For I don't wish to give her up altogether, not even to such a vehement loving heart as he sounds to have."

"He sounds to me a bigot and a bully," said Miss Winkworth bluntly.

Mrs. Gaskell put her head on one side and narrowed her eyes thoughtfully. "The bigotry is the chief problem," she said. "The bullying she will like."

"How? Like to be bullied? What sort of a woman is that?"

"Miss Brontë's sort. She would never be content with a man who did not rule her and order her well. Even his rigidity of temperament may militate in his favor in the end. What she could not have borne would have been a *bending* sort of man, who would not exact obedience and give firm direction; then she would have had her own way while despising him. No, his sternness will be bad only for her friends."

Meanwhile Mr. Nicholls's sway was not yet set up, and Charlotte was free to enjoy herself with the "heretics." Both Catherine Winkworth and her sister Emily, who was now married, had become very fond of her (chiefly by correspondence) since their meeting the year before, and they were longing to gossip with her and find out all her love story. Rather to their surprise (they had found her so reticent before) she seemed eager to talk.

In the intimate surroundings of the big bed-sitting-room Mrs. Gaskell had appointed her, they all sat chatting over their sewing.

"It will be a great happiness to you to have someone to care for and make happy," said Catherine.

"Yes, it is a great thing to be the first object with anyone," Charlotte answered, but a little dubiously, they thought.

"And you must be very sure of that with Mr. Nicholls; he has known you and wished for this so long, I hear."

After a moment's silence, Charlotte suddenly said, "But Katie, it has cost me a good deal to come to this."

"You will have to care for his things, instead of yours, is that it? But you have been together so long already that you know what his things are very well. He is very devoted to his duties, is he not? And you would like to help him with those?"

"I have always been used to those, and it is a great pleasure to me that he is so much beloved by all the people in the parish; there is quite a rejoicing over his return. But that is not everything, and I cannot conceal from myself that he is not intellectual; there are many places into which he could not follow me intellectually."

"Well, of course," put in Emily, "everyone has their own tastes. For myself, if a man had a firm, constant, affectionate, reliable nature, I should be much better satisfied with him than if he had an intellect far beyond mine, and brilliant gifts, without that trustworthiness. I care most for a calm equable atmosphere at home."

"I do believe Mr. Nicholls is as reliable as you say, or I wouldn't marry him. Still . . . such a character would be far less amusing and interesting than a more impulsive and fickle one. It might be—dull." Charlotte looked around at them all with a questioning, anxious expression that they found very touching and pathetic.

"For a day's companion, yes," said Catherine, "but not for a life's. One's home ought to be the one fixed point, the one untroubled region in one's lot. At home one wants peace and settled love and trust, not storm and change and excitement. Besides, one might supply the fickleness required oneself, which would be a relief sometimes."

Her sister let out a little squeal, and both the older women tried hard to look shocked, but neither succeeded and in the end they all burst into giggles.

"Oh, Katie, if *I* had ever said such a wicked thing!" exclaimed Mrs. Gaskell, and Charlotte echoed, "I never thought to hear such a speech from *you!*"

"You don't agree with it?"

"Oh, there is truth in it," said Mrs. Gaskell. "So much that I don't think I could ever have been so candid. There is danger that one might go too far."

"I think not. The steadiness and generosity on the other side would always keep one in check."

"Take no notice of her," said Emily. "She likes to say shocking things. I'm sure you'll never really flirt when you're married, Katie, and I'm doubly sure Miss Brontë never will, however stiff Mr. Nicholls is."

"He is a Puseyite," said Charlotte, growing solemn again. "I fear it will stand in the way of some of my friendships. But I shall always be the same in my heart toward them: I shall never let him make me a bigot."

"Perhaps, too, you may do something to introduce him to goodness in sects where he thought it could not be."

"That is what I hope. He has a most sincere love of goodness wherever he sees it. I think if he could come to know Mr. Gaskell it would change his feeling."

Charlotte suddenly fell to asking questions about Emily's recent marriage, whether she was happy, how she had felt beforehand—what doubts and fears she had had, if any. "Surely," was the answer, "no one could be exactly always lighthearted at such a time who was not very young and thoughtless. Our mother tells us how nervous she was before *her* marriage, and well she might have been, having wed with only the most confused notions of what such a step meant—as many poor girls still do today, due to the ridiculous prudery of their mothers. I believe it is better to marry at a more mature age, when your expectations are more reasonable and your former ignorance quite done away with by talking to others."

Charlotte tried not to blush. Such topics disturbed her. She almost wished she *were* ignorant of what lay before her. Yet by the time Mrs. Gaskell had gently and affectionately praised her own husband and given a good reference to the institution of marriage generally, Charlotte felt somehow greatly comforted.

One thing Mrs. Gaskell said, however, disturbed her in a different way. "I have few fears for Charlotte Brontë. But what's to become of Currer Bell? You had better do all your writing before you are married, my dear, for you will do none after."

In May she spent a week at Brookroyd.

Her quarrel with Ellen was made up. How could it continue? But although they had resumed writing to each other, they had not met for some months, and, their estrangement having intervened, Ellen still felt inwardly bruised when she hugged and kissed Charlotte on her arrival.

Charlotte had loved being with Mrs. Gaskell, but there was something even more comfortable about this old friendship, which she drew around her like a well-worn shawl. Ellen's family, who had always loved her, now lavished particular kindness on her, decorating her room with spring flowers till it looked like a bower, deferring to her lightest wish in everything, and, best of all, showing the highest enthusiasm for her wedding plans.

Only Ellen seemed more quiet than usual, and at last Charlotte said, "What is it, Nell, dear? Are you still against it? Say what's in your mind."

"What's the use? It's all settled now."

"Yes . . . nothing can change it now," echoed Charlotte with a curious, doubtful emphasis, as if trying to make it real to herself. "But still I should like you to be open. You think the match less than brilliant, is it that? Of course you are right, but—"

"Oh, Charlotte . . ." Ellen burst out. "It is not that at all! Had it been a brilliant match, as you call it, I suppose I should be even more hatefully jealous than I am!"

Charlotte sat stunned. "Jealous? You—of me? Is that possible?"

"Oh, forgive me! I've disappointed you. . . . I was never worthy of you. I am so ordinary, a prey to every low, commonplace feeling —feelings so far beneath you that you cannot be expected to sympathize with them—"

But Charlotte could only stare at her and repeat, "Jealous? You —of me?"

For in her mind was the picture of Ellen at Roe Head School—pretty, well-dressed, rich, and, above all, calm in mind and pure in spirit. Charlotte had not, to her knowledge, been jealous of her since then; but those first days had set a stamp upon her mind, so strong that it had never once occurred to her that envy might be felt on the other side.

"Nell . . . Was it *this* that made you side with Papa last winter, saying he knew best and that we ought to bear our lot to the end, whatever it is?" Some measure of her indecision at that time was evident in the fact that Ellen's views had deeply unsettled her. It was a pity she had not had Mary by her, who would certainly have told her briskly that if she had not previously considered her own pleasure in a matter so important, it was high time she began to make the experience more common. But then, Mary firmly believed in seeking for happiness and making one's own decisions regardless of friends and family alike; neither Ellen nor Charlotte had ever aspired to such ruthless independence.

"I expect so. I always liked Mr. Nicholls, and I always knew he liked you. Do you remember, years ago, when he first came, I told you I observed some interesting seeds of goodness in him. You laughed at me then and said all that *you* saw was narrowness of mind."

"I see that still."

"I always supposed, when one loved, one no longer noticed the loved one's faults."

"It isn't so with me. I wish it were."

"Yet you see his good points more clearly?"

"Yes—even Papa sees and acknowledges them now. It's strange—his outraged paternal pride made him quite irrational. But now he has conquered that, his organ of justice has woken up from its stunned sleep, and he is full of praise and even complacency about his future son-in-law." Charlotte, who had been staring out of the window, turned and met Ellen's eyes. "We both call him Arthur now," she said, and burst into tears.

Ellen, who had been crying herself a few moments before,

rushed to her and took her in her arms. "Charlotte! What is it? What *is* it?"

"Nothing . . ."

"But tell me!"

"The Duke of Wellington's name—was Arthur—" was all Charlotte could say.

chapter 7 A STRANGE AND PERILOUS THING

*W*hen she arrived home after a shopping trip to Leeds, Charlotte was greeted by her father with more genial enthusiasm than he had shown since the whole quarrel about Mr. Nicholls began.

"My darling! I am so happy to see you. How I missed you! Well, never mind. Tell me all about it. No, first let me tell *you*. The parish is apprised of the wanderer's imminent return, and you'll be very gratified at the royal welcome awaiting him. He was ever a favorite—as indeed he deserved." Charlotte raised her eyebrows, and Patrick, with an only slightly sheepish look, went on, "Indeed, there has been some injustice done the man. But all is put right now. And I"—he rubbed his hands gleefully—"have given Mr. de Renzi his warning! How I pity whoever gets him next—no matter. The relief to me is enormous, quite immeasurable. Your husband-to-be is to return to us on June the eleventh, and Mr. de Renzi must stay on until you return from Ireland."

Ireland was the place chosen by Arthur for the honeymoon. He had his heart set on showing her the setting of his childhood, and introducing her to his adopted family, who had raised him and his brother since Arthur was seven. Then he planned to show her the glories of the West Coast. They were to be away six weeks, a thought which pleased Patrick so little that he grew gloomy.

"You know, my dear, I can't help being concerned about Arthur's health. His rheumatism is getting worse and worse. Poor fellow, it was ever a sad sight when he had an attack, to see him limping about, trying to conceal his pain. Does it not alarm you, Charlotte? You know what can come of severe rheumatism—terrible suffering! Complete ultimate helplessness!"

Charlotte shuddered. An aunt of Ellen's had died like that. "If he is doomed to suffer," she said, "all the more will he need care and help."

"What a lucky fellow he is, to be sure! Come—I want to show you the little room. All that is lacking is the curtains. Your betrothed is most satisfied with all our arrangements."

Charlotte could not help smiling to herself. Papa had come around so completely to the marriage that he did not even see the ludicrousness of his own inconsistencies. A lucky fellow, indeed! It was Papa, Charlotte thought, who was the lucky fellow, and subconsciously he had realized it.

While he showed her the new decorations, he was chatting on happily about the wedding. "Arthur is insistent on your having your way in everything, my dear. I think he would have liked to invite a good number of his clerical friends, but as you want a quiet wedding, he is willing to forego all but the Grants and Mr. Sowden. Of course Miss Ellen will be your bridesmaid?" Charlotte nodded. "And may I put in one request? Pray do invite that dear lady, Miss Wooler. I need a bridge between our two generations, and besides, I find much in common with her."

"Will you promise to try to prevent the exact date leaking out in the village? I would so hate it if everyone came to stare at us."

"As you wish, my dear," said Patrick, all but pouting with disappointment. He would have loved the whole population to turn out with laurels and banners to cheer his sweet darling child (the more passionately beloved now for having been so long out of favor) on her wedding morning.

The marriage date was set for June 29th. Mr. Nicholls returned to Haworth two weeks before. Charlotte, who had been worrying about whether she would be properly glad to see him, dropped her sewing at his knock and ran to the door and into his arms and found herself remarkably pleased to be there.

"Charlotte—" He kissed her cheek soundly, then, more diffidently, her lips.

"Oh, Arthur! It is good to see you!"

She led him in by the arm, and once the door was closed they embraced with less restraint. Charlotte found such kisses puzzling. It was not thrilling at the time, though they warmed and comforted; it was thinking about it afterward that sometimes sent the authentic shivers through her.

"And how is your rheumatism, Arthur?"

"Ah. Who told you? I did not mean to trouble you with it; I was hoping it would pass. Seemingly the excitement of the coming event has wrought on me, bringing it on to a pitch where my landlady at Kirk Smeaton became somewhat alarmed at my groans and sent for a specialist."

"And what did he say?" asked Charlotte, now thoroughly frightened.

"Why, he said I must not get too wrought up, that nervous tension can affect the muscles as much as rheumatism—"

"What?" cried Charlotte in quite a different tone. "You mean to tell me that he found you are *not* rheumatic?"

"Of course I am rheumatic, Charlotte!" he exclaimed indignantly. "I have suffered *torments*. Surely *you* do not doubt it?"

"Tell me, are you suffering now?"

"No," he said, adding naively, "When I am with you, all pain leaves me."

"You mean you do not need to make others sorry for you!" said Charlotte. "Your landlady at Kirk Smeaton did you great harm by pampering and fussing over you. I shall give Mrs. Brown fair warning of your terrible affliction, so that she may laugh at you whenever you begin to groan."

"Charlotte! Have you no pity for me?"

"Not the least bit. If the specialist said it was all nerves, why, I've seen a lot of what your nerves can do to all around you, and I tell you the sooner you take command of them the better."

For a moment longer he favored her with his most "Puseyite" look, compounded of severity, dignity, and wounded male pride. Then he saw she was trying not to laugh, and he reached out his big hand for her. "The sooner you take command of me the better. For this much is true: when I am married to you, I cannot conceive of feeling pain any more than one anticipates suffering in heaven."

The day before the wedding, Ellen and Miss Wooler arrived together early, and helped with the last-minute preparations. Mr. Nicholls was staying at the Grants, whence he would come over the fields with Mr. Sowden for the service, which was to be at eight in the morning to avoid sightseers.

There was time for a break after tea, despite the frantic last-minute bustle, and Charlotte took "the ladies" (as Mr. Nicholls called them) up to her room to show them her new dresses. The dress she was to travel in the next day was, in Ellen's eyes, the sweetest—lilac shot-silk, with wide sleeves and little lace trimmings, most delicate and well-suited to Charlotte's figure. "It is like a doll's dress!" Ellen exclaimed. The wedding gown was white embroidered muslin, and the veil had a border of ivy leaves. They reverently laid it out on a chair and gazed at it.

"You will look like a little snowdrop, my dear," said Miss Wooler.

They worked till suppertime, packing, cooking, and arranging. Patrick kept to his room. They did not see him until it was time for the evening ritual of family prayers, conducted in the parlor.

"I hope your dear father is not indisposed?" whispered Miss Wooler as they prepared to file in.

"I think he *is* a little upset. Mr. de Renzi—the curate, you know —was expected to stay on until we return from Ireland, but he has suddenly taken himself off, and in no very pleasant fashion, so Mr. Nicholls has had to provide a locum. Papa does not like strangers and he is understandably put out."

Prayers, attended by Tabby, Martha, and her sisters Hannah and Tabitha, who were helping, passed off quietly. Only Charlotte noticed that Papa did not look at anyone, and mumbled a good deal more than usual, as if his thoughts were elsewhere than on God.

When the servants had left the room and "the ladies" were smoothing the kneeling-creases off their dresses preparatory to withdrawing, Patrick suddenly electrified them all by announcing shrilly that he would not be coming to church in the morning.

"Papa! What can you mean?"

"It is not to be done, Charlotte. That is all there is to it. It is not—to be done."

Ellen took Miss Wooler's arm and they hastily left the parlor, closing the door. Charlotte stood still.

"It is of no use to look at me like that, Charlotte!" Patrick burst out. "I cannot help it."

"But Papa," she said faintly. "If you do not come, who is to give me away?"

Patrick did not seem to hear. He stood with his back to her, tapping his fingers irritably on the desk. They stayed there without speaking for about five minutes, each waiting for some move from the other. Abruptly Charlotte whirled and left the room.

Ellen and Miss Wooler were waiting for her across the hall. They both rose as she came in, distressed by her pallor and the proximity of tears. Miss Wooler hurried to embrace her.

"There, there, Charlotte, don't mind too much! He is old, and this is a very difficult moment for him. Perhaps he really cannot bring himself to see you married."

"Perhaps," said Charlotte thinly. "But we have a more solid

problem. Someone must give me away. It is Papa's duty, which he will not—very well, cannot—perform. Am I then not to be married?"

Ellen rushed to the bookshelves. "Where is the prayer-book, Charlotte? Let us see what it says. It may not have to be a parent, and it certainly does not have to be a man, for I saw a friend once given away by her widowed mother."

They found the place and all three bent their heads over the page.

"There! Not a word about who may or may not do the office. It could be any older friend."

Charlotte turned slowly to her old teacher. "Miss Wooler. . . ?"

"I? My dear Charlotte, what a great honor! I should be delighted."

The wedding was over. Patrick recovered, now the deed was done and not to be undone, and was geniality itself at the wedding breakfast, paying court handsomely to Miss Wooler and persistently addressing Charlotte as "Mrs. Nicholls." Mr. Sowden, who had performed the ceremony, was very attentive to Ellen; Martha, Hannah, and Tabitha Brown happily adopted the role of handmaidens, and old Tabby sat in a corner and cried every time her eyes fell on Charlotte in her diminutive white dress.

At last Arthur came up and took her hand. "You must change, my love. The cab is waiting for us, and we have a long journey ahead."

With Ellen's help, Charlotte put on her lilac dress. Her box was loaded onto the cab which waited at the garden gate. A little knot of villagers, to whom the news had leaked out by now, were gathered at the foot of the lane to see her off, and the few favored guests who had attended the breakfast, together with the servants, came crowding out to kiss Charlotte, shake the groom by the hand, and wish them well.

Ellen hung back, so as to be the last. "God bless you!" she whispered tearfully as she hugged Charlotte tightly. "Write to me. You will, won't you?"

"Dearest, dearest Nell!"

They drove through fitful periods of sunshine to Keighley station and there took a train to Conway, where they were to spend the night. Charlotte's natural nervousness and her inevitable tiredness increased all day, and were exacerbated by a trying cold. By the time they reached Conway, the weather was dark, wet, and wild. Over dinner at the inn, neither of them could find much to say. For her part, Charlotte could only wish the night well over, her cold and headache dispelled, and honeymoons in general uninvented. She had never felt less bridal in her life, and as Arthur led her up the stairs to their comfortable but dauntingly unfamiliar inn sitting-room, her strongest impulse—if she had had energy enough left—would have been to turn and flee.

"You're tired, my love," said Arthur quietly when the heavy oak door had shut them up alone together.

She looked up at him piteously. He gathered her in his arms. She leaned against him, limp and trembling. Whatever demands he made of her now, she had nothing to offer. She was exhausted.

"Come and sit with me," he said.

To her initial confusion he lifted her off her feet, carried her to a chair by the fire, and sat down with her on his knees.

"Listen to the storm," he said. "The wind is 'wuthering' almost as it does on the moors. . . . It should make you feel at home."

She said nothing. She sat stiffly, primly, her hands clenching each other with the sheer unaccustomedness of their proximity and the strange, intimate position. As he went on speaking, very gently his arm urged her to lean more against him.

"And soon we will be at *my* home. I wonder what you will think of it. It is partly a school, as I told you. But first we will see Dublin, and I'll show you Trinity, where I studied, and take you for a boat-ride on the canal which my brother manages—I do hope he will meet us when we get there. I'm sure he will, for he is longing to meet you, as are all my dear family. . . ."

Now she was leaning on him, and as he felt her slight figure against him the agitation he had so far mastered began to tell in his voice, which lost some of its measured depth and rose unsteadily.

"My aunt, you know, has been like a mother to me, since my

uncle adopted me and brought me, with my brother, from our native Scotland as orphan children. My many cousins treat me as their brother. You will like them, especially Mary Anne, who is so much an admirer of your books."

Charlotte did not interrupt. Let him talk as long as he liked. His voice, shaking now, and stilted, nevertheless had a strangely soothing effect on her—perhaps it was more the warmth of his big body. The flickering of the firelight and the steady glow of the lamp were also, in some way, calming her. They seemed so home-like, so ordinary. . . . After all, millions of women had passed through this (though not many for the first time at her age!). He was kind and gentlemanly. He would be good to her. Slowly she relaxed. Her head fell on his shoulder and her hand crept into his.

As if this triumph of trust over timidity proved more than his overwrought nerves could bear, Arthur stopped speaking abruptly and stood up, almost pushing her off his knees.

"It's late," he said. "Will you—would you care to go in first?"

Charlotte, feeling the loss of his closeness, did not understand what he meant at first. But he glanced at the bedroom door and she started and then said faintly, "As you wish."

He lit a candle for her. His hands shook so much that she had to steady them. The touch of her hands, cupped round his, seemed to unman him completely. "Charlotte—" he said sharply, the word bursting out of him.

"Yes, Arthur."

"I do not think—I—"

He stared at her wildly across the candle-flame. She found her-self, completely against her will, wanting to smile. All the lurid tales she had heard of brutish husbands overcome by passion re-turned to her as she looked at the helpless, wild-eyed figure of her own, looking as terrified as if he were about to be pushed off a cliff.

Suddenly all fear for herself left her. All she wanted was to comfort him, put him at his ease, as she had been a moment before when he had held and talked to her.

She reached up and laid her hand on his bearded cheek for a moment. "My husband," she heard herself say for the first time—and saw a change in his face, in his body, which gave her a most heady and beautiful taste of her womanly power. He straightened, swallowed, and said firmly, "Call me when you are ready."

"Yes, Arthur," she said meekly, and left him.

In the big strange bed, Charlotte's mind was alert, noticing everything. She was amazed at the way his body weighted down the bed beside her, at the strange smell of his skin and hair and breath, so different from a woman's smell. She divined his fears: under these unpropitious circumstances, they were the masculine equivalent of her own (it was his first time, too), and she understood intuitively how to reassure him.

"We have all this night, Arthur," she whispered, "and all the rest of our lives. There is no hurry." And she leaned to him, kissing him and touching him softly on the face and neck. Gradually his frantic trembling ceased, as hers had done before the fire; the warmth, the unfamiliar but marvelous consolation of her small, soft, delicate body touching his through the two thin layers of cloth, relieved his tormented manhood of its mysterious restraints, and the long, fraught dream began to become a reality.

For him, from then on, it was simple. But for Charlotte it was not simple at all, for nothing emotional was ever simple for her. She had had many thoughts, half-suppressed, about how she would meet this experience. In youth she had desired it, had all but been through it in the dark depths of adolescent imagination. Later, when real men had entered her sphere of consciousness, she had scarcely allowed herself to recognize the meaning of her body's urgings, for there had seemed no hope of a permissible outlet. Certainly she had never approached—in waking hours, at least—a contemplation of Monsieur Héger or any other as a lover in the true sense.

But now a whole lifetime's inhibitions must be set aside. Knowing in advance, and now having very active proof of the exceptional strength of her husband's feelings for her, she was all but overwhelmed by the importance of casting off all the bonds she had imposed on her natural sensuality, and responding to him without restraint or shame. However, that was easier acknowledged than achieved. Very strongly had those painful flushes of desire, experienced when reading Byron at thirteen, or writing of Zamorna a few years later, been suppressed; and heavy were the layers of control she had laid above them. Now, after twenty years she must prize up those gravestones of conscience and self-preservation and peer into the depths of her nature to see whether that lovely, burning, demanding urge was still alive, or whether it had been crushed and stifled there in the lonely dark.

At first it seemed dead. All she had to help her was duty, affection, and a strong desire to comfort and satisfy her husband. But that was enough, she found, to begin with, though it was hardly what Byron had seemed to promise. When Arthur had fallen asleep, with many broken protestations of love and delight, she lay close to him, wide awake now and with no symptoms of cold other than a parched mouth, and thought it all over. As she relived the experience, setting aside as well as she could all prudery and false modesty, the recollections fused together in her mind into something she had been too deeply anxious to feel at the time. A glow, proudly sensed and profoundly remembered from long ago, began to suffuse her body, and she thought with rising elation, "I am not too old! It will happen—it will happen!" and was aware of the beginnings of a new, unlooked-for happiness.

chapter 8 THE DARK STAR LIGHTS UP

*P*atrick had been accustomed to refer scathingly to his curate's account of his origins and connections as "the Irish fiction." He had implied by this that Mr. Nicholls was no better in these respects than himself, and his prejudiced notions of the young man's home and family had communicated themselves to Charlotte.

She was therefore rather more than pleasantly surprised to be met in Dublin by three well-dressed and cultivated young people instead of the outlandish Irish countryfolk she had been half-expecting. They were Arthur's brother Alan and two Bell cousins, Joseph and Mary Anne, all so courteous and charming to Charlotte that her nervousness disappeared, and she was able to enjoy the principal sights of Dublin for two or three days quite unhindered by her usual shyness.

At the end of each day, spent making calls on her husband's relatives or visiting his old college or in some other way exploring his past, Charlotte retired with him to their own sanctuary to explore the new world of the senses which was gradually opening up for both. His initial crippling tensions overcome, Arthur began to emerge as a lover not only passionate, but generous and sensitive to his wife's needs. She had helped him at first; now he helped her, and soon the sensual happiness Charlotte had foreseen was a reality for her. During the days also, Arthur lost no occasion to demonstrate by a hundred little courtesies his satisfaction at having her with him, his joy in possessing her. To Charlotte, one of the greatest delights was having someone with her all the time, to cherish and protect her: the knowledge that she need never be alone again.

A week after the wedding, they traveled to Banagher, and here an even greater surprise awaited Charlotte. The house where Arthur had grown up from the age of seven, after he and his brother Alan had been adopted by their Uncle Bell and brought thence from Scotland, was a fine big property, set in woodland and surrounded by a walled garden. It had been built in late Stuart times, and endowed as a school in the seventeenth century. The school itself, now being administered by another of Arthur's cousins, stretched out in the rear of the house, adding to the impression of settled prosperity and respectability which struck Charlotte from the moment they turned in to the wrought-iron gates.

The inmates fulfilled the promise of those they had sent ahead as emissaries. Mary Anne led her around, introducing her to the large family as if Charlotte were her own discovery, and then inveigled her away to look over the house.

"This will be yours and dear cousin Arthur's room," she said, opening a door on the ground floor. "Oh, please don't be upset at its being so big and gloomy! Mother insisted upon the best bedroom for you, though I told her you would surely prefer something cozier. I somehow knew, from reading your books, that you would feel lost in this."

Charlotte looked around. It was a high-ceilinged room, with a great curtained bed dwarfed by the proportions surrounding it. But in the wide fireplace burned a bright fire of turf and logs, and Mary Anne was hurrying about with a taper lighting candelabra on every surface to drive back the shadows.

"It is a noble chamber," said Charlotte, "not so much too big as too magnificent for me."

Mary Anne returned to her slowly, still carrying her taper. She was a sweetly pretty girl, something over twenty, Charlotte guessed, with dark curly hair and bright dark eyes. She limped rather badly, and seeming to guess Charlotte's thoughts, said quickly, "You must not mind my lameness, for I don't in the least! I fell off a horse when I was a child, out hunting, and became a hobbledehoy. But I find I am not the less loved, and that is what matters to me." She stood close to Charlotte and looked into her eyes. "Arthur loves you," she said quietly. "One has only to watch him for a minute or two to see how much. You are indeed fortunate. But then, after so many years' acquaintance, you will think me impertinent to tell you that."

"It delights me, nevertheless, to see how highly he is regarded by others," said Charlotte.

"Well! You mustn't judge only by his family—of course, we all think the world of him. But you will meet those from the neighborhood, whose judgment is less biased, and they will fill you with satisfaction at having captured the heart of such a treasure as our Arthur."

Why, you love him yourself, thought Charlotte with a sudden flash of insight. The idea of this young and pretty creature being fond of Arthur in a romantic way gave Charlotte a strange thrill of possession. It also warmed her doubly toward Mary Anne, who far from evincing any jealousy was treating her with the warmth of a sister.

That night, in the canopied bed, she and Arthur lay together and talked. This was a new delight, one she had never envisaged— snug and comfortable, her head pillowed on his shoulder, their friendly whispers meeting in the dark. The curtains of the bed

seemed to cut them off from all the world, and the sense of intimacy and security was blissful to her.

"I must say, I am delighted with my new relations," she said.
"They are all so amiable and pleasing."

"Confess you did not look to find them so civilized."

"I'll own they seem more—well, more English in their manners
than I expected. Why did you not tell me what cultivated connections you have, and what a fine home?"

"One doesn't boast of such things. Whenever I mentioned anything about my family to your father, he showed his skepticism
clearly. And then, I was afraid you might marry me for my
headmaster-uncle, my canal-managing brother, or my pretty lady-
like cousins, instead of for myself alone."

Charlotte laughed into his neck. "I am more likely to have married you for your enchanting Aunt Bell. She has all the port and
manners of a great lady, and yet she is so unpretentious. Tonight
we chatted by the fire together like old friends, and she said, 'Sitting like this with you, I quite forget I am talking to a celebrated
authoress!' But I am at home with all of them, and I must say I'm
most impressed with everything I see. So much English order and
repose about the household habits and arrangements!"

"Why? Had you expected chaos?"

"One had heard so much of Irish negligence," Charlotte murmured.

"Ah! But we are Scots," said Arthur complacently.

Before long, not only was Charlotte quite recovered from her
cold, but Arthur himself—now wholly relaxed and with not a trace
of rheumatism—had gained several pounds in weight, his carriage
straightened, and his whole bearing altered for the better.

This physical improvement was just one of several factors in the
speedy change in Charlotte's whole view of him. He was like a
different man here, and she began to realize that she had *never*
seen him to advantage in Haworth, subservient as he had neces-
sarily been there to her father, and functioning also under the
most trying constraints and oppressions. No signs appeared of a
deeper intellectual affinity with herself; but there were many

lesser revelations, among them his gentlemanly reception of the many who came to call on them, and a positive passion for wildlife and nature.

When they finally reached County Clare, that rugged and spectacular coastline appealed almost as deeply to Arthur as to Charlotte. She feared he would think her affected, to want to drink in these natural marvels without the distraction of talking or walking; but he allowed her to sit on the clifftop above Kilkee, with her legs wrapped in a rug which he tenderly arranged, and be left quite in peace to commune with the surging Atlantic as long as she liked. Only when she edged too near the brink did she realize —from the immediacy with which his hands grasped her shoulders from behind—that he had not gone far from her, and must have been as quietly and profoundly absorbed with the scene as herself. This endeared him to her more than ever, demolishing another barrier that she felt might have existed to true understanding between them.

From then on, whatever glorious sights they saw—and the West Coast of Ireland is a natural paradise—they saw them together, usually hand in hand.

They traveled for a fortnight, from Kilkee to Glengarriff. But Charlotte's growing happiness began to be overshadowed by a growing sense of guilt and uneasiness about her father. Sometimes, even in moments of the purest joy, arising either from the matchless beauties surrounding her or from the devotion and protection which accompanied everything she did, she would be overtaken by the strongest longing to cut the trip short and go home immediately. She hated to mention this to Arthur; when she thought of how he must feel about returning to a species of slavery in Haworth, dutybound to serve out a further sentence for the old man whom *she* loved but whom *he* had every reason to dislike and resent, her heart ached for him. So she put off her request until something happened which broke the smooth unspoiled idyll and made a return home advisable.

One day they went riding, a thing Charlotte had never done before. Both she and Arthur were at the peak of good health and good spirits, and to be mounted on tall horses on a fine bright blowy day seemed only fitting. Charlotte felt literally "on top of the world," full of buoyancy and confidence, quite unlike her usual timorous self. So much so, in fact, that when they came to a bad place, rocky and narrow, and the guide advised her to dismount, she said, "I don't believe I will—I am sure my horse will carry me safely."

The mare she was riding was in fact more nervous than she, and as it picked its way past the dangerous drop, it trembled, and once its hoof slipped on a large smooth stone which clattered down into the river tumbling below. Charlotte clutched the pommel of her sidesaddle in a quick spasm of fright, but kept her seat, and the place was passed.

She straightened and took a breath, glorying in her relative fearlessness and new daring, which came, she thought, from knowing that Arthur was nearby. How different was every venture, now that she was no longer alone, from what it had been before! She had just time to savor this new, inner security, when her mare suddenly, without apparent reason, seemed to go mad.

It reared up, whinnying. Charlotte grabbed its mane, and managed to save herself falling; but the mare, once on four legs again, continued to buck and plunge, and Charlotte caught her breath and screamed. Arthur, riding ahead, leaped from his horse and rushed back to lay hands on the mare's bridle. Just as he did so, Charlotte lost her balance and slipped from the saddle.

Several moments of the most acute physical terror she had ever known followed. Arthur, facing forward, did not notice at first that she was on the ground. She lay cowering, not knowing whether she had been hurt by the fall, only conscious of the kicking, trampling hooves that flailed about her. She closed her eyes in an agony of fear, and in that moment she *saw* her own body, in its borrowed habit, stretched bloody-headed upon the stones, felt Arthur's overwhelming grief, and (almost worse) the horror of his having to report her death or injury to her father.

At this she found breath to cry out, "Arthur! Arthur! Let it go!"

Arthur whirled, saw her, and released the struggling mare, who sprang over Charlotte and shied away. There it stood in a nervous lather while Arthur and the guide lifted Charlotte to her feet.

"My dearest—my beloved—are you hurt? Dear God—!" Arthur cried, white to the lips with shock.

"I think I'm all right—" replied Charlotte shakily.

Careless of the staring guide, Arthur held her close, trembling wildly. "If I had lost you—" he gasped. "If I ever lost you—"

They arrived back in Haworth at the beginning of August, after only a month away.

Martha, forewarned by a letter, had laid out a royal tea, with three kinds of cold meat and every other delicacy she could think of. She was waiting at the door when the cab discharged them at the gate, and fairly hugged Charlotte. "Oh, Miss Charlotte! How we've missed thee!"

"And I all of you, believe me! Tell me quickly, how is Papa? You can't imagine how anxious I've been—"

"Now don't upset thisen, if I tell thee 'e's not been too well. 'E's pined a bit, which is only natural, but Hannah and me's took care on 'im as best we could."

The parlor door opened and Papa appeared in it. His looks shocked her; he seemed to have aged visibly; his wasted chin was now deeply sunk into his cravat, which it was his odd fancy to swathe with bands of white silk until the whole stood up nearly to his ears. His spectacles slipped down his nose and his clothes hung on him as if his flesh had shrunk on his bones.

"Papa!" Charlotte exclaimed. "Oh, dearest Papa—I am so glad to see you!"

She flew to him and he held her pressed to his breast for a long moment. He did not ask about her journey or do more than nod to Arthur, standing near the door. He only said, "You are home."

But Charlotte knew that her fears had not been false. Her long absence had been a severe infliction, and she vowed to herself that she would never leave him again as long as he lived.

chapter 9 **BURYING THE PAST**

*D*uring the racking years of the recent past, Charlotte had become profoundly convinced that whatever happiness she was fated to know in her life was over. The enchanted years before Roe Head, the first ecstatic months in Brussels—dead and gone; she must expect no more.

Yet now a new happiness came to her, a warm, steady, growing happiness of a kind she had not anticipated. In her romantic youth she had supposed marriage must be an ecstasy or a disaster; when she had contemplated marriage to Arthur Nicholls she had been miserable through knowing it would not be either of these but something in between—a compromise, a defeat. (This had caused her angry quarrel with Ellen, who had touched her on the raw by saying that the very act of marrying would be inconsistent with Charlotte's life and goals; it was too true.)

Yet here indeed was her "mixed cup," and she drank it down gladly. The burden of loneliness-present and the terror of lone-liness-eternal were lifted, and in their place was normality. She had joined the ranks of the lucky ones—the loved, the protected, the unafraid; and she found, to her relief and quiet delight, that for this blessing she was prepared to sacrifice much that had once seemed essential to her as a lone woman fighting for independence and against despair.

The leisure which had once enabled her to write, to commune with herself—and to sink into morbidity and grief—was quite done away with now. She was busy from morning till night, be-cause the whole burden of parish duties had been quietly accepted by her husband and he expected that she would help him full-time like any ordinary parson's wife. The total freedom she had had hitherto, to form her own routine and make her own decisions, was also gone: Arthur was the head of the household now, and such decisions, even in small things, rested with him.

This was irksome at times, but, just as Mrs. Gaskell had fore-seen, no other kind of husband would have suited Charlotte. She generally fell in with his wishes and secretly relished his authority, though she maintained a check, in the form of some salutary mockery, on any attempt to dominate her. She was also learning the time-honored feminine tricks which she had once thought were not for her, whereby women "manage" their husbands; and if he did go too far sometimes, she could weather it patiently because he loved her. This love, which strengthened from week to week, gave her quite a new idea of herself.

How could she think herself ugly when such a good (and, she now thought, handsome) man adored her and assured her several times a day by looks, words, and actions that she was the very light of his eyes? This release from a crippling sense of her unattrac-tiveness was for a long time enough to balance the petty restric-tions or annoyances which marriage inevitably brought.

And there was another cause of gratitude. Papa was safe, too. He was really too frail all that autumn to take any church duty, and to see Arthur putting on his vestments each Sunday while the old man sat smoking by the fire gave Charlotte deep contentment. All antagonism between the two seemed ended. In fact, this was largely due to Arthur's tact and forbearance and to Patrick's having got what he basically wanted. But Charlotte took it literally for a miracle. God, seeing that misery was impairing her faith, had given her a sign, for which she did not neglect to thank Him night and morning.

Arthur was offered several good livings, one by Sir James Kay-Shuttleworth himself, who would have been very pleased to have the husband of the famous Currer Bell established on his estate and pressed his offer home without restraint; but Arthur steadily refused.

"I have promised my wife that as long as her father is alive, I will stay in Haworth as his curate. And so I shall."

Charlotte's premarital fears that Arthur would put a blight on her friendships were not fulfilled—largely perhaps because she was kept too fully occupied to keep them up! As far as Ellen was concerned, Arthur liked her and found her in every way an unexceptionable companion for Charlotte. During that autumn, they even tried to make a match between her and Arthur's friend Sutcliff Sowden.

Ellen visited them in October and Mr. Sowden was invited to join them for walks. Once or twice he came, and then their moorland strolls were even-numbered and enjoyable, at least to the newlyweds. But Ellen was not very taken with the scheme, which she quickly saw through.

"He is a curate like other curates," she said flatly. "I don't want to join you in your anticlerical campaign, Charlotte, but I've come to believe you have carried off the only marriageable curate in the whole of Yorkshire."

So they took their next walk in a trio, and this was less comfortable. Arthur walked between them, while they tried to talk across him. After half a mile, Charlotte stopped. "Walk on my right, please, Arthur," she said firmly. "I want to be next to Nell. Even you shall not come between us."

He laughingly assured them that he had no intention of trying.

Yet it was hard as never before for the two women to get time alone together. Charlotte's many activities did not stop for visits, and during leisure moments Arthur was nearly always there. However, at last they found themselves alone one evening by the dining-room fire, as in the old days, with Flossy stretched between them.

"Well, Charlotte? And how is—marriage?"

Charlotte gazed into the fire. "Very full of new things," she said.

"Are you not going to be more specific?"

"I will say one thing. Married women who unthinkingly urge their entire female acquaintance to marry are to be censured. It is a very strange and solemn and perilous thing for a woman to become a wife. Her life is not her own anymore. It is far different with men—their lives go on as before—but their wives must cleave to them in *every* way. It is as though marriage were not just a union of two individuals, but a matter of the woman being attached to the man and henceforth having to follow him in everything."

"I should like that," said Ellen simply.

"Would you, Nell? Then marry Mr. Sowden!"

She shook her head with a wry little smile. "I find him uninspiring."

"Marriage, they say, is all the better for starting with a little aversion."

"Did yours?"

"Yes. But it has gone. I love my dear one heartily."

"So, despite not being so free, all is perfect?"

"Nothing is ever *that*. There is still no intellectual compatibility. But we are indulgent to each other. And my freedom is well-lost, so far as it *is* lost. It is a wonderful thing to be so constantly needed."

"But you will not write."

"Oh, yes, I will! I have a novel started now."

But she spoke so lightly that Ellen shook her head.

"I fear for your career, Charlotte. Before, your writing was all in all to you—it justified your existence, in your own eyes. But now you are happy, you may not need to write."

Charlotte stared at her, frowning. She did not look for wisdom and profound insights from Ellen, and when occasionally she got them, she was disconcerted.

"Nonsense! When the evenings draw in, I will get down to work."

"They have drawn in already," said Ellen quietly.

After she had gone, they had other visitors, less pleasing to Arthur, and the occasion was so distasteful to him, he announced that while of course Charlotte might invite whom she chose to visit her, the next time certain callers arrived, he, Arthur, intended to bolt.

It was while Charlotte was writing a lively account of all this to Ellen that the first crisis of her marriage occurred. Arthur, leaning over her shoulder to read what she wrote, suddenly exploded. "Really, Charlotte! You are too indiscreet! Don't you realize such letters are dangerous as lucifer matches if they ever fell into the wrong hands?"

"Oh, Arthur! Come now. I've always written so, and I intend to continue. If one holds back, there is no point in writing. Letters become more dead messages, as men's usually are. Mine to Ellen are communications. I write as I speak to her."

"Speaking is one thing: words float off into the ether and are heard no more. A letter can be a permanent source of trouble." He straightened up and looked Puseyite. "Now, Charlotte, hear me. You are to add a postscript telling Miss Ellen to fire this and every letter of yours, past and future. Or there will be no more! I am resolved on that."

For a moment, Charlotte felt rebellion seethe within her. But looking at him, standing there so stern and masterful, her eyes brimmed with sudden laughter. "Oh, dear! Well, if you are *re-solved*, Arthur, there is no more to be said." And she smiled an obedient smile which he did not at all trust, picked up her pen, and added the required instructions, knowing very well that Ellen would not dream of carrying them out.

But Charlotte grew uneasy, nevertheless. The more often Ar-

thur persisted in trying to restrict her correspondence, the more
her thoughts turned to Ellen's old remark, "But you will not
write." Mrs. Gaskell had said that, too. Charlotte began a close and
repetitive examination of her inner self, which preoccupied her
even while her hands were busy arranging Sunday-school teas,
packing baskets for Arthur's rounds of the needy, ironing his sur-
plice, or working on a new altar-cloth. This was undemanding
work, but tiring and time-consuming. While using but a fraction
of her potential, it yet excluded all the rest. It reminded her, in a
way, of her first employment, at Roe Head School. Then she had
been in a continual ferment of rebellion, burning to get back to
her imaginary, creative world. Now she was quite content. But as
soon as she realized her contentment, worries began gnawing at it.
Had Arthur, with his love, and his firm, well-justified demands on
her time, actually destroyed the thing in her which had given her
her uniqueness? Was she—instead of expanding into mature and
fulfilled womanhood—dwindling into a mere country parson's
wife?

This thought began to work upon her in a way which frightened her. For the first time since her marriage she found herself
not sleeping well, but lying awake at Arthur's side in the big bed
which had been her parents', thinking all manner of strange, disturbing thoughts. She thought of Papa next door. . . . It was sometimes hard to forget his proximity when Arthur made love to her.
Deafness was one affliction he had never suffered from. The delights of the honeymoon fluctuated now. Sometimes all was well;
at others, inhibition seized her. Her body became a thing not her
own, and not to be moved to feeling or response. At such times
Arthur was unfailingly patient and tender, but she sensed his disappointment.

One night he whispered, "Have you any fears, my darling, that
you haven't told me?"

At the word "fear," a secret she had been hiding from herself
sprang into clear sight in her brain. She had never wanted children. She had never—except with Julia Gaskell, and, for that brief,
happy time in Brussels, the little Hégers—liked children or known

how to cope with them. The thought of a small, helpless, infinitely demanding creature of her own was like contemplating an eternal millstone hung about her neck, weighting her down to domesticity forever.

Once, long ago, she had had a dream, which she had incorporated into *Jane Eyre*—a dream in which she ran through darkness, impeded by a cold, clinging, wailing infant. Now she relived that dream again. Fear brought it, she knew that. Yet when Arthur asked her, "Have you any fears?" she replied quickly, "Of course not! What could I fear, now I have you?" It was the answer he had wanted, and he was happy to accept it. But she in her turn was disappointed in him; for, loving her as she knew he did, should he not have guessed she was lying, should he not have persisted?

Between these two great qualms—that her unique faculty of creation was shrinking, and that she might conceive—Charlotte's unexpected happiness might have been seriously undermined. But she had learned to master and override so many morbid inner weaknesses that she tackled this threat to her newfound stability and health as strongly as she knew how.

In the case of the fear of child-bearing, she put it firmly from her, half-laughing at herself: "At my age! A stunted thing like me! Unless God has me in view as a second Sarah, I can hardly be said to be at risk." As to her other fear, there was definitely something to be done about that, and one afternoon when Arthur was out visiting in the parish, she set herself to begin a new novel.

She had not quite told Ellen the truth, for it was barely more than a vague notion in her head when she had described it as "begun." But now she made her lie come true. She wrote ten pages and it had started to flow when she heard Arthur's voice calling her from the hall, "Charlotte! Is my tea ready?"

Jerked back to the realities of life, Charlotte's racing pencil stumbled, halted, then went on.

"Charlotte?"

"Ask Martha!" she called down without raising her head.

"I am asking *you*," his voice came back, with a touch of severity.

Charlotte stopped dead, her eyes wide and fixed. No. No, this came first. This was her work. *This was herself.* But although she did not rise and go downstairs, neither could she force herself to go on writing. And after a minute or two she heard his footsteps coming upstairs. He opened her door without knocking.

"Charlotte?"

Had there now been a hint of imperiousness, of masculine authority in his voice, she would have rebelled. But it was merely querulous. She turned slowly. He stood in the doorway, looking at her in loving inquiry. His eyes were tired, his shoulders stooped, his boots covered in mud. She jumped to her feet.

"My dear, forgive me! I will come at once."

That evening they sat together by the fire. He was reading, she sewing. Every now and then he would make a remark about his book, or the day he had spent. It was companionable, it was delightful. Yet the feeling returned, and at last Charlotte said, "If you were not with me, I would be writing now."

He looked up sharply. "Is that what you were up to this afternoon?"

She said nothing, but went up to her room and fetched the pages. When he saw them he put his book aside and sat in patient expectancy. With a strange sense of nervousness, she read him what she had written. It was about a plain-faced, well-dressed little girl brought to a school by an apparently wealthy father, and left there, to be fawned on and pampered by the avaricious headmistress and despised by the other girls. It soon evolved that the man had not been either rich or her father, for he disappeared, leaving no money for the child's fees. The headmistress's attitude speedily changed, and the child's situation was saved only by the arrival of an eccentric bachelor who said he would sponsor her.

When she came to the place where she had been interrupted, Charlotte looked up anxiously at Arthur. He was staring into the fire and did not move for several minutes. Had he been listening at all? But at last he looked at her, smiled, and said, "The critics will accuse you of repetition. The child is like Jane, or even Lucy."

"Oh it's only a rough beginning," said Charlotte lightly. "I shall change all that." And she ran upstairs again, put the pages away, and came down again at once so that he should not guess how badly she wanted to stay up there. For what? To weep with exasperation, with disappointment at his failure to respond as she had wanted? To write more? She did not clearly know. She only knew that to go down to him again was, for the first time in their marriage, an effort.

He put out his hand to her as she came into the room. She put hers into it, smiling brightly.

He was no fool, and he truly loved her. He saw the smile, recognized its forced quality at once, and interpreted it rightly. "Charlotte," he said quietly, "come and sit close to me."

He drew her onto his knee and gazed into eyes suddenly brilliant with tears.

"I have hurt you, my dearest," he said. "I should be flogged."

"No!" She pressed her face quickly down on his shoulder to hide it.

"I say yes. But I did not mean it. Will you believe my only wish is your happiness? I would never try to stop you writing, if that will make you happy. But the truth is, my love, that I want the happiness of Charlotte Brontë, clergyman's daughter, not that of Currer Bell, the celebrated writer. It was not her, with all her fame and laurels, that I courted and married. She may fly to heaven whenever she pleases, so I may keep the sweet unspoiled creature that I cherish."

Charlotte's innermost heart seemed to freeze. And when Arthur kissed and petted her, though her blood stirred, that icy place remained, unwarmed and full of fear. In the days that followed, she shut that cold place up and hid knowledge of it from herself. But the ten pages remained ten pages, and no more.

There came upon her after that the need—unacknowledged, unexpressed—to do other things of her own in which Arthur had no share. Private things, belonging to the inner world he could not and would not enter.

One day she was tidying some of her papers and she found herself standing very still, staring at a box containing packets of letters. Arthur had not given up his campaign to elicit from Ellen a written promise to burn letters Charlotte wrote, and so suddenly these letters—not those she had written, but those she had received from loved ones, and those who had loved her—seemed to have a peculiar, almost illicit importance. She felt a desire to read them, but—not now, not today when Arthur was in the house! She remembered guiltily how she and Emily used to carry Byron's poems out onto the moors, there to read them and savor their sensual delights far from Papa's inhibiting aura. It was the same now! Struggling to assure herself there was nothing wrong, she nevertheless waited till Arthur had to travel some distance on parish affairs and was not expected home till evening. Then she shut herself up in the little study which had been Emily's, and read the entire contents of the box.

Perhaps she had expected the letters—from George, from James Taylor, even from Monsieur Héger—to have lost their potency, now that she was soundly loved and married. But they had retained it, and to their former power was now added an aching poignancy. Though they spoke of long past dreams and sorrows, they retained, like bees, the ability to sting even after death.

Guilt grew on her as she read. Her love for her husband should have armored her against these nostalgic tears, these flights of remembered emotion. Just to have kept them seemed an act of disloyalty. Such things might be hoarded, surely, only until the present and future became more important than the past. . . .

And what to do with them now? Evening was coming, and Arthur would soon return. At last she put all the neat packets into the wooden box and carried them out to the back of the house, meaning to burn them. But when it came to doing the deed, when she crouched by the box with a lighted spill in her hand, ready to fire all those tokens of pain and hope and pleasure, her hand would not obey her order. The letters directed in Monsieur Héger's writing lay on the top, tied with faded silk ribbon. She turned them face-downward and tried again, and the ribbon was scorched. But then she snatched the flame away and threw the spill down. It was not to be done.

Eventually she went back to the kitchen and fetched a shovel.

She would make truth follow fiction, and bury them, as "Lucy" had buried the letters of "Dr. John." The moor was the place for them! But the tough, resistant turf refused to yield. Just at dusk she returned, the box still under her arm and tears running down her cheeks, and dug a deep hole in the front garden near the old holly tree. It would guard her treasures, and its roots would finally obliterate them.

Smoothing the earth tenderly above them, she remembered how Emily had burned her papers the night before she died. Charlotte shivered briefly, and hurried back indoors to wash the soil from her hands.

chapter *10* THE LAST STORM

*"C*harlotte! Are you busy?"

"I was about to write to Ellen. Why?"

"I have half an hour to spare. Come for a walk."

She glanced through the window. There had been a thaw over-night, and the first heavy snowfall of winter had melted. The sky was blue with little round white clouds being bowled across it by a buffeting wind. She laid down her pen.

"Here's your cloak—we won't go far."

But the moors were so invigorating that half an hour proved insufficient for Arthur. "Let's go to the waterfall! After the thaw it should be a grand sight."

Charlotte tucked her arm through his and they strode on, the wind tugging her cloak and forcing Arthur to carry his tall hat in his hand. They talked animatedly all the way; but when they reached the cataract they stood as they had stood before the wild splendid Atlantic, silenced by their mutual joy at the sight of the foaming torrent "raving over the rocks, white and bountiful," as Charlotte thought. Standing close to her husband's side, Charlotte was aware of an additional blessing. For the first time since Emily's death she could look at "her place" without anguish.

While they stood there the little clouds were darkening and conjoining, and the rain began to fall in long sharp darts. Arthur started as if waking. "Come! This won't do, you'll get wet. We must hurry back."

But it was not a path that could be hurried over, and it was more than an hour before they got home. They were both soaked to the skin.

Arthur fussed so much about her changing every stitch immediately instead of just drying out before the fire that Charlotte became a little impatient. But by the evening she knew she was going to get one of her colds: her throat ached and she was shivering.

This cold, certainly no worse than many another she had had, affronted Charlotte somehow. She had never in her life been so bloomingly healthy as since her marriage, and she had come to believe that the act of love—and the condition of being loved and cared for—had had a fully tonic effect upon her whole system. She had gained weight and complexion and been full of well-being and energy.

To find she was still subject to the trying humiliation of a cold was infuriating, and it had inconvenient side-effects. Mrs. Gaskell had been promising a visit, which was now put off, as was Charlotte's "bridal visit" to Brookroyd. These seemed mere postponements; but the cold proved stubborn, and lingered on till Charlotte determined to go to Ellen whether she were perfectly well or not.

"You will not go until I pronounce you fit enough," decreed Arthur.

Charlotte was prepared to ignore this, but suddenly word reached her through Miss Wooler that Mercy, one of Ellen's sisters who lived at home, had typhoid. Arthur flew into a panic.

"That settles it! You shall not stir abroad until winter is safely over and all infection dispelled."

Charlotte was frantic too, on Ellen's account, and would have gone at once, but in this Arthur was adamant. And soon enough another infliction was added which really did make traveling impossible.

She began to suffer from faintness and nausea.

It came upon her after the turn of the year, and at first she thought it was just her normal winter weakness and was disappointed with her body for this betrayal of her hopes of permanent good health. She could be very little help to anyone in her present state, for every time she ate she was sick, and every time she stood up she felt faint. Arthur, torn between alarm and a dawning anticipation, urged her to take to her bed; but Charlotte fought this off as long as she could.

"Why are you so obstinate, dearest? You must take care of yourself—for my sake if not for yours!"

"There is nothing seriously wrong with me."

Arthur took her hand and held it to his face in silence for a few moments. Then he said, "Have you thought—that the cause may be natural?"

Charlotte's mind went blank and her body became perfectly still. "It cannot be that."

He looked at her quickly, frowning. "Why not, Charlotte?"

"I am too old."

"You—" He swallowed his emotion, and went on very quietly, "You do not love like a woman who is too old. The body has its own mysteries. As you have awakened late to love, but awakened completely, so it may be you will awaken to motherhood."

For another moment she sat rigid, eyes glazed, alone with her fear, her deep unwillingness. Then suddenly she turned to him and flung herself into his arms. As he clasped her, it seemed to him that his whole mind was one yearning prayer—of gratitude, of hope, of hunger for the total fulfillment of their marriage.

"My dear love—! If it were so! I thought no further than having you for my wife. Further blessings were quite beyond my dreams."

Muffled against his shoulder, she got out the words, "We cannot be sure. Pray don't tell Papa!"

But the natural joy Arthur felt was soon overlaid by anxiety and pity. All the healthy flesh she had gained fell away as the sickness grew worse and worse. Before long it was impossible to keep Patrick from noticing, and one day, when Charlotte did not appear at breakfast, the old man suddenly banged on the table and shouted at his son-in-law, "Something's being kept from me! Why does my daughter not come to her meals? Why does she keep seated all the time while you fuss about her like a hen? Tell me the truth!"

"We think she may be going to have a child, sir," said Arthur quietly.

The old man stared at him for a moment, then abruptly buried his head in his hands. "I knew it," he said brokenly. "I knew it." He looked up again, and now the face he turned to his curate was as it had been during the days of enmity, white and quivering with hatred and sorrow.

"You have killed her, Nicholls."

Arthur gasped and half-rose to his feet, his hands on the table-edge.

"Yes. She will not survive. Marriage—childbirth—they are destroyers of women! I should never, never, never have allowed it! Fool that I was—selfish, wicked old fool! Now you have killed my darling, and I am to blame, for I should have been strong and resolute, and protected her from you and from all men till she was past the age of danger...."

Shaking his head and mumbling to himself, he got up and shuffled from the dining-room, leaving Arthur dazed with sudden fear, as if the old man had the power of prophecy.

At the end of January, Arthur decided that Haworth did not contain medical advice good enough for Charlotte, and summoned the best doctor in the region, Dr. MacTurk from Bradford.

After the examination, the two men conferred.

"Well, sir, you are going to be a father."

Arthur lifted his head and drew in his breath, but said nothing.

"You suspected it, of course. It's quite true. Her confinement will be at the end of September. In the meantime this sickness must be brought under control, although it is perfectly natural. The best thing is for her to lie in bed and rest until it passes off, and I will give you a calming medicine for her. Only the lightest food, of course."

"She is in no danger—?"

"No, no, I don't think so. Of course she is not in her first youth, and her health in general is not what one might wish, but I have seen less promising pregnancies turn out well. Meanwhile your local doctor, Ingham, will take care of her. I'll instruct him personally, and he will keep me informed."

When he had gone, Arthur went into the bedroom. The sight of Charlotte, lying so weakly on her pillows, smote his heart. He sat on the bedside and took her hand. "Did he tell you?"

She nodded, and smiled wanly.

"Darling—my darling little wife—" He put his face down and kissed her tenderly many times. She lay under his embrace, unmoving, smiling feebly. "We must take such care of you—and our precious little one—"

"Have you told Papa?" asked Charlotte faintly.

"He knows."

"He is angry."

"When the child is born, he will be so happy."

"Yes . . . but that's far ahead. . . . Arthur—"

"Yes, my dear love?"

"I feel so very ill—"

"Come! The doctor gave me medicine for you. It will make you better."

But the medicine had no noticeable effect. Throughout February the sickness grew worse, until Charlotte could keep nothing down and began to vomit blood.

The first time this happened, only Martha was in the room. "Oh, Miss Charlotte—what's to do?" she cried.

"Sh, Martha, don't make a fuss. Wash it away quickly. Keep it covered on your way down—don't tell them, *please*."

"But what's it mean? It's never the consumption! They do spit blood wi' that—"

"No, no, Martha. This is from my stomach. It's because I have had nothing to eat, and the straining on emptiness is harmful. Bring me a cup of warm broth—"

But the mere mention of food made her ill again. Her poor aching stomach-muscles griped as if some great clawed hand were clenching and unclenching on her vitals. The nights became indescribable and the worsening of her condition could not be hidden from Arthur, who attended her then, hardly sleeping at all, but sitting up beside her with basin and damp cloths and the draughts of cold water which were needed to wash out her mouth, and of which she could sometimes drink a little. But on the whole she ate almost nothing, and this Martha took upon herself like a cross.

"Tha must eat, Miss Charlotte! Oh, do eat, be it ever so little, for if tha doostna, 'ow cansta keep thy wee bairn from clemming? Think on 'im, Miss, as depends on thee for life, and tak' a cup o' this beef tea—"

And sometimes Charlotte could, though most of it came back later.

"What she eats wouldna keep a wren alive!" Martha groaned to Tabby in the kitchen. But Tabby could not hear her anymore, and soon she had to be moved to her sister's house in the village. There she sat out her last days, mumbling occasionally to herself, "I'll be gone afore long, and none to see me off—none on 'em left of all me childer to walk through t'gate after an old body—"

Late in February, Martha brought Charlotte the news. "Old Tabby's gone, Miss. She were took in t'middle of t'night."

Charlotte turned her head and looked at her wonderingly. "Our dear old Tabby—dead?"

Martha wiped her eyes on her apron. "Ay. But ye're not to fret, Miss Charlotte. The Lord takes away, but to you 'E's giving." She put her sadness hardily from her and began bustling about the bed, bunching the pillows and smoothing the sheets. "Ye must think o' that foremost, Miss. Why, think, what a bonny little thing

it'll be most like, a girl p'raps, dainty like thee but wi' Mr. Nicholls's dark wavy 'air and eyes like parson's, blue and lively . . .
Ee!" she said when no flicker of a smile appeared. "Do fettle thisen
up a mite, Miss Charlotte! Tha looks that down, it breaks fowks'
earts to see thee! Doostn't tha look forrard to thy bairn?"

"I can't imagine it, Martha—so many months of this—how can I
get through it? I dare say I shall be glad sometime. But I am so
ill—so weary—"

Still she did not know that her life was ebbing. Weak, ill, and
suffering as she was, it never occurred to her that God, who had so
unexpectedly heaped blessings on her, would take them all away
and leave those who loved her desolate.

Inside her emaciated body, her mind functioned on—more
effortfully every passing day, but usually clear. She knew how
weak she was growing. Sometimes she would lift up her hand and
look at it in some astonishment. It was almost transparent; her
arms were sticks; her face must be like a skull, for they would
never let her see it now, even after her hair had been combed. She
stared for hours on end at the sky through the window, still taking
some shadow of her former pleasure in its changing moods. Arthur
spent all the time possible with her, reading her the letters that
came, and helping her, very occasionally when she felt able, to
scribble replies in pencil, faint and brief.

To Ellen, she wrote, "I must write one line out of my dreary
bed. The news of Mercy's probable recovery came like a ray of joy
to me. I am not going to talk of my sufferings—it would be useless
and painful. I want to give you an assurance, which I know will
comfort you—and that is that I find my husband the tenderest
nurse, the kindest support, the best earthly comfort that ever
woman had. His patience never fails, and it is tried by sad days and
broken nights. Papa—thank God!—is better. Our poor old Tabby
is *dead* and *buried*. May God comfort and help you."

An effort like this exhausted her, and Arthur would have liked
to keep her from writing anything. But he feared now that she was
dying, and since he could not bring himself to write the truth to

Ellen or any of Charlotte's other friends—for such news would bring them crowding to see her, which he could not bear—it seemed only right that if she wished to write them valedictory notes, he should allow it, for their sakes as well as hers.

Once a day, Patrick forced himself to go and see her. He did not want to. He wanted nothing but to die before she did. He could not in the least understand how it was that he went on living. He tried to numb his heart before he entered her room, for truly it seemed he could bear no more; he felt grief alone would kill him, when each day as he opened the door she would strain every feeble nerve to raise herself up in the bed and whisper with a fixed smile, "I am better today, Papa!" He would come and sit by her and stroke her hand and try to find things to say, but often his mind wandered and he would sit there in silence until someone came to lead him downstairs.

He never thought of praying. He left that to *him*—his son-in-law. Sometimes, from habit, his mouth formed words that had now, through association, become more terrible to him than any others: "Thy will be done."

But he was not resigned in any religious sense. He was merely worn out by sorrow till no power or hope remained to fight it off. He could not even be angry with *him*. In a sense, he felt they were both paying the price of original sin.

Easter was coming, and spring, and suddenly, toward the middle of March, there was hope.

Word went out to the anxious villagers that Miss Charlotte was hungry. She lay there, Mrs. Brown reported (for Martha and her sisters had told her), like a little throstle, opening its mouth for food, and those who longed for her recovery sat round her like parent birds, putting in pitiful spoonsful of pudding, sips of wine and water, bread sopped in broth. She ate ravenously everything she was able to eat, but her shrunken stomach could not accept much. And even while her body was given the means to strengthen itself, her mind began to give way. She fell into a shallow delirium.

All parish duties were in abeyance. None were looked for. The village seemed to go about its business with held breath, waiting, and many prayers were said for Charlotte by those who passed by the grim old parsonage and looked up at the sickroom window.

Arthur sat by her bedside constantly, holding her hand. There was little else to do for her now. He tried not to think of their child, whose life was fading before it had begun, because when he did he imagined it living, a baby in his arms. When he dropped asleep, his head down on the bed, he dreamed he was baptizing it with all sorts of fine, noble names.

Late one night he was on his knees beside her, praying aloud, as Patrick, in the days when he had faith and hope, had used to pray. His prayer was fierce and harsh, "Let her live! I want my wife—I earned her—I want our child! Let it taste life before You take it to Yourself—spare them, Lord, spare them!"

A movement from the bed stopped him. Charlotte's eyes were open and she was sensible. "Arthur," she whispered incredulously, "I am not going to die, am I? God will not separate us—we have been so happy."

And a great pang of guilt scorched her—the fiercest and the last.

That March was true to its reputation. Lionlike, it roused itself at the end, and its gales rampaged over Yorkshire in their fullest fury.

Whether due to her lifelong susceptibility to the equinoctial changes, or from some inner cause, Charlotte relapsed. She ceased to eat; she no longer recognized Arthur or any other. Unnourished, she sank swiftly; and on the last wild night of that savage month, she and the barely formed child within her died.

In attendance at the end was not Dr. Ingham, but his new young assistant, a Dr. Dugdale. When he had made sure of death, he sent Arthur away to wake and inform Mr. Brontë, and himself roused Martha, who was sleeping in the house. "Do you know how to do what must be done now?" he asked.

"I should do. I've done it enough times in this house."

Dr. Dugdale put away his things, and then, bag in hand, looked down at the candlelit bed and the skeletal body from which Martha had just drawn back the covers. He sighed heavily. "I would have been very proud to bring that child into the world," he said. "The ways of the Lord are strange."

"Ay," said Martha. " 'Tis a sad pity. Poor lass. Poor bairn!" And then shrilly, as realization came, and anger, and grief, "Doostn't tha wonder sometimes, doctor, seein' t'way God runs this world, if tha couldna do better thisen?"

The two men kept vigil all that night on either side of the bed. Arthur sobbed despairingly from time to time, but Patrick sat, dry-eyed, livid, and stark, as cold as the corpse between them.

Morning came—Easter Sunday morning. Arthur rose stiffly. He looked aged with grief and exhaustion. The old man opposite him jerked into a sort of alertness.

"Where are you going?" he asked agitatedly.

"To order the bell tolled."

"You'll come straight back?"

Charlotte's widower looked at her father. He might live on for years. . . . Years in this house, without warmth, without love, without companionship or hope. . . . But he had given her his word.

He looked about him for a moment, as if seeking her in the grayish, chilly air. Then he dropped his head in resignation.

"Yes," he said, "I will come."

POSTSCRIPT

*P*atrick survived for another six years after Charlotte's death. He managed to stay quite active till the end, and his pride in the extraordinary nature and achievements of his children grew. He drew comfort from a belief that his own eccentric character and method of upbringing had had a great deal of influence on the evolution of their genius.

Arthur Nicholls fulfilled his promise. He stayed on as curate in Haworth until Patrick's death in 1861. He may well have expected to inherit the incumbency, but some of the church trustees did not care for his formal approach to his calling and he was defeated by one vote.

Arthur gathered up all that remained of Charlotte and her sisters, including portraits, manuscripts, letters, and a boxful of the "little magazines" they had written together in their childhood, which he had never tried to decipher. He also took Martha Brown and the last of the Brontë dogs, and returned to his family home in Banagher, Ireland. There, in time, he married his pretty "hobbledehoy" cousin, Mary Anne. The marriage was happy, though they had no children, and Arthur lived to see the beginning of this century.

Ellen Nussey, too, lived on to old age. Till her death, her friendship with Charlotte remained the central interest of her life, the remainder of which she spent in enhancing and, where necessary, defending Charlotte's memory. Unlike Mary Taylor, who had destroyed nearly all Charlotte's letters, Ellen kept hers—over five hundred of them. They were the basis of much of the scholarship and legend which built up around the Brontë sisters.

Charlotte's power as a writer and as a personality seemed to grow with her death. Many tributes were written, including some which so offended those close to her with their misconceptions that Ellen suggested to Patrick that he should commission Mrs. Gaskell to set matters straight. Mrs. Gaskell, who had been deeply grieved to hear of Charlotte's death, was persuaded to take on the loving task of writing Charlotte's *Life*. The result was a biography which still rates as one of the greatest in the English language.